O, Juliet

ROBIN MAXWELL

 NEW AMERICAN LIBRARY

New American Library
Published by New American Library,
a division of Penguin Group (USA) Inc.,
375 Hudson Street, New York, New York 10014, USA
Penguin Group (Canada), 90 Eglinton Avenue East, Suite 700, Toronto,
Ontario M4P 2Y3, Canada (a division of Pearson Penguin Canada Inc.)
Penguin Books Ltd., 80 Strand, London WC2R 0RL, England
Penguin Ireland, 25 St. Stephen's Green, Dublin 2,
Ireland (a division of Penguin Books Ltd.)
Penguin Group (Australia), 250 Camberwell Road, Camberwell,
Victoria 3124, Australia (a division of Pearson Australia Group Pty. Ltd.)
Penguin Books India Pvt. Ltd., 11 Community Centre,
Panchsheel Park, New Delhi - 110 017, India
Penguin Group (NZ), 67 Apollo Drive, Rosedale, North Shore 0632,
New Zealand (a division of Pearson New Zealand Ltd.)
Penguin Books (South Africa) (Pty.) Ltd., 24 Sturdee Avenue,
Rosebank, Johannesburg 2196, South Africa

Penguin Books Ltd., Registered Offices:
80 Strand, London WC2R 0RL, England

First published by New American Library,
a division of Penguin Group (USA) Inc.

First Printing, February 2010
1   3   5   7   9   10   8   6   4   2

Cover painting: *Flowers on a Balcony* by Jean Capeinick/Fine Art Photographic Library, London/Art Resource, NY. Inside cover painting: *Romeo and Juliet* by Sir Frank Dicksee/© Southampton City Art Gallery, Hampshire, UK/The Bridgeman Art Library.

 REGISTERED TRADEMARK—MARCA REGISTRADA

Library of Congress Cataloging-in-Publication Data:

Maxwell, Robin, 1948–
O, Juliet/Robin Maxwell.
p. cm.
ISBN 978-0-451-22915-1
1. Verona (Italy)—Fiction. 2. Families—Italy—Fiction. 3. Vendetta—Fiction. I. Title.
PS3563.A925403 2010
813'.54—dc22   2009032469

Set in Bembo
Designed by Elke Sigal

Printed in the United States of America

PUBLISHER'S NOTE
This is a work of fiction. Names, characters, places, and incidents either are the product of the author's imagination or are used fictitiously, and any resemblance to actual persons, living or dead, business establishments, events, or locales is entirely coincidental.
The publisher does not have any control over and does not assume any responsibility for author or third-party Web sites or their content.

O, Juliet

"I love this novel! A reigning queen of historical fiction takes on the treasured tale of Romeo and Juliet."

—Michelle Moran, national bestselling author of *Cleopatra's Daughter*

"An intimate historical retelling of the timeless classic."

—C. W. Gortner, author of *The Last Queen*

"Robin Maxwell turns her talents toward Shakespeare's ultimate heroine of romantic love, but Maxwell's Juliet emerges as a clever young woman and poetess from Florence, betrothed to her father's diabolical business partner. Maxwell takes a well-known story and introduces her own set of twists, using historical detail, her vivid imagination and real people to great effect."

—*New York Times* bestseller Lalita Tademy, author of *Cane River* and *Red River*

"Not many writers would dare to compete with William Shakespeare but Robin Maxwell pulls it off. Her star-crossed young lovers are just as unforgettable as the bard's, and now readers get to see what happened offstage."

—*New York Times* bestseller Sharon Kay Penman, author of *Devil's Brood*

Signora da Vinci

"A glorious novel of fifteenth-century Florence, utterly engrossing and glittering with color. Lorenzo the Magnificent, Leonardo da Vinci, and his courageous, passionate mother, Caterina, walk through the pages of this book, radiating life and touching the heart. I will never see the *Mona Lisa* with the same eyes again. Robin Maxwell has a stunning achievement in *Signora da Vinci*." —Sandra Worth, author of *The King's Daughter*

continued . . .

"Reading Maxwell's brilliant new novel, it's easy to see why Anne is the 'Boleyn girl' who changed the course of history, and why she is the source of never-ending fascination. We are finally able to catch a glimpse of Anne Boleyn before her enemies vilified her, while she was still just a young woman looking for true love. I couldn't put it down." —Michelle Moran

"Anne Boleyn fans will cry 'Huzzah!' when they learn that novelist Robin Maxwell has returned to her Tudor roots. In this saucy romp, a prequel to her *Secret Diary of Anne Boleyn*, Maxwell writes in the remembered voice of a child—a tricky feat indeed. Readers will find much to delight in, from finely drawn secondary characters like Leonardo da Vinci to scintillating descriptions of the French glitterati and the royal court. Frothy and French in its main setting, Maxwell's work nevertheless conveys a gravitas that foretells Mademoiselle Boleyn's eventual fate."

—Vicki León, author of *Uppity Women of the Renaissance*

"Historically plausible account of Anne Boleyn's adolescence in France as a courtier of King François . . . lavishly imagined . . . [an] accomplished rehabilitation of the much-maligned Anne as an empowered woman."

—*Kirkus Reviews*

Praise for the Other Novels of
Robin Maxwell

"The powerfully lascivious intersections of sexual and international politics, combined with Maxwell's electrifying prose, make for enthralling historical fiction." —*Publishers Weekly* (starred review)

"History doesn't come more fascinating . . . than the wife-felling reign of Henry VIII." —*Entertainment Weekly*

"Another satisfying historical epic from Maxwell, [who provides] a sweep of powerful emotion." —*Irish American Magazine*

A compelling, exhilarating, and thought-provoking account. . . . All of the characters are richly drawn, and the saga of Grace O'Malley sears the imagination." —*Boston Irish Reporter*

"Maxwell brings all of bloody Tudor England vividly to life."

—*Publishers Weekly* (starred review)

For Max

⁓

My bounty is as boundless as the sea
My love as deep; the more I give to thee
The more I have, for both are infinite.

—WILLIAM SHAKESPEARE from *Romeo and Juliet*

O, Juliet

Chapter One

Golden light of afternoon on honey-colored stone,
enclosing Eden down below my balcony and room.

Stone? Room? Might there be a better rhyme? Perhaps. There was always a better rhyme. Yet the sentiment was perfect. This balcony and walled garden were my private heaven. My room as well. Together they were an incomparable refuge for a Florentine girl.

Well, no longer a girl at eighteen, but a woman ripe for marriage and motherhood. Oh, but I *did* feel girlish in ways. Gazing down at the wild green of the square garden, I recalled the times when my brothers chased me, a giggling child, along the broad path that wound between trees and flowering bushes, the three of them flicking me with water from the pretty central fountain, Mama looking up all smiles from her embroidery, warning her boys to take care of their little sister.

The path was overgrown now, the fountain dry. My mother and father had let the garden fall to ruin when their sons died. I always believed its demise was a kind of penance they chose to pay for sins they were sure they had committed. Sins so vile that God would take from them all their male children.

My heart had broken, too, when they died. Though it was small consolation, their deaths had meant the bestowing of my eldest brother's room to me—the sweetest bedchamber in the house, for with its gracious balcony, it looked down upon the garden. And while I missed the burbling fountain and the ease of walking well-tended paths, I saw something wonderful in the green overgrowth. The *wildness* of it, the secrets hidden beneath the thick vines and roots and bushes. And how birds and small animals had more made it their home since its desertion. That garden sent me into flights of fancy and imaginings. Every day I would stand at the balcony rail and ponder its mysteries, let the sight of it drive me to visions of small worlds and great worlds and exotic, faraway lands.

The balcony was ten feet by ten, the half near the bedroom, door and proper Venetian glass window a covered loggia, the other jutting like the prow of a ship over the garden. Through a wooden door was my room, quite large, high-ceilinged, and gracious in proportion. There was a second window, this one overlooking Via della Colonna, the street upon which our house fronted. The furnishings were those that were found in all wealthy merchants' homes—a fine canopied and curtained bed—though mine, I thought, was hung more beautifully than most, my father the city's finest seller of silk.

There were the requisite chests that surrounded the bed and lined the walls, in which all belongings were stored. I had one unusual piece—a high cabinet in red lacquer that Papa had had brought from China, one in which the pieces of my gowns could be hung and not folded.

But of all my furnishings, those that I most cherished were my wooden desk and chair. Unremarkable as they were, they were sacred to me. Some girls took great pleasure in their prettily painted marriage chests that grew fuller every year with linen and baby clothes, gold plate, and fine pieces of glass they would one day take with them into their husband's house. Some loved their beds, their cushions and coverlets so cozy, pulling down the curtains to find comfort, like animals in their dens.

But for me the center of the world, the universe itself, was my desk. For here it was that I read and I wrote, and more than in my bed and sleep, did here I dream. I had with the privacy of my room and balcony and inspiration of that walled garden all that I needed to travel unhindered in the Kingdom of Words.

Ah, precious words! While reading was my joy, writing was—dare I say under threat of blasphemy—my religion.

It was time to leave for Lucrezia's ball, but I stayed one moment more to enjoy the garden. Happy thoughts of this night and my dearest friend's betrothal warred with unhappy ones, for her marriage meant that mine was also ahead. And that would mean losing the garden, the balcony, the room, the desk. I would go to my husband's house, and this would prove an end to my private joys.

Growing up, I had always been a girl like any other, good and obedient and loving God. I wished, as all young ladies did, for a wealthy husband and many healthy children. I'd been betrothed at the age of five to the son of my father's best friend, but then the fever had come and claimed him along with my brothers. There had been such mourning in both our houses that all talk of my marriage ceased. I was moved from the nursery down the long upper hall to my new room, and began to watch the garden where we'd all played grow wild.

Only in the past year, when Papa had found the need of a partner to fill his sons' place in the silk works, had plans for my marriage been placed once more on the table. This partner, Jacopo Strozzi, whose family's standing and wealth was in Florence second only to the Medici's, had made it known that he would consider me for a wife.

Jacopo. I cringed at the thought of him. The occasions we had met at my father's house had been grating in every way. His pinched mouth and furrowed forehead bespoke a constipated soul. The air that blew from between his dark ivory teeth onto my face as we conversed was faintly putrid, and his voice—oh, of all his attributes, that was the most distasteful. It was high-pitched and nasal, and his words were spoken with a whine, an affectation I think he believed a sign of nobility. It made me want to slap him silent. Then I curbed my thoughts, tearing my eyes away from the garden, and walked into my room.

This was Lucrezia's day, a celebration of her marriage to come—a happy occasion of the rarest match. She and Piero de' Medici, betrothed since childhood, were fond of each other, and as friendly as a boy and girl were allowed by convention to be. There was more than a fair chance that Lucrezia and Piero's arranged marriage would blossom over the years into love. Perhaps not the kind of love of which I secretly dreamed. Not Guinevere and Lancelot, nor Tristan and Isolde, nor Dante and Beatrice. But good and strong, and as enduring as we in our society did allow.

I peered at myself in the glass for the briefest moment, knowing my curled and braided hair was in place, Mama's jewels glistened at my neck, and my gown of Papa's finest silk was perfectly beautiful, and left my sanctuary.

I walked the long hall, dark even now in the afternoon, and several doors closed on rooms that mocked our family with their emptiness. My brothers' rooms. At the hall's end near the stairs was my parents' bedchamber.

The door was ajar. From inside I could hear the irritation in Mama's voice, chiding a servant. "Must you slop water all over the floor? Look at that, you've spotted my dress!"

I hurried past, not wishing to engage with Mama in one of her moods, and saw a glimpse of poor Viola, a young kitchen maid who had carried many pails of hot water up the stairs for her mistress's bath. Now she was worriedly examining the skirt of my mother's ball gown set upon a headless dressmaker's form, searching for the water stains she had been accused of making.

I hurried down the steps, but halfway to the ground floor began hearing a heated conversation echoing out from Papa's study.

"But why, Jacopo? Why would this family—one whose name I barely recognize—have done such a thing to me? To sink an entire cargo of silk . . ."

"And vandalize the factory."

"You have evidence of that as well?"

I had come to one side of the open study door and again did not wish to converse with my parent, clearly in the throes of unpleasantness. So I stopped and stood still, waiting for a moment to pass by without being seen.

Jacopo Strozzi spoke with a strident tone. "Proof positive. The Monticecco, for some unnameable reason, have become the avowed enemies of the Capelletti." Suddenly his voice grew smooth and oiled. "And now, Capello, any enemy of yours is an enemy of mine."

"What can be done?"

"What is always done to saboteurs, wretched criminals. They will be exposed and they will pay for their crimes. In blood, if need be. Monticecco blood."

I chanced a peek around the doorframe to see the men's eyes locked in a fierce brothers-in-battle gaze, and scurried past. I was out the front door in a moment and found waiting outside it the family litter, its four bearers snapping to attention at the sight of me. As one of them helped me in, I told him my destination and pressed a lavender-scented cloth to my nose to block the mild stench rising from the summer street and settled into the cushioned compartment. We were off.

It was a short distance across the city of Florence from our house to Via Bardi, but one affording me sufficient time to clear my head of the dark furies of home, and begin contemplating what would surely be a pleasurable evening ahead.

Chapter Two

"Juliet Capelletti, here to see Lucrezia Tornabuoni."

The smile of the Palazzo Bardi's doorman spread so wide I felt myself instantly welcomed into the rarefied world of the Medici. He stepped aside and bade me enter the pale green marble vestibule, pushing me back with a protective arm as a servant rushed past, half-blinded by a huge urn bursting with fresh flowers.

"You must forgive us, signorina. We have never had such excitement in the house before. I will take you to the lady . . . our lady. . . ." He chuckled with embarrassed delight. "Soon-to-be our lady."

As the doorman led me toward a grand stairway, we passed a long snaking line of men assembled before a closed door. Each of them was splendidly dressed, their heads crowned with huge flared turbans in brilliant hues of silk and satin and brocade. The grouping seemed strange to me, their demeanor more reserved than their fashionable costumes. Indeed, they were remarkably silent and inward for a gang of Florentine men, who, by their very nature, talked and laughed loudly and with generous gesticulation, conducted business and deal-making at every turn.

They barely took notice of me, for as we approached the door, it opened and everyone came to attention. The first man in line went in, passing one coming out, and I could see inside the room, which appeared to be a fine study with many shelves lined with books and scrolls. In a chair, sitting comfortably, was a bareheaded Cosimo de' Medici, his kindly face wreathed in a smile. He put out his hand to the newly admitted Florentine, clearly a supplicant, who knelt to kiss the offered hand, murmuring, "Don Cosimo." Then the door shut on the odd tableau.

"Juliet!" I heard the rich, throaty voice of my friend calling from above. At the top of the stairs was Lucrezia, holding around her a dressing gown and excitedly beckoning me up to her.

As I ascended, I passed two chattering maids, one in front of the other, carrying between their shoulders a long folded tapestry, and a liveried manservant, his arms full of unlit torches. Arrived at the landing of the noble floor, I felt myself instantly embraced, the warm fragrance of Lucrezia's jasmine oil enveloping me.

"Oh let me look at you, friend!" she cried, and held me at arm's length. But as she gazed at me, I was also gifted with the sight of her. She, too, was eighteen, and, like a rare flower just opening for the first time, at the freshest peak of her beauty. She had delicately wrought cheeks and chin and nose, a generous mouth. Her hair was a thick flax, this evening arrayed in intricate twisted braids and soft curling tendrils. The green of her sparkling eyes was wonderful.

"You are lovely! Turn, turn," she ordered me, and I obeyed.

"A gown I've never seen. The dusty rose suits you. And the neck-lace. Let me see. Juliet! These are diamonds and rubies. What is your father thinking?"

"I'm meant to make an impression tonight," I said with a dolorous sigh.

Lucrezia took me by the hand and pulled me down the hall past a massive, dome-ceilinged ballroom where, by the look of its decoration—velvet and gold-shot draperies, hundreds of yet-unlit tapers in their candelabrum, flowers, and festoons of greenery—much of this evening's festivities would take place. I could see Maestro Donatello, the city's finest artisan, flinging his fingers to the left and right, sending his apprentices to their various tasks. "More torches to the garden!" he cried. "Pull up the hem of that curtain!"

Farther on was a carved door through which Lucrezia led me into a bedroom, large, though not as sumptuously appointed as I might have imagined a Medici sleeping chamber to be. Two maids were emptying a steel tub, sending pailfuls of used bath-water down a well shaft. I had never seen such a thing before.

Plumbing of the rich, I thought.

When Lucrezia closed the door, she turned to me. "So you're to make an impression? On your betrothed, I assume?"

"Jacopo Strozzi is not my betrothed," I insisted, my voice sulky. "Not yet. He hasn't even signed the partnership papers with my father."

I looked around me. The bed upon which Lucrezia's clothing and two fabulous feathered masks were laid out was enormous and gorgeously curtained, with wine-colored velvet brocade and ermine trim. I realized with quiet delight that it was draped with my papa's wares. And while the headboard was high and painted with fantastical birds, and great wooden chests surrounded it on every side, no colorful frescoes decorated the walls, just sections of painted patterns in dark, muted colors. The only furnishings were a single cushioned chair, a plain writing desk, and a small altar to the Virgin.

"This is the conjugal bedroom?" I asked.

"Not Don Cosimo's. Only Mona Contessina's."

I was surprised. I'd not heard of married couples with separate bedchambers. Rudely, I nosed about the room. "No books," I said. "Your mother-in-law-to-be does not read?"

"Her husband doesn't expect it of her. They're old-fashioned in that way. Come, help me on with my things."

We went to the bed and I picked up the long-sleeved white silk *camicia* that had been embroidered with pomegranates and posies. Lucrezia laid aside her dressing gown to reveal a body of the sweetest feminine form—small breasts high and rounded, waist narrow, and hips flaring with womanly curves. I could hear the maids tittering as they carried the tub from the room, leaving my friend and me to our private conversation. She raised her arms and I slipped the garment over her head, careful to leave the hairdresser's every curl and tendril in place.

"Have you seen Piero today?" I asked her.

"No. My father-in-law insists it will be bad luck."

"This is your betrothal ball, not your wedding day," I told her.

"Don Cosimo had my horoscope drawn."

"And that is where he derived such superstition?"

"Yes, but also that I'm to have an extraordinary life."

"You're becoming a Medici, Lucrezia. One doesn't need an astrologer to deduce a brilliant future." I picked up the yellow silk brocaded *guarnacca* studded with gold stars. The gown was ungainly for its weight, and the bodice and sleeves hung down limp over the front of its skirt. "Raise your arms," I commanded, and dropped it on from above. "What were you thinking just then? You were somewhere else."

"I was thinking I would rather be marrying Don Cosimo."

I barked a laugh as I tightened the laces in back, cinching in Lucrezia's already waspish waist. "And you call *me* outrageous," I said.

"He's a true gentleman. Polite. Affectionate. And such a scholar."

Lucrezia was right. Five years before he had single-handedly set all of Florence afire with *Rinascimento*—a rebirth of the antiquities. Afterward, any man who counted himself a member of the Medici Faction educated his sons in the classics.

It had taken hardly any convincing of Lucrezia Tornabuoni's father by Cosimo to hire for his heir's thirteen-year-old wife-to-be both Greek and Latin tutors, and even one for mathematics. He wished for her to be a very great lady, he'd said. And while such an education for girls was not yet the fashion, Lucrezia had wished—and asked very sweetly—for her dearest friend, Juliet Capelletti, to receive the same benefit.

"He has the most wonderful library in his study," she said.

"I saw a glimpse of it when I came in."

"He owns some of the rarest Greek codices that exist."

"*Your* fancy," I observed. Lucrezia had taken to that ancient language like a bird to flight, delighting in its myths and pantheon of gods and goddesses. No one but me and her tutor knew how enamored she was of it all, as her parents believed her devoutly and altogether Christian. Those pagan leanings would have appalled them.

I plucked the silk undergarment through the slashed shoulders and sleeves of the *guarnacca*, blousing them prettily.

"There's something in that library that would set *your* heart fluttering," Lucrezia teased.

"And what would that be?" I said with more than a touch of skepticism. I had enjoyed my education, but the Greek language had strained my intellect. I much preferred Italian.

"A manuscript of *Vita Nuova* . . . from the time of Dante himself."

My arms fell uselessly to my sides. Lucrezia had known very well the effect of her words. The poet Dante Alighieri was like a god to me, and *Vita Nuova*—the story of his boyhood love for Beatrice—the stuff of my dreams.

Lucrezia turned to face me, smiling like a cat. "When I am a lady of this household, I'll take you in to see it. You can pore over it. Weep over it. Allow it to inspire you."

I hugged her and kissed her fragrant cheek. "Thank you!" I whispered passionately. "Thank you." In her reciprocal embrace I felt Lucrezia's joy in the simple art of giving. I had much to learn from the lady's generous nature.

I sought to regain my composure. "Guests will be arriving soon. We should see to your jewelry."

"No jewels tonight," she demurred.

"For what reason?" I demanded.

"Because I am marrying into a great but altogether unostentatious family. I wish to show them I am one with them in this." She saw my disappointment. "But I have not decided on my shoes yet." Lucrezia seated herself on the bed and opened a chest displaying half a dozen pairs of varying colors, styles, and heels. She stuck out a foot in my direction and I fitted it with a sheath of gold velvet raised on a high platform.

"I'll just say no to marrying Jacopo," I said with firm defiance.

"And what will you do with the rest of your life? Take to a nunnery—a hopeless romantic like yourself?" Lucrezia was altogether unperturbed, knowing well it was idle talk.

We both knew as surely as we breathed that a woman was bound to do what best benefited her parents, her husband, her children, and her church. "Her own desires"—well, no woman I knew allowed herself that luxury, nor even wasted a moment of rumination on such devilish indulgences. Lucrezia turned her foot this way and that. "This one is too high. I'll stand as tall as Piero."

I next chose a soft flat slipper with a Turkish curl to the toe in pale yellow that matched her overdress.

"Perhaps I'll go the way of Saint Margaret of Cortona and spend my youth in fornication," I said.

"I don't suppose you'll be 'touched by Grace' as she was, and spend the rest of your life in your bedroom crying for your sins."

"Ha!"

I put the second yellow slipper on Lucrezia's other foot.

"These are pretty," she said.

"I hate Jacopo Strozzi," I announced, knowing that my flippancy sometimes bordered on the ridiculous.

"It is your mother-in-law you will need fortitude to tolerate," Lucrezia said.

I groaned loudly at the thought. Allessandra Strozzi was famously harsh and renowned in all of Florence for the ruthlessness of her matchmaking. No one was good enough for her sons.

"Besides, you barely know Jacopo Strozzi," she added. "I'm sure you'll grow to love him, like I'll grow to love Piero."

"I thought you said you did love him already."

"I do." She looked suddenly pensive. "But he is so . . . so . . ."

"What?"

"Unwell. Barely twenty-five and he is already called 'Piero the Gouty.' "

"Surely the most important of his limbs does not have gout."

"Juliet!"

I picked up a pair of scarlet shoes that matched the pomegranates on Lucrezia's *camicia*, but when I moved to place them on her feet, she stayed my hand. "Juliet . . . ," she repeated, this time her voice pleading.

All the jesting had gone out of me. "My father told me, 'Even if it breaks your heart, you will marry this man.' " I sniffed back emotion. "But that is the way we live, I suppose. At least it will make an end to my father's nagging and my mother's harping at me for grandchildren."

"You're not going to say you don't want children now."

"Of course I want children," I said, "as long as they don't kill me on the way out."

"Childbirth kill *you*? Never! You're strong as Don Cosimo's mule . . . and twice as stubborn. And here's the best reason to marry. We'll be matrons together—the queens of Florentine society." She picked up the two feathered fans and handed me one.

"We'll rule with exquisite grace and style," she said, playfully putting the hawk's face before her own. "Raise large and beautiful families. Our feasts will be the most splendid, our patronage to hospitals and orphanages and artists legendary. We will have private rooms of our own. You will write your poetry."

I began to smile. "In secret," I said, holding up my own mask. "I think Jacopo would forbid me writing." I handed Lucrezia a small looking glass, and she regarded her feathered visage.

"It's good to have some secrets from your husband. And you will always have me to read your verses."

I was overcome with gratitude. Tears were threatening. "No one has ever had a better friend than I do."

We removed our masks and gazed at each other.

"You're wrong," Lucrezia said. "*I* have."

"The red or the yellow?" I said quickly, not wishing for sentiment to overwhelm us on this night of celebration.

Sniffing loudly, she said, "Let me see the high gold ones again. I'm thinking that Piero de' Medici may need a wife who is his equal."

Chapter Three

I was avoiding my parents, very easy to do in so large and loud a crush of celebrating people, with musicians playing. And I was masked, my feathered face a happy disguise. I caught glimpses of them—my mother, Mona Simonetta, short and plump as a partridge, and Papa, Capello Capelletti, a rangy beanstalk. To confer as they were now doing—looking this way and that, no doubt wondering at my whereabouts—Papa needed bending at the waist and Mama craning her neck to give him an ear.

I sidestepped behind a marble pillar and leaned back, sighing. This night of Lucrezia and Piero's betrothal, one that I wished to celebrate joyfully, was sure to be spent either cat-and-mousing with my parents, or trapped in a corner with Jacopo Strozzi, me pretending his conversation scintillating, his breath sweet, and his manner delightful. And several times this night I had noticed Allessandra Strozzi, dark complexioned and severe in countenance, peering with great intensity into the crowd, probably looking for me.

Rein yourself in, I ordered myself. Jacopo had never been unkind, and Mama said he often asked after my likes and dislikes. He plied me with compliments, though I always felt they would have been the same for any and every other girl in Florence he might be courting. He brought me small gifts—a silver crucifix, jade rosary beads, and a Book of Hours—all, I supposed, to remind me of the pious woman I was expected to be. Well, I told myself, I had best come to grips with my future husband. I must find a way to make the thought of sharing Jacopo's home and bed and bearing his children somehow less revolting. Lucrezia was right. Nothing could be done to change it.

"Cosimo and Contessina de' Medici!" I heard announced as the music died. There was great shuffling of feet and rustling of fine fabric as everyone turned to the front of the ballroom. Guests pulled the masks from their faces in a respectful gesture and fell silent as the smiling Godfather of Florence, his wife on his arm, waved beneficently over the crowd.

"Good friends!" he cried, and everyone crowed back at him—"Don Cosimo!" He laughed, delighted at the warmth and fellowship flowing forward and back. "What a day of glad tidings this is," he continued. Now there was hardly a sound that could be heard. "Our son Piero has not only made a match in the beautiful Lucrezia Tornabuoni. He has *met* his match!"

Everyone roared their approval, and I thought how overbrimming with pride my friend must be, honored so by so honorable a man.

Lucrezia and Piero appeared then, he looking darkly handsome and quite elegant in a black velvet tunic piped in silver and, eschewing a dramatic turban, wearing instead a flat cap with a long, upward-curving white feather. Lucrezia, clutching his hand, eyes fastened on her betrothed, glowed with a look that proclaimed, "I am the luckiest girl in the world!"

"May the joining of our two houses, and the heirs that spring fat and healthy from her womb, prove a blessing to Florence," Cosimo intoned, "and all the citizens of the Republic!"

The cheering at that was loud and raucous. I watched as Cosimo gently herded the now shy couple onto the floor that had cleared for them. Musicians struck the first chords of the *pima*, and Lucrezia and Piero took their poses. At the precise moment they swooped into motion, their gazes locked, and all could see that Cosimo's words were not the empty praise and platitudes of any proud father. These two on the dance floor were something marvelous. Important. Radiating a glorious destiny. And we were the fortunate witnesses.

"Well, there you are," I heard my mother say inches behind my ear, and cringed. I had been caught. "Let me see the mask Lucrezia gifted you."

I turned and, pulling the feathered creation that hung on a ribbon from my waist, dutifully held it up to my face.

"Oh, it is very fine. It must have been expensive."

Through the eyeholes I saw my mother appraising me from foot to head. She fluffed out a slashed sleeve and smoothed my skirt. Then her eyes fell disapprovingly on my bodice. "Much too low," she muttered.

"It is the fashion," I said. "You saw the dress before I left the house."

Undeterred, she took a fine silk handkerchief from her sleeve and began tucking it between my breasts.

"Mother!" I pulled back farther behind the pillar. "Do you wish me to die of embarrassment in the middle of the Medici ballroom?" I wanted to resist her ministrations but knew it would create more of a scene.

"I will not have you meeting your husband-to-be looking like a prostitute."

"Don't be horrible!"

"There, that's better."

I looked down. The pretty curve of my bosom was now concealed under poufs of silk. It looked quite ridiculous.

"Come with me," my mother said.

"May I not even watch my friend dance the first dance with her betrothed?" I was ashamed of the petulance in my voice, but it caused my mother to relent.

"You see where your father is?" She nodded across the room to where he now stood with his future business partner. His face was red and angry.

"Can Papa not enjoy the evening?"

"Not with all the trouble brewing at the factory. The Monticecco . . . ," she began, but her voice trailed off. "But that is none of our affair. You just meet us over there in a quarter of an hour."

"Yes, Mama."

She gave the silk handkerchief another upward tug.

"Will you *leave* it?" I moaned.

She tottered away on her high platform shoes with an alarming lack of grace. A stiff breeze would have knocked her over.

I made a slow circle around the dance floor behind the crowd. I could see that all the girls and women had their eyes fixed on the happy couple.

Maria Cantorre appeared the saddest. At fourteen she was about to be married to a wealthy Roman wool merchant fifty years her senior. His last wife and every one of his children had died in the plague of 1438, and poor Maria had been chosen among all the marriageable females in Florence for the fertility of her family's women to provide a new parade of heirs for the old man.

Chaterina Valenti, a pretty but dull-witted girl of my age, had just married below her rank, as her father's intemperate business dealings had left her with a pitiful dowry. She was so openly seething with jealousy over Lucrezia's good fortune I was tempted to tap her on the shoulder and advise her to perhaps hide her envy for fear of shaming herself, her husband, and her family.

Constanza Marello, a wisp of a woman with a sharp beaky nose, was the infamous Spinster of Florence. Despite an immense dowry, the Fates had continually mocked her, killing off one after another of Constanza's prospective bridegrooms, so that now, at almost thirty, she was too old to begin childbearing. No one would wish to marry such a woman. I had recently heard gossip that she was headed for a nunnery, her dowry used to endow the holy house of San Lorenzo. If Constanza's family could not raise its worth through her marriage to a wealthy man, it could nevertheless reap spiritual riches and great respect by its generous patronage of the church.

With the final chords of the first dance played out, the virgins of Florence were called to the floor. As we formed a circle, bracelets of tiny cymbals were thrust into our hands. How many times I had joined this *roundele* I could not count, but as I took the hands of the girls to the left and right of me, I tried to forget it was bound to be my last. It was a joyous dance, very sprightly, with steps and snakelike weaves and swift turns that made the most of a young lady's grace and lightness. Eyes sparkled with promise. Arms raised above our heads, wrists twisted with delicate flicks that jangled our cymbal bracelets in fetching rhythm.

The Virgins' Dance made everyone smile, and as we circled and twirled, I found myself laughing, felt my soul soaring and free from care, as though music—not blood—was coursing through my veins. All around us revelers clapped to the beat that quickened, our feet skipping faster, faster, faster, the cymbals, the drums, CRESCENDO!

We fell together, arms about one another, gasping happily. But there was no respite. Another dance had already begun. The gentlemen joined in now, and the rest of the ladies, too. We were circle-within-circle—the men without, women within. In this way, in the space of a *quadernaria*, we would come face-to-face with every person of the other sex at the ball, politely touching hands, smiling, nodding, bowing, and turning.

We had danced thus for only a moment before I stood opposite my father. His sour mood had not lightened even a fraction, and I was further assailed by a disapproving look that said, "Why did you not come to me when I called?" I replied with the downcast eyes of a chastised daughter and was much relieved when the stanza moved him on, putting in his place the city's current *gonfaloniere*, a fat and jolly guildsman who, with a delighted belly laugh, gave me an extra twirl that nearly undid the perfect symmetry of the double-circle dance.

Coming back to my place in the circle, I found myself before another friendly face, though this one my age. My father's nephew Marco was a happy, boisterous young man known and loved for his clownishness.

"What's that stuck between your bosoms, good cousin?" he

demanded, improvising an extra hop and a spin. As he bowed, he reached out and gave my mother's silk kerchief a tug.

"Marco," I whispered threateningly.

"It looks very silly," he said in a loud voice. "Poufs on your poufs!"

Before I could bean the boy, he had danced away, and to my dismay I now stood before Signor Strozzi. My husband-to-be, clutching my hand with the long, tapering fingers of his own cold, clammy one, was silent and stultifyingly formal. His steps were stiff, as though a pole were lodged in his *ano*. I nearly laughed aloud at that thought. But what he did next stifled the sound in my throat.

He smiled. Smugly. Possessively. With long yellowing teeth.

I thought I might faint.

Never had I been gladder for a cast-off to a new partner than I was when the stanza changed, and no more delightful a partner could I have wished for. It was our host. Cosimo de' Medici's eyes sparkled so impishly and his feet stepped so lightly that he seemed a much younger man. I suddenly understood why Lucrezia loved him so.

"Ah, Juliet," he said, beaming, "what a joyful occasion. Tell me, is your friend happy?"

I executed the slight swivel of a *campegiarre* and gazed back at him over my shoulder.

"Only walking on air. How could she feel otherwise?"

With the *quadernaria* drawing to a close, we made our final bows, but as before, the musicians had barely finished with one tune before striking up another. These were the chords we all recognized as a *bassadanza*, a slow and stately procession of couples. Everyone took a moment to place their masks on their faces.

Don Cosimo had moved forward to partner with the lady next to me. Suddenly I felt my hand grasped by strong, warm fingers and turned to greet my partner. All I could see of him behind his sleek wolf's mask were his eyes, deep brown and soulful, a firm angled chin, and lush lips.

Facing one another, broken into two lines—men and women—we began the graceful rising and falling motion of the *undagiarre*, but I found myself quite unnerved.

My partner's eyes would not leave mine.

There I found myself, imprisoned by a stranger's gaze and oddly longing for the moment he would grasp my hand again. His lips parted. Revealed was an even line of pearl white teeth. We came together, palms touching palms, and then he spoke.

"'Such sweet decorum and such gentle graces attend my lady as she dances.'"

"What did you say?"

We separated again. My mind reeled. The voice itself was rich and mellifluous, a kind of music unto itself. But it was the *words* that had rocked me. Now I took his arm, and facing front, we promenaded forward, stepped and pivoted, stepped and pivoted.

I could not contain myself, but I kept my voice low as I said, "The line reads, '*Such sweet decorum and such gentle graces attend my lady's greeting as she* walks.'"

"Yes, but you are dancing."

"You dare amend Dante?"

"When it suits me," he said, his tone simple and sincere. But I was flummoxed.

"You are outrageous, my lord!" I cried, losing my step and my footing. Then to my horror I stumbled. I saw myself careening into the back of Cosimo's partner, but in the moment before

I collapsed the entire procession, those strong hands cinched my waist and gracefully propelled me out of harm's and humiliation's way.

The dance went on without us, and in moments I'd been guided from the ballroom floor down the stairs to the vestibule and into the palazzo's scented garden.

It was torch and moonlit, deserted but for my wolfman and me.

I was strangely light-headed and clearheaded all at once.

"Will you unmask?" he said in a low, husky tone. The way my body felt, he might have uttered, "Will you undress?" I wondered if he knew I ached to see the face that matched that voice.

"Will you?" I whispered.

"For my dancing lady?" he teased. "Anything she pleases."

"Then on the count of three," I said, sounding, I thought, like a mathematics tutor, and, closing my eyes, nodded thrice.

The cool night air tingled my damp cheeks as the mask came off. A vein thumped in my neck. Slowly I raised my eyelids.

He was right before me, having moved closer, this audacious young man, he who took liberties with Dante Alighieri.

Oh, he was beautiful! The hair that flowed to his shoulders was chestnut and thick with waves. The dark windows of his wide-set eyes dared me to enter at my own risk. His cheekbones were broad but finely chiseled, and the nose was straight and perfectly shaped—more Circassian than Italian, I thought.

Then I smiled, thinking, *I am no stranger to that mouth.* Instantly I quashed the thought.

Too late.

"Why do you smile that way?" he asked.

I stood speechless, as I did not wish to lie to him. Yet the truth was deeply mortifying. He was a stranger! One whose impudence had made me stumble in the promenade.

"What? Suddenly mute?" he prodded. "Inside, you chastised me. Now you refuse to speak."

"I do not refuse," I finally said. "I simply wish to choose my words more carefully."

"You needn't be careful with me," he said with unexpected gentleness. "I lived with sisters. I'm used to teasing them." Then he went silent, his head tilting slightly, examining my face. He was quiet for a long while.

"Now you're the mute," I accused.

He laughed, and the sound of it fluttered my heart. So sweet was it, I silently determined, that I must make this young man laugh again and again. Those eyes refused to release me from their locked grip. I wished desperately that my mother's handkerchief was not stuffed in my bodice.

The full lips moved and he said softly, *"'I found her so full of natural dignity and admirable bearing she did not seem the daughter of an ordinary man, but rather a god.'"*

I was awed at his grasp of our favorite poet, indeed, my favorite of his books—*Vita Nuova*—and I wished with all desperation to reply in kind, though without revealing my soul too deeply.

"Good sir," I finally said, "*'you speak without the trusted counsel of reason.'*"

He was delighted at my choice of quotes.

"Now it is you who is guilty of changing Dante's words," he said, "and, moreover, changing his meaning."

"Not so!" I cried. "I simply chose a phrase, a part of a phrase. One that follows your own in chapter two."

"And what is the rest of that phrase?" he probed, taking half a step closer. We were in dangerous proximity now.

I could hardly breathe. I closed my eyes to recall the words as they stood on the page. "*'And though her image,'* " I recited, "*'which remained constantly with me, was Love's assurance of holding me, it was of such pure quality that never did it permit to be ruled by Love without the trusted counsel of reason.'* " I opened my eyes, mortified that I had been the first to speak of that most poignant of emotions.

"You see, you *did* change the meaning," he insisted. "Dante was saying that in his love for Beatrice he was always blessed by reason." His face fixed itself in a noncommittal expression. "Though when it comes to the love *I* feel, I might not be so blessed."

I thought I might swoon and had to take a step backward. But with a small smile, the gentleman took one forward.

It was a bold challenge and though he had not touched me, a strong but pleasant shock reverberated through my body. I strove to remain calm.

"Who are you?" I said. "Why do I not know you?"

"I have been in Padua. At university. Before that, I lived with my uncles in Verona for several years." Pain flickered across his features then. "There were many deaths in my family—all my elder brothers, and my sisters. . . ." He shook his head. "The family business here in Florence will one day be mine."

"I lost all my brothers, too," I said.

Both of us looked down at our feet, yet too unfamiliar to share that black misery.

"And your name?" I did ask.

He grinned, then closed his eyes, as though trying to remember a particular line. *"'Names follow from the things they name, as the saying goes. . . .'"* He hesitated and I jumped in, so we spoke together in unison, from chapter thirteen:

"'Names are the consequences of things.'"

We both smiled, utterly pleased with ourselves.

"So I am the consequence of my father's and mother's 'thing'?" I asked.

His laugh was bawdy this time. "I imagine your father would not approve of your speaking of his 'thing.'"

"Come, tell me your name," I begged.

"Romeo," he said. "And yours?"

"Juliet."

"Ju-li-et. It lies gently on the tongue."

"And your family's name?"

He spun suddenly on his heel and with a flourish bowed low before me.

> *What matter is my name if my mind has shattered*
> *in a thousand pieces and my heart,*
> *where the soul resides, has grown*
> *to the size of the sun?*

My brow furrowed. "That is not Dante. Or if it is, I cannot place it."

He pressed his lips tightly together, then spoke. "It is my own verse."

"You're a poet!"

"That I would never claim."

"Why? They were pretty words, carefully composed. I had to think a moment. They *could* have been Dante's."

"You are far too kind, Lady Juliet." His eyes narrowed. "Indeed, I think you mock me."

"No, no! Romeo, I am an honest woman. There is much I cannot claim for myself. But straight talking is one that I proudly do. And when it comes to poetry, sir, I fancy myself of strong and fair opinion. And I tell you your verse was pleasant to the ear."

He sighed happily.

"Here, listen to mine," I said.

> *Am I mad to judge a man by the shape of his hand,*
> *square and strong, the way he holds my face so tender in his*
> > *palm.*
> *Warm, enchanted fingertips that magic make upon my soul,*
> *All of that, all of that, in the shape of a hand.*

Romeo fixed me with a blank gaze.

"*You* wrote that?"

"I did. What's wrong with it?"

"Nothing."

"Then why do you stand there like a stag just struck by an arrow?"

"Women . . . ," he began, but could not finish.

"Women do not write poetry?" I finished for him. I bristled, insulted, and started turning away.

"No, please, Juliet!"

He grasped my hand in both of his, not unaware of his presumptuousness. I could not deny that despite my strong words, his touch had, alarmingly, turned me soft inside. Yielding.

"Forgive me. I have never known a woman poet. The verse was . . . brilliant. And the verse was *yours*."

"Brilliant?"

"I thought it so. Dante, were he here in this garden, would agree."

I gently released myself from his grip, aware that pulling away was what I wished least to do. "You teased me before," I said, surprised to hear my voice grow low and husky. "You tease me again."

He shook his head. "Who has read your poems?"

"Only my friend Lucrezia."

"Others should read your work."

"Oh no. That would cause a world of unhappiness." I fell silent, suddenly miserable. "My future husband would never approve."

Romeo's features crumpled, and a certain light faded from his eyes. I understood his disappointment.

As much from my own anger at the Fates as his, I lashed out at him with as much sense as a hedgehog. "What, did you not expect a woman of my age to be betrothed? Do I look like a spinster to you? Am I so hideous?"

He was amused at my intemperance, refusing—like a stubborn fish—to take my bait.

"Ah, I see. You test me," he said. "You wish me to versify on the subject of your beauty."

"That was not my intention," I insisted. He nevertheless said:

> *Her color is the paleness of the pearl*
> *She is the highest nature can achieve*
> *And by her mold all beauty tests itself.*

I smiled at the well-chosen lines of our favorite poet.

"Ah, she is mollified."

"Not entirely," I said, enjoying the game. "I require one of yours."

"On the spur of the moment?"

"Well, certainly you've written of other ladies' beauty."

He was very quiet and displayed a look of bafflement.

"Come, a winsome young bachelor like yourself . . ."

"I am not a bachelor. I'm a scholar, only recently come from—"

"Padua, I know. But you have written of love—your heart 'the size of the sun.' Is beauty so hard?"

A slow smile bowed his lips and his eyes swept over my face.

"No, my lady, not when the beauty is that of an angel."

I was growing keenly aware of the sensations this man's near presence was having on my body. I strove to remain serene.

He continued slowly, as the words flowed into his head.

> *Not when the name evokes a precious stone.*
> *Who is Juliet? How does her smile manage*
> *to foretell the rising sun, her eyes*
> *the brightest stars in the southern sky?*
> *Who is Juliet, a lady on whose sweetly scented breath ride*
> *surprising words that illumine the night and make*
> *a poet's heart sing with wonder at his good fortune to know her?*

"I am more than satisfied," I said, deeply impressed with his agility and flattered by the sentiment.

"But I am not." He looked unhappy. "Who is your be-trothed?"

"My 'nearly betrothed' is Jacopo Strozzi."

Romeo's face paled.

"Do you know him?"

"I know of him."

"*What* do you know of him?"

My young courtier was growing more uneasy by the moment, the magic vapors surrounding us suddenly evaporating.

"What is it?" I asked.

He remained stubbornly silent.

"I have been honest with you, sir. You must do me the honor likewise. What do you know of Jacopo Strozzi?"

"That he will soon be partners with an enemy of my father."

A sharp breath escaped me. "That enemy's name is Capelletti," I whispered.

"It is. How do you know this?"

"My father is Capello Capelletti." I found myself anguished at speaking the next words. "Our families are at war with one another."

He turned where he stood but did not walk away. I could see his body trembling. My own felt suddenly weak.

"What are you doing in this house?" My voice was urgent. "The Medici bear no more love for the Monticecco than do the Capelletti."

"I came to change that," Romeo said, turning back to me. "These are ancient rivalries, and Don Cosimo is a reasonable man. He claims to want peace in Florence. I sought an audience with him. I was too late to see him before the ball, but I will speak to him before the night is over."

"Ah, Romeo . . ." Now it was I at a loss for words. I was a girl with knowledge of my father's business with this family. I was not a traitor, yet I felt compelled to say: "Are you so sure this feud is ancient?"

"What do you mean?"

"What do you know of a sunken cargo ship?"

"Nothing."

I could say no more. "I must go."

"No, wait."

He took my arm in a desperate grip. I looked down at his hand, square and strong, and wished my poem alive—*Oh, that Romeo held my face tender in his palm*—but I pulled from his grasp, refusing to meet his eye.

Lifting my skirts, I ran from the garden. The palazzo vestibule felt small and stuffy, its pale green marble suddenly sinister in the torchlight. I hurried up the stairs to the ballroom, rearranging my face to hide the chaos of feeling and lies.

And not a moment too soon.

My father reared up before me like a jagged mountain peak.

"Where have you been!" he demanded, having to shout above the music and the mass of people dancing.

"I'm sorry, Papa, I felt ill. I went to the garden for a breath of air. I'm better now."

His eyes were in line with the doorway and I thought suddenly that Romeo might enter just behind me—a dangerous coincidence. I took my father's arm and brought him around, facing away from the door, then turned on my girlish charms, those he had always delighted in, in my younger years.

"Did you dance with Mama?" I asked, smiling up at him. "You know how she loves a *saltarello*."

"No," he growled, unamused, "I was too busy consoling Signor Strozzi, who was unable to find my daughter."

"Well, he mustn't have tried very hard," I answered with a flash of peevishness. "Perhaps a single flight of stairs was too hard on his poor old bandy legs."

"Juliet!" Papa swung me around to face him. His expression was as red and ragged as it had been while he'd talked of his sabotaged business. He did not seem to care that people were staring.

But then neither did I.

His voice was low and threatening. "I am taking you to speak with your betrothed."

"He is not my betrothed *yet*," was my rebellious retort.

I thought my father's face might explode with his fury, but now he was aware of the scene he was creating in the Medici ballroom, and he reined himself in. His voice remained threatening.

"We will speak of your unruliness later. But now you will begin comporting yourself like the noblewoman you seem to have forgotten you are, and you will make your apologies to Signor Strozzi for your absence. Then you will satisfy him that he has chosen for himself a proper Florentine wife and not some wild, willful child that will bring him nothing but ill fortune in his life. Do you understand?"

"Yes, Papa."

As he pulled me around the dance floor's perimeter, I heard him muttering, "This is your mother's fault. . . . Too permissive . . . the price of educating a girl . . ."

I smiled to myself. *Too late. Knowledge is inside me. It cannot be unlearned.*

Then I was standing before Jacopo Strozzi. He was not, as my father had indicated, waiting with bated breath to see me. Clearly he was straining to hear a conversation being carried on by two bankers nearby about the papal curia's treasury deficit.

"She was dizzy," my father told Jacopo. "Needed some air. Please excuse me." He disappeared into the crowd.

"Good evening, signorina," Jacopo said, hard-pressed to tear himself away from the financial gossip. He forced himself, however, and bowed to me with great formality.

"Good evening, signor," I answered in kind, and curtsied perfunctorily.

"You're looking lovely this evening."

"Thank you."

Suddenly he stiffened so sharply at the sight of something behind me that I turned to see what had alarmed him. It was his mother, her eyes fixed on the pair of us with such blatant interest that even I grew uncomfortable. I turned back to Jacopo, taking pity on the poor man.

"A beautiful evening," I said, striving for levity. "The night air was cool. It cleared my head."

"Why did it need clearing?" he asked, forcing himself to recover from the embarrassment.

"Three dances without stopping. I was overheated." I looked down at my gown. "The brocade is a bit heavy."

I caught him staring at my chest and imagined him enchanted with my bosom. But his next words disabused me of the thought.

"That is a rare weave," he said of my dusty rose bodice. "The warp, I would say, is the pink, the woof a soft gray, or perhaps tawny." He seemed to be warming to his subject, his mother forgotten. "Whichever, the effect is soft and elegant." He fixed me with one of his ghastly smiles. "You wear it well, my lady."

"How kind of you to say so," I replied. I searched for any reasonable conversation. "Are brocades your specialty?" I seemed to remember my father had decided to bring the man into his textile business for some talent or another.

But Jacopo's concentration had been drawn elsewhere, as the pair nearby who discussed the curia's holdings mentioned an astonishingly large sum of money.

"And you were saying? Signor Strozzi," I prodded him, annoyed at how tenuous was my hold on the attentions of my future husband.

"I was saying . . . ?" He became flustered with his complete lapse in memory of our conversation.

"Brocades are your specialty?" I prompted.

"Brocades and wool," he said, composing himself. "Many find wool a dull cloth, but I find it exciting." He spoke the last word with little conviction, but in fact a dull gleam had come into Jacopo's eyes. "It is all in the sheep, you see. . . ."

Just then I saw Romeo enter the room. I struggled to hold my attention on Signor Strozzi, who was now droning on about the grazing habits of English ewes, while I followed the movements of my lithe and handsome young poet as he wove single-mindedly through the crowd toward Cosimo de' Medici.

"Have you noticed that? Lady Juliet?"

"Oh, ah . . . so sorry. Have I noticed . . . ?"

"That English wool is softer, less scratchy on the skin?"

"You know, I have actually. I own a wine-colored wool gown that feels as smooth as silk."

"My point exactly," he said with what, in this gentleman,

must pass for delight. "If you show me that dress, I will be able to tell you the very county in which those sheep grazed."

"Really?" I coughed, covering my mouth, so I could turn away from Jacopo, for Romeo was now standing by Don Cosimo's side, waiting patiently while he spoke to his wife, Contessina. Then she moved away. I coughed again. "Signor Strozzi," I said in a weak voice, "would you be so kind as to pat me on the back?"

"Of course, of course," he said, and complied, though I noticed he took the opportunity to lean in the direction of the two men discussing the pope's finances.

Romeo had succeeded in gaining Don Cosimo's attention. From the Medici's expression I could see his young petitioner had wasted no time getting to his point. The older man's look was grave, but he was nodding his head as Romeo spoke, passion animating his face, his hands—those beautiful hands— expressively slicing and chopping the air before him.

"A few more pats and I will be fine," I said to Jacopo, who was as distracted as I.

Now Don Cosimo was speaking to Romeo, who listened with rapt attention to every syllable uttered. He looked as though he wished to reply, but Cosimo's monologue had become a lecture—one that was, in fact, growing louder so that even across the room, with music still playing, I heard several fragments—"ancient hatreds" and "unlikely reconciliation."

The two had attracted attention to themselves, and now I saw a group of young men pointing to Romeo. A snarling face. A fist raised. He had been recognized—Daniel in the lion's den!

Commotion ensued and as the room erupted, I used the diversion to slip away from Jacopo's ministrations. Romeo was making for the double doors, a gang of noble thugs gaining on him. I darted in from the other side, coming face-to-face with him for the briefest moment—long enough for him to revel in my need to see him.

His smile was brilliant. "The cathedral, noon on Wednesday," he said, then darted away and down the marble stairs.

I planted myself square in the middle of the doorway with an innocent smile on my face. The toughs were forced to stop short to keep from knocking me down. I cried out, as if terrified by the sight of them bearing down on me. They moved to the right and I feinted right. They tried the left and I, with a girlish giggle, moved left, guileless and confused.

By now Romeo had certainly made the street. I curtsied prettily and let the frustrated ruffians pass, satisfied with my impromptu performance.

I sidestepped to a window overlooking the street to claim one more vision of this daring soul, but was greeted by nothing more than sight of his pursuers bursting from the front door and running out into the empty, torchlit street, with futile looks this way and that.

Then all at once a white horse exploded from an alleyway into their midst, scattering the men like a handful of dice thrown on the ground. They loudly cursed the rider.

It was Romeo!

I thrilled as the mount reared up proudly on two legs and crashed down again. Then amid a terrible clattering of hooves on cobble, horse and master sped off into the dark.

I wondered how I could calmly return to Jacopo Strozzi—his grazing ewes and monetary distractions. All my thoughts were of this Monticecco man, so recently a stranger, now a star at the center of my universe. And I wondered at the time and place for the future assignation he had announced—the cathedral at noon on Wednesday. *Why the Duomo? And why in broad daylight?*

And then I knew. I sighed happily. Romeo. My poet. My friend. *Vita Nuova.*

A New Life!

Chapter Four

How many times that Wednesday morn I rushed between my bedroom's window on the street to its garden balcony, I do not know. The window was to see the arrival of Lucrezia in her litter come to fetch me, and the balcony to cool my brow, receive a chestful of calming air.

She could not be late. Not today!

I had many times pleaded with my father for leave to go to the cathedral, and just as many been refused. It was not to Mass I wished to go—for that purpose they surely would have given me leave—but to Friar Bartolomo's weekly "Symposium" on the subject of Dante Alighieri's works. It was a popular lecture, one attended by hundreds, sometimes a thousand, it was said, so beloved were his poems with his Florentine brethren.

It was this gathering to which Romeo Monticecco had invited me as he'd fled the Medici ballroom. I'd thought of nothing else since then, and worried myself sick with the thought of my father's certain prohibition.

Then a miracle on Tuesday.

The sinking of his ship full of goods forced a sudden trip to the port town of Pisa. I was left blessedly alone with Mama, who, while strict in many ways, was in others very malleable. I proceeded to bandy about the name of my friend Lucrezia, whom I had begged and convinced to come along to the symposium.

"Lucrezia has asked me to accompany her to the Duomo at Wednesday noon," I lied. "To the symposium," I reminded my absentminded mother. "Dante."

She had perked up instantly, for she approved very heartily of my friendship with a soon-to-be Medici, and the more time I spent in her company, the better. Then Mama's face fell.

"You know how often your father has said no to this."

"But we'll have a chaperone—hers. And we'll go in the Tornabuoni litter." I spoke conspiratorially. "The whole town is still talking about the Medici ball. Lucrezia is so admired as a great lady."

"Yes, she is." Mama pursed her lips into a tight bud as she did when she was thinking hard. "Well, I suppose it will be all right. But you must dress properly. Something demure."

I had won my permission.

Now I was peering out my front window in nervous anticipation. I wore a sky blue silk *guarnacca*, its bodice so high that not an inch of bosom could be seen, and a thick rolled headdress that covered my hair. I bit my lips to pink them, and slapped my cheeks to do the same. The use of cosmetics was frowned upon in my father's house, and in any event none would be proper for a visit to the Duomo at noon.

Then I saw them—four liveried bearers carrying the wide, gilded Tornabuoni litter. I raced down the steps, calling good-bye to Mama, and was out the door and settled breathlessly next to Lucrezia in the space of a minute. Our chaperone, old Signora Munao, sat across from us and stayed very silent, as was her place to do.

"Very ladylike," Lucrezia said, noting my perspiring face and already lopsided headdress.

"Fix it, please." I turned to her. She righted the rolled coif, tucking a lock that had gone astray back under it. With her handkerchief she blotted my brow and upper lip.

I felt suddenly guilty. I'd not told Lucrezia of my rendezvous with Romeo. Indeed, I had told her nothing of him at all.

"I wonder what circle of hell Friar Bartolomo will be expounding upon today," I said, rather than reveal my true reason for our outing.

"No wonder you're warm," she muttered, seemingly unconcerned with the subject of Dante's *Inferno.* "Any higher and your bodice would be up to your eyes."

"Mama worries endlessly about decorum."

"Why did she even let you come?"

"Well . . . I . . ."

"And why, suddenly, is the symposium something you so desperately need to hear?" Her tone was suspicious. Lucrezia Tornabuoni was a young woman of rare intellect and spotless instinct. Something was afoot and she knew it.

This was the time for my revelation. But I could not bring myself to reveal it. Instead I quoted, full of passion:

> *O you possessed of sturdy intellects,*
> *observe the teaching that is hidden here*
> *beneath the veil of verses so obscure. . . .*

"All right, all right," Lucrezia cried in mock despair. "To the Duomo, then."

The litter came round a corner into the cathedral square and we exited into the great circular shadow of Brunelleschi's architectural masterpiece. I had been nine years old the day of the famous church's consecration, its massive egg-shaped dome the grandest in the world. Pope Eugenius had come from Rome for the celebration and spectacle, as had two hundred thousand souls from everywhere.

Now as we entered the enormous marble edifice, the crowd seemed sparse in comparison with that day, yet every face seemed eager and cheerful, and all moved quickly to the front altar in order to better hear the friar's lecture.

There were some men who looked askance at us, two young ladies—not matrons—in this place, but we moved quickly, speaking to no one. With our chaperone trailing behind, I steered my friend to the right where the now-empty choir was, and we took our places near the side aisle.

I had no knowledge of Romeo's plan, indeed no promise of his coming. If he did come, would he find me? If found . . . what then? All I knew was a heart thumping insistently in my breast, my senses afire, and memory of a strong, warm hand clutching my own.

Now came Friar Bartolomo before the altar, with tonsured head and humble in his rough brown robe. "Welcome, all," he began with a broad smile.

The crowd replied in kind with friendly, familiar ease. I thought it strange, a man of God in the Lord's House, more kindly tutor than priest.

"As I told you when we last met, we would today diverge from our usual travels." He went on in a playfully tremulous voice. "We have spent many tortured weeks in all the circles of Dante's hell."

This caused the audience to laugh with delight.

"So we shall climb up from the bowels of the earth to the maestro's other masterwork, *Vita Nuova*."

I think my jaw dropped then, for there was no doubt that Romeo had known this day's agenda. Known it would please me no end.

A perfect invitation.

I chanced a look around for him but saw only a sea of faces smiling with anticipation. I craned my neck the other way and found myself caught in Lucrezia's stare.

"Looking for someone?" she said. That tone of suspicion again.

"Before you settle into complacency," the friar continued, saving me from another lie to my friend, "before you feel yourself freed entirely from darkness and pain, let me tell you the subject of our explorations this day." He opened a small volume I took to be *Vita Nuova*, turning to a page marked with a ribbon. "The subject is death."

The jovial murmurings of the crowd were silenced as all attended the cleric's words.

"Have we not—every one of us—suffered at the cruel hand of the Reaper?"

There were numerous utterings from the assembled, agreement and consensus.

"Dante, himself, suffered a most wrenching loss with the

death of his Beatrice. The poet wrote"—the friar read now—
" *'So much grief had become the destroyer of my soul.'* He was a man who," he quoted, "*'died a death of tears.'* "

The gentleman beside me nodded with deep understanding.

"He was so bereft he became *'jealous of whosoever dies,'*" Bartolomo went on. "And yet, my friends, Dante Alighieri, torn apart by grief, gave us instruction in graceful acceptance of loss. In the depths of his misery he writes of seeing Beatrice's ladies covering her head with a white veil and it seemed that his deceased lover's face was—listen to these words—'*so filled with joyous acceptance that it said to me: I am contemplating the fountainhead of peace.'*" Friar Bartolomo looked up and smiled beatifically at his students. "Death is a '*fountainhead of peace.'* Can we not all take comfort in that image?"

From everywhere I heard men calling, "Yes, yes."

The teacher found another ribboned page. "His Beatrice, he said, '*has ascended to high heaven into a realm where angels live in peace.'*"

A long sigh was heard behind me.

" *'Her tender soul, perfectly filled with grace, now lives with glory in a worthy place.'*"

A man in front of me put his face in his hands and wept unabashedly.

Bartolomo went on.

> *The pleasure of her beauty,*
> *having removed itself from mortal sight,*
> *was transformed into beauty of the soul*
> *spreading throughout the heavens. . . .*

He looked up. *"'This lady had become a citizen of eternal life.'"*

Suddenly a voice from the choir rail a few feet before me called out, "Good friar, why of all his subjects in a book Dante titled *New Life* do you choose to speak only of a lady's death?"

My heart leapt nearly from my chest.

It was Romeo.

That deep, melodious voice had come to be familiar to me in one short meeting. I twisted sharply to see him, but then many did the same, for they wished to know the face of the man who spoke out so boldly in the friar's symposium.

And there he was! My Romeo dressed in a short blue tunic with wide flowing sleeves.

"Why not speak of love?" he persisted. *"'Joyous love.'* What our maestro called *'the very summit of bliss.'"*

"Only because, young sir," the friar answered mildly, "my chosen topic was death."

"But perhaps the good people of Florence have had enough of death. They might prefer a happier topic." Romeo looked around at the assembled.

Everyone was silent, unused—it appeared—to one of their ranks defying their teacher.

"Are there none here that are"—and Romeo quoted—*"'utterly consumed for the sake of a lady'*? Who *'travel on the road of love'*?"

I felt a gush of words unbidden, yet unstoppable, burst from my throat. "Here is one *'on the road of sighs'* who is calling, *'Love, help your faithful one'*!"

Romeo turned to find me. He was beaming and triumphant. Our eyes met and held.

A horrified Lucrezia whispered, "Juliet . . ."

But now the congregation, shocked that a young, unmarried lady was here and, even more so, that the lady had spoken and knew Dante so well, was all agog. Excitement rippled the room. And grumbling, too.

But I had grown very bold and asked the friar, "Did not Dante write in the vernacular so his words might be understood by ladies who found Latin verses difficult to comprehend?"

"Yes, that is true," Bartolomo said.

But this audience of men was not at all happy. They began to talk loudly among themselves.

"Let her speak!" Romeo cried.

The place reluctantly quieted.

My mouth was dry cotton, but I rose to the occasion. *"I have a vision of love . . . ,'"* I recited, my voice echoing grandly in the cavernous chamber, *"' . . . a miracle too rich and strange to behold.'"*

"'Here in my unbearable bliss . . . ,'" Romeo shouted in exultant reply, *"' . . . all my thoughts are telling me of love!'"*

Someone cried, "Go on, go on!"

"'Whenever and wherever she appears,'" he spoke in a voice filled with wonder, *"'in anticipation of her marvelous greeting, I hold no man my enemy.'"*

The place rumbled with agreement of that sentiment. Love did make a heart more peaceful.

All fear fled my soul and now in the midst of hundreds I spoke with Dante's words, but only to Romeo. *"'Love's power is insane'*!"

He threw back his head and laughed.

"Brava! Bravo!" someone called. Then other voices of approbation joined them.

"Good people," called the friar. "Good people, attend me!"

Everyone quieted.

"I can see that the topic of love makes many hearts race. But take pity on a poor old man who has prepared his lecture on a somewhat more grim note, but one most worthy of discussion. Perhaps next week we will take up the subject of Dante and Beatrice's romance. But for now . . ."

We did return to Friar Bartolomo's chosen theme, and for the rest of the afternoon Romeo and I remained silent and respectful. As the talk was of *Vita Nuova*, it was infinitely pleasurable, and I learned many things that I had not, in my solitary study of it, observed before.

So engrossed had I become that when the session ended, I had not noticed Romeo's departure from his place at the choir rail. I looked all around for him as we made for the cathedral door, but found no one but my cousin Marco.

He fixed me with an impish grin. "You kept your love of Dante, and Dante's love, very quiet, cousin. I never knew."

I kissed him on both cheeks.

"But did you know your sparring partner was that interloper we chased from Don Cosimo's ball? A Monticecco?"

"Was he?" I said, pretending ignorance. "You must not have caught him, for he seemed unscathed."

"If he comes close to any of us again, I promise you he will be very scathed." He eyed my high-necked gown. "Who is dressing you these days? The Sisters of Mercy? My aunt must believe you're in danger of becoming a fallen woman."

Marco was too close to the truth for comfort.

"I have to find Lucrezia," I said, and left him. Making my

way through the crush, I was suddenly, delightfully confronted by Romeo, his gaze warm and enveloping.

"You are magnificent," he said, and without flourish slipped something into my hand. I briefly looked down, only to find, when I had lifted my eyes again, that he had disappeared into the crowd.

It was a rolled paper I now held in my hand, which I surreptitiously and quickly unfurled. Its written title was "Dante's God of Love," and the well-drawn sketch of colored chalks above it showed the virile, handsome God of Love holding in his arms a woman, naked except for a filmy red robe trailing to the ground.

I quickly rerolled it and tucked this most subversive drawing into my sleeve before hurrying after Lucrezia, all the while my heart threatening to burst the confines of my breast.

Romeo

$\mathcal{I}$ ndeed, Juliet had been magnificent. Like no other woman I had ever had chance to know. I stood, invisible at the cathedral door, rendered still and stunned by the memory of this great lady's being.

She had proven bold at the Medici ball, conversing unabashedly and alone in the garden for far longer than was seemly, and then cleverly held off those ruffians at the door. As I'd ridden away, my pursuers shouting curses after me, the clatter of furious hooves on empty cobble streets, the cool wind stinging my flushed cheeks, the feel of racing blood and tensed sinews that had powered my dangerous escape, all fell away. Sounds grew muted. Vision blurred. My mind stilled even as I crossed the river and my mount took us up into the southern hills.

This girl I had met, this woman, daughter of my enemy—Juliet—it was memory of her in the Medici courtyard that had silenced the city sounds, disappeared the world around me, rendered me empty, yet filled to overflowing. Blissful and terror-struck all at once.

Juliet. Those eyes that had steady held my gaze, never shy, never downcast. Unflinching. The curve of her rosy lips as she spoke, no *bantered*—audacious as a university boy. Her throat, long and pale in the moonlight. The round pillows of her breasts that heaved so gently as she laughed.

I had known girls before. Some beautiful. Some plain. But all ordinary. They simpered. They giggled. They failed to excite. But this Juliet, standing there so bold in that garden, was infinitely thrilling, brighter than the brightest star in the blackness of heaven.

Then I remembered my own stars. The woman they'd foretold for me. Is it possible? *This, my family's enemy, my wife-to-be?* All of a sudden like a dam bursting, blood came rushing through my veins in a great torrent, roaring in my ears. *Juliet, my fated one.*

Then in a mysterious passage of time I was home, my horse groomed and stabled for the night. I had walked through the door, my mother smiling a welcome, her long hair loose about the shoulders of her night shift. The sight of her shocked me. She was the only woman I had, in my life, ever loved.

"Mama," I'd whispered and kissed her cheeks, blushing behind her sight, strangely mortified. *Am I worthy of Juliet*, I wondered, *worthy as my father was of my mother?*

Now as I stood in the shadow of the cathedral door I recalled the sight of Juliet Capelletti under the great dome amid all of Dante's devotees, so brave she would shout aloud, replying to my plaintive calls. She shocked me. Truly rocked the ground beneath my feet. Made the air shimmer with her power and grace. This woman had slipped free the prison of rules that governed us all and met me halfway to paradise.

I am in love, I thought. *For the first time, in love!*

Then I saw him—Jacopo Strozzi—exiting the church with the last of the Dante crowd. He moved within it, but his eyes said *he was unmoved*—that our poet had made no mark on his soul. Why was he here? Surely he could not have known of Juliet's unplanned attendance. Had he come to win her affection? Perhaps he knew of her love for Dante and wished to make his bride happy by teaching himself the words of love.

Then I grew cold. He had not expected her to be at the symposium. Yet she *was* there. And she had proven herself a public shame, exchanging loving barbs with a stranger. Had he also seen me running like a fugitive from the ball? Certainly he must have heard later that the fleeing man had been a Monticecco. His partner's enemy.

And yes, now I saw his eyes were black with fury. *He did know.* What a danger to Juliet! The Strozzi claimed nearly the strength and riches of the Medici but unlike Don Cosimo's family, it was infamous for its ruthlessness, even brutality. Now I could see in this Strozzi's face a terrible choler, one that my beloved lady and I had, by our actions, unknowingly provoked.

Then all of a sudden that expression changed—anger to fear, almost cowering. And I saw its cause.

A matron in the finest somber brown silk, her face shades lighter but still muddy, approaching him.

"Mama," Jacopo said, and kissed her hand. "Coming to confession?"

I hid myself half behind the great door with one ear to the conversation.

"What is wrong with you, Jacopo?" Allessandra Strozzi demanded. Her voice lacked any of what I knew to be maternal warmth. "You look as though you've swallowed a melon whole."

"It's nothing," he said.

"I saw your 'bride' leaving." She said the word with unaccountable disdain. "With the Tornabuoni girl. Now, *that* one would have been a wife worth having."

Jacopo sighed, then set his face in a stony grimace.

"I hear the dowry is enormous. Oh, if I had just moved more quickly, more cleverly . . ."

"Mama, please . . ."

"Your brothers wish you to attend them at their office this afternoon."

"I cannot. I meet with Capello within the hour."

This time her look was closer to disgust. She sighed dramatically. "I fear you have chosen your new partner as badly as you've chosen your wife. But who am I to say?" She turned to the cathedral doors. "Your brothers will be disappointed."

She disappeared into the church, leaving Jacopo shaken, and I thought near tears. Humiliated twice in the space of an hour, he managed to compose himself, and his trembling reasserted itself into bitter black.

"Women," he cursed, and strode away.

Danger, Juliet! I silently cried. *This man is poison.*

Then I cringed, thinking of my family's hatred of hers. Was I any less lethal to her well-being than Jacopo?

Emerging from behind the door, I let the sun beat down on my head, praying for its power to gift me with intelligence, a way to win Juliet and live with her in the light, blessed by all, cursed by none.

I would find a way. I would.

Chapter Five

"Have you any idea what a spectacle you made of yourself?" Lucrezia was bristling as we put distance between ourselves and our chaperone, walking down to the Arno as our bearers set a simple picnic on the riverbank. On a normal day my friend and I would be strolling arm in arm, our heads together, sharing a story or a laugh. But this was no ordinary day.

And I was in no ordinary state of mind.

"What harm have I done?" I replied, more a retort than a question. "I spoke with intelligence of Dante in a Dante symposium."

"No, Juliet. Before a huge crowd of Florentines, you engaged quite passionately in a dialogue with a stranger . . . about love."

To this I had neither answer nor retort, for it was altogether true.

"He *was* a stranger, was he not?" Lucrezia asked, prescient distrust creeping into her voice.

The moment of truth had arrived.

"No, not precisely."

"O, sweet Jesu." She turned me to face her. "Friend, what have you done?"

"Nothing. *Nothing.* Honestly, Lucrezia, there have been no improprieties." I couldn't help smiling to myself. "At least not yet."

"Juliet!"

"You asked for the truth. Now you have it."

"Who is he?"

I was rendered silent again, anticipating a further explosion at my answer, but there was no avoiding it. Lucrezia was searing me with her eyes.

"His name is Romeo."

"I know no Romeos. Is he Florentine?"

"His family is. He's been away at university. In Padua. Before that, he lived in Verona with his uncles."

"I cannot believe this. Next you will be telling me the size of his foot. How do you know this man?"

I swallowed hard. "I met him at your betrothal ball. We spoke for a time in the garden."

"Unchaperoned?"

"Yes, unchaperoned. But all we did was talk. Nothing untoward happened."

"How could 'nothing untoward' have happened that night if its consequence was your outrageous display this afternoon?"

"There is something . . . ," I said very softly.

"What?"

"There is something you should know about Romeo." Then I went quiet, paralyzed with trepidation.

"Tell me, Juliet."

"He is Romeo Monticecco."

Lucrezia grew suddenly flushed. She said nothing, but I knew her mind was working furiously. Then she said, "That disturbance at the ball. I heard it was a Monticecco whom our kinsman chased from the house."

"That was he."

"*After* you and he spent time alone, unchaperoned, in the Medici garden 'simply talking'!"

Defiance suddenly flared in me. "If you want the whole truth . . . something more did happen." I held Lucrezia's searching gaze. "Love happened."

My friend turned away then, confused and overcome. I gathered my thoughts, for I knew there must be further explanation.

"Oh, Lucrezia, I did not go seeking for this. It found *me*." I went around to face her. She looked ill with worry.

"You laid yourself open for this disaster," she said, "refusing to be satisfied with the marriage your family arranged. Seeking private conversation with a stranger in a dark garden . . ."

"I stumbled in the *bassadanza*. He took me out for air"—I was grasping for explanations—"but when we unmasked—"

Lucrezia groaned.

"When we unmasked, I discovered before me the most beautiful man, not only of face and form, but of mind. Oh, my friend, there was such . . . concordance between us. He seemed to *know* me, and I him." I was lost in remembering that scented evening and spoke as if in a dream. "We met on the common ground of *Vita Nuova* and danced the sweetest dance there."

"Until you learned his name."

"He'd come that night to seek audience with Don Cosimo," I said, trying to make sense of things.

"And what could his business have possibly been? His house is deeply mistrusted by the Medici, and despised by yours."

"He came to make peace on his family's behalf."

"He was sent by his father?"

"I think he came of his own accord."

Lucrezia sighed heavily. I took both her hands in mine.

"Please, please do not judge me harshly."

Her eyes flashed with hurt and anger. "Should I not judge you for using me without my knowledge today to help you meet your lover? You made me your fool."

"I'm sorry for that, truly I am! I've been wild with such longings since I met him. I have not slept except fitfully, and then I dream of him. And I dream in verse, words flowing into words, streams and rivers of them, and all with the theme of love. When I wake, I try to remember the poems, but they're gone, disappeared. And all I have left are memories of the feel of his hand, the sound of his voice, the shape of his lips. I remember every word spoken in the garden. Every syllable. And when I am not lost in memory, I'm raging against the Fates for having placed before me the perfect man, the ideal lover—and he is my father's greatest enemy!"

Lucrezia regarded me with a steady eye. "Juliet, forgive me. I have been hard on you when, indeed, the Fates have dealt unfairly with your happiness and future."

I felt tears welling with her words of sympathy.

"But you must think seriously about what you must do . . .

and what you must not do. The more your father feels your re-belliousness, the harder he will make it for you."

Signora Munao called to us to come back to the blanket on the ground, now laid with our meal. Lucrezia waved her away.

"But"—I was growing agitated—"I desire Romeo. I want him in my bed!"

"Shhh!"

Signora Munao was staring at the pair of us, wondering about the commotion.

I tried to calm myself as I said, "Everyone knows that for a woman to conceive in the act of coition she, as well as the man, must be satisfied. Is that not true?"

"Of course it's true."

"I know that I will never be satisfied with Jacopo Strozzi. I can barely stand to have him touch my hand. So he will not give me children, and what is a marriage without children?"

"Juliet," she pleaded.

"So why marry him at all?"

"And what do you propose instead? Disown your family? Forget your blood? Run away with your lover? Live in poverty and disgrace?"

"Do you think I am not haunted every moment by those thoughts?"

Signora Munao was almost upon us, looking very cross.

"Just promise me you will not see him again before you marry. Please, I am your true friend, and I know that what you most desperately wish for will only bring tragedy down on your house. Promise me."

"Signorinas," our old chaperone snapped in an aggravated tone, "I am seeing a lack of decorum here. Raised voices. Flushed cheeks." She addressed Lucrezia: "Your mother and your husband-to-be would be most displeased if they learned of this public display. Now come and have your meal quietly and begin acting like the gentlewomen you are."

"Yes, signora," Lucrezia said.

"My humble apologies," I added, and we followed her back to the blanket.

In the end, I realized, I had promised Lucrezia nothing.

Chapter Six

Here I lie in the arms of Love red robe trailing down O sweet God
of Love lift me high let me fall let me drown in your sea in your sighs
whispered now whispered soft as I die . . . I awoke from the rushing
river of verse to the sound of muted thumping. I opened my
eyes but saw nothing save moonlight streaming in through my
balcony window. Another thump . . . on that door.

I rose, pulling a light robe over my shift, and padded across
the cool stone. The screech of the handle and hinge was loud in
the silent night. The air that struck my face and breast was very
soft, very mild.

With my first footfall outside I stepped on a fig. Saw half a
dozen at the base of the door, fallen from an ancient tree whose
several muscular limbs hung languorously over my loggia. The
thumps had been figs falling on the door. The thought of that
fruit made me crave one. A nearby branch was groaning with it,
and I reached out.

A sudden darting hand snatched my wrist and held it tight.

I shrieked in fright.

"Juliet! Do not fear."

I knew the voice at once. I looked into the shadow of the leafy limb and there lay Romeo, all spread along the length of it. He released his grip. I stepped back.

"You've been lying in wait," I accused, regaining my composure. "Throwing figs at my door."

"Guilty."

I was lost for words, an unusual state of affairs.

"Are you angry?" he said.

"No . . . perhaps worried you are deranged."

He laughed at that.

"Keep your voice down."

"Sorry."

"Should I ask why you're here?"

"Do you need to ask?"

I nodded.

"I find it useless trying to sleep," he answered. "I'm kept awake by thoughts of you."

I suddenly felt myself naked and pulled the robe around my thin shift. His eyes were on me, unrelenting.

"You look like a wood nymph," I said. "Come down from there." I backed away and let him jump to the balcony. He was graceful as a cat. Now we were face-to-face. But there was no Medici ball up a flight of stairs here, nor a church full of Florentines surrounding us. We were alone.

"So my missiles woke you?"

I was unsure how to act. I felt I should be indignant at his overbold visit, embarrassed at my state of undress.

Alarmingly, I was neither.

"I was dreaming a love poem when you woke me," I admitted.

"*Dreaming* a poem?"

"Have you never done that?"

"No. Verse comes hard to my mind." The moonlight was cool, but his gaze was searing. "Tell me your poem."

"I cannot. It was an endless stream of words." Then I remembered. "But the God of Love was holding me in his arms. I wore a trailing red gown."

"Like the sketch—chapter three!" he cried, then recited, "*'In his arms there lay a figure asleep and naked except for a crimson cloth loosely wrapping it.'*"

"Oh dear, I seem to plagiarize, even in my sleep."

But Romeo did not smile. "Did the God of Love also bid you eat my burning heart?"

My breath erupted in a sharp gasp. "You leap very handily from Dante and his beloved to you and me," I said.

"Should I not?"

"You should slow down."

He looked chastised and backed away. Sat on the balcony wall. "What should I say, my lady?" he asked with courtesy.

"Tell me what Don Cosimo said when you talked to him about peace."

"He spoke of history," Romeo said, remembering. "Bad blood between the Guelf and Ghibelline factions all those years ago. What a senseless conflict that was—country folk who followed the emperor, city folk who gave allegiance to the pope. Meaningless hatred. Centuries of feuding."

I nodded for Romeo to go on.

"That war was done a hundred years ago, but when Cosimo

came to power, the hatred flared again. Two camps formed, jealous ghosts of the Ghibellines and Guelfs: those who rallied round the city-bound Medici—your father is one of these—and others, like my family, who lived outside the walls, hating Don Cosimo and all his friends and retainers. But he says more fault is rightly laid at my family's doorstep."

"Is that true?"

He looked downcast. "I fear it is."

"What did he tell you to do?"

"If I manage to cool tempers enough—my father, my uncles, the other anti-Medicians—Don Cosimo will bring them to his table, broker a peace."

"Did he say how this could be done? Was any sage advice given?"

"It might have been forthcoming, but I was chased from the room before I could hear it." He grinned now. "And thank you, Lady Juliet, for helping my escape."

I smiled flirtatiously. "How could I allow those ruffians to injure a peacemaker?"

His laugh was rueful. "Some peacemaker . . ."

Gently I said, "You spoke to your father?"

"And was threatened with disownment if I uttered another word." He looked down at his feet, mortified. "And yes, he did sink your father's cargo."

"Oh, Romeo!" No words could have wrenched my heart more.

"Never mind," he said. "Let us talk of pleasanter things. You are a *poet*. That amazes me."

"It should not. Women own brains, and fingers to hold a quill. Have you never heard of Christine de Pisan?"

"Of course. We studied her at university."

"Was she not a woman?"

"She was, and a great writer. A contentious writer. A poet. But Christine de Pisan was a widow," said Romeo, "who only began writing to support her children. Even she believed a woman's place was in the home—that public discourse was a male domain."

"She thought her life 'a mutation of Fortune,' " I agreed. "She claims she became 'an honorary man.' "

Romeo moved closer to me. Without invitation he threaded his fingers through my hair. "Is that what you wish for yourself?"

Something melted inside me. "I have no wish to be a man," I said, "honorary or otherwise. I only wish to write."

"Do you wish to love?" he whispered.

He was so bold. Yet I nodded.

"Close your eyes, Juliet."

Without thought or fear I did as he asked. I believed I would soon feel his lips on mine. But instead he lifted my hand and, with infinite delicacy, pushed back the sleeve of my gown. Then I felt warm breath on the tenderest inside of my forearm.

"I believe in the senses," he murmured, sending tiny waves of air across my skin. "Here is touch."

I shivered with delight. "Give me another," I demanded.

"This one is mine," he said, releasing my hand and moving away, but in the next moment he was behind me, his face buried in my hair at the back of my neck. He inhaled deeply. "Aaahh," he sighed. "The natural perfume of Juliet."

I tilted back my head to lean upon his and there we remained, still and breathing. Did he know that I wished his hands to circle my waist, slide across the naked skin of my breasts?

"Listen," he said softly into the shell of my ear.

I did, my eyes still closed. "It is the nightingale," I said. Its trilling notes in the darkness had never sounded so sweet to me. How was it that all at once I heard magic in that song?

I felt his arms on my shoulders, turning me a half-turn. Then with both hands enclosing my head, he tilted it skyward. "Open your eyes."

I did as I was told. There before me at what seemed as close as arm's length was the full moon, a dark brace of clouds skittering across its bright and shadowed surface.

"Touch. Smell. Sound. Sight," he uttered. "All so easily gratified."

"What of taste?" I said, pressing him.

"Ah, now you become greedy."

I turned to face him. "It *is* one of the senses."

"True."

Again, I thought that he would kiss me, to this way prove the fifth sensation. Instead he turned and, searching the fruit-heavy branch, snapped from it a fat ripe fig. When he faced me again, he held in his hands its two halves.

"Were there more light," he said, "we would see the luscious . . . pink . . . flesh." His voice caressed the words. Then holding my eyes with his, he took a half in his palm and brought it to his mouth. I grew suddenly alarmed as he buried his lips in the soft fig's center and closed his eyes, ecstatic.

"My lord!" I cried, breaking the spell.

His eyes sprang open and he gazed without apology into mine. "I think I should go. I've overstayed my welcome."

"No, no."

But he had leapt to the balcony wall and swung his body

up into the tree. Hanging loose from the branch by one arm, he leaned down and held out his hand to me. The fig's other half was cupped in his palm. "For you, my lady—the final sense."

I took it, words failing me once again.

"When you taste it," he said, "think of me."

Then he was gone, all rustling leaves and shadows.

I stood stupidly, staring at the half fruit, and, smiling, brought it to my lips.

Chapter Seven

It was the custom that all women friends of a bride should keep her company during the first meal at the house of the bridegroom. In the case of Chaterina Valenti, this was the house of her bridegroom's father, where the couple had taken up residence.

It was a run-down house, dark and badly furnished, the faint smell of mold and rot pervading all. As we silently ate our meal at the long wooden table, Chaterina's father-in-law, grunting as he chewed, threw bits of meat and whole bones to two mange-ridden dogs lounging in the straw at his feet. Her husband, Antonio, who had clearly learned manners from his loutish father, smiled at the poor girl with bits of food stuck between his teeth.

His mother, Mona Ginetta, to which neither man paid the slightest attention, was a grim harridan who regarded all her guests with equal disdain. Her house was poor and her men coarse, and I guessed she wished that they were not so embarrassingly on display to the gentlewomen of Florence.

Making the occasion bleaker still was the dour priest who had been invited to share the meal—another custom recently popular—as though a man of religion at a family's table made them pious. This cleric, after he had spoken the blessing, never said another word. He did not bother to hide his boredom, nor had he bothered to wash. He was rank with perspiration and smelled as though he had stepped in excrement in the street.

Chaterina was much relieved when Antonio and his father, trailed by the dogs and the priest, left the table with barely a "*Buona sera*," but I watched her face crumple with disappointment when her mother-in-law stayed firm in her chair. The sour-faced woman had, for the first time, been given leave to assert her dominion in the household. Chaterina was, from this moment on, the dominated.

"Has everyone had enough to eat?" our friend asked us, the first words she had spoken the whole meal through, and reached for a slice of bread. In a flash her hand was slapped away by Mona Ginetta, who fixed the girl with a withering glare, silencing all of us before we could answer.

"You've had two pieces already," she accused. "And a double portion of macaroni. My son will not look kindly on a wife going to fat." Then she looked around the table, wondering, I supposed, if she dared insult any of the rest of us.

"Sorry, Mona Ginetta, sorry," the daughter-in-law said. "I'll be more attentive to what I eat."

"It's funny," I said lightly but pointedly, "Chaterina is always the one we worry is too thin."

"That is true," Lucrezia piped in with an encouraging smile at our beleaguered friend. "She's got the tiniest waist. We're all jealous of her."

As everyone else chimed in with their agreement, Mona Ginetta began to seethe.

"I have a gift for you," Elena Rinaldi said, drawing the conversation onto pleasanter ground and pushing a small wrapped box toward her hostess. When the rest of us began speaking excitedly, Mona Ginetta pushed back her chair with a decisive scrape and stood. To Chaterina she said, "I will leave you to your guests." In a moment she was thankfully gone, but her leave had not purged the room of darkness. We were horribly aware that this shrew stood at the center of Chaterina's future.

And all I could think of was Allessandra Strozzi.

"Dare we ask about the wedding night?" Maria piped in, keeping her voice low. Antonio might come from a boorish family, but he was half the age of Maria's betrothed.

I did not think Chaterina's face could fall any further, but I was wrong. She pushed her lips tight together to keep from crying, but tears still sprang to her eyes. "Awful," she managed.

Lucrezia reached out and placed a hand on Chaterina's.

"I was afraid," she went on, "and I told him so . . . expecting that he would . . . be gentle." She hid her face in her cupped hands. "He was not. He pounded hard. Went on and on. It seemed like forever."

It pained me to hear her continue, for I knew I had no bright banter to buoy her, no advice to share.

"It hurt. Terribly," she said, her voice cracking. "Then he . . ." She hesitated. ". . . pulled away. Out. He was angry. Disgusted. Told me I was 'dry.' Told me I had hurt *him*."

Chaterina went silent then, and we were all still, battered by her account.

"I have just the thing," Constanza Marello suddenly said.

What in heaven's name could the Spinster of Florence have to offer the miserable newlywed?

"I have four sisters," she went on. "All married. They talk among themselves. Endlessly. About what goes on . . . under the sheets." She leered so lasciviously we broke into laughter, and the unhappy spell was shattered. Constanza beckoned to us and we leaned in to the center of the table. "There is an oil they use . . . for lubrication. My eldest sister's husband is endowed like a stallion, she tells us. This oil 'eases the passage.' "

A hopeful smile played on Chaterina's lips. "Could you get me some?" she said, then added with a conspiratorial grin, "Though I shall never have to worry about a horse-sized *cazzo*. More like a billy goat."

Everyone roared at that, and the evening went on in much better cheer.

Later, Lucrezia and I stood outside waiting for our litters to be brought around. It was a mild evening that reminded me of another such night.

"Why are you smiling like that?" she asked me.

I hesitated before answering. "He came to my balcony."

"Oh no . . . Juliet!"

"It was lovely, Lucrezia. He was a perfect gentleman."

"Alone on your garden balcony in the middle of the night?"

I said nothing.

"And you would therefore have been in your shift?"

"With a robe."

She made a huffing sound.

"It's all right, Lucrezia."

"It is not all right. Nothing has changed. You are soon to be betrothed to another man. The Monticecco and the Capelletti are still enemies."

"I know that. And I know how these things are. Have always been. But suddenly it occurs to me—a strange thought perhaps—that people who love each other should marry each other. That *this* is how it should be."

Lucrezia stared at me as though I were raving, then said, "You're always going on about Dante and Beatrice and their great romance. But in truth, he barely spoke to her. His love was in his head. In his breast. In his verse. And that was enough."

"It's not enough for me!"

Lucrezia shook her head sharply. "Dear God, could you have found any young man less suitable for this . . . this . . ."

"Affair of the heart," I finished for her.

"How can it end well?"

"End well!" I cried. "Has Chaterina's arranged marriage ended well?" I faced Lucrezia squarely. "So you, my dearest friend, wish for me the sad nuptial bed I will certainly share with Jacopo Strozzi? You wish me a life altogether barren of love? I will not thank you for that!"

I was glad my litter had arrived. I flung myself and my anger into its darkness, but Lucrezia's words had begun to smother me, smother all my bright hopes.

No, I ordered myself, *you must fight to keep them alive!* Dante was right. Love's power *was* insane. Suddenly there was strength flowing into me, through me. I felt my fists clenching and my spine straightening. Tears of passionate resolve flowed down my cheeks.

"I choose madness," I said aloud, in hopes that the God of Love was listening. "I choose madness."

Romeo

The surgery was proving brutal, and the patient was unforgiving. My saw was finding resistance, and I heard the screeching of the blade on dry, brittle wood as an old man's shrieks of pain. I had not wished to cut such a gracious limb from so majestic an olive, one of the few in our orchard that was perhaps alive when the boy Plato was still following Socrates around Athens as his student. But the large branch was dead and hung so high above the ground that it would certainly kill a worker if it suddenly gave way and fell on him.

Discomfiting as this chore was proving, I could not help but revel at the perfection of the summer day, the joy of my homecoming from Padua to the orchard of my youth, and thoughts of Juliet, which on the one hand soothed me as did a bath in the warm mineral springs of Abano Terme, and on the other inflamed my senses like a hard ride through the hills on my beautiful Blanca.

It had surprised me how easily I had resumed my place here

and how little I missed the life of learning at university. Perhaps it was facile of me, but in my heart I believed there was more to be learned from the countryside, the Tuscan weather, the olives and the vines of my father's farm, than from a Latin master droning on inside the airless walls of a classroom.

I did not disdain my education. Without it I would surely have been a dolt. I would never have known Dante or tried my hand at poetry, and would, therefore, never have found the perfect way to court and win the affection of Juliet, sweet Juliet— the woman my stars had, on the day of my birth, promised me.

I had ruminated much on that thought of late. How a scholar versed in the science of the heavens could, with his charts and numerical calculations, using the moment and place of a person's birth and the movements of celestial bodies, foretell with such accuracy the disposition of a person's mind, and what his life had in store for him.

Of all the things Paolo Toscanelli had told my father of his youngest son's nature and future, my finding "a woman of great fortitude" had intrigued me the most. As a boy who had no interest in girls save teasing his sisters, I was baffled by the prophecy. As a youth at university finding comfort in the arms of the few prostitutes I could afford, Toscanelli's remarkable woman seemed as far away as the stars that had foretold her.

When I'd brazenly taken myself that evening to the Palazzo Bardi to remonstrate with Don Cosimo, she was the very last thing on my mind. And yet when I first laid eyes on Juliet swooping and spinning as she danced the Virgins' Dance, heard her laugh above all the others, thought the flick of her cymbaled wrists the most graceful and her face the most astonishingly lovely, I knew that she was my woman of great fortitude. She was the woman fated and foretold.

She was mine.

The making of peace between my family and the silk merchant Capelletti had at first been a mere challenge to overcome. Why my father had become a vandal was a mystery to me, and an annoyance to my soul. The quiet and gentility of our lives had been defiled by senseless violence.

Every time I had tried to discuss the feud with Papa, he had slammed the door closed, shutting me out as if I were a child. It angered me, certainly. At twenty-five I was man enough to be privy to any and all family business.

But once I met Juliet, had fallen into the deep well of those eyes, sparred playfully with her in a way that a man does only with another man ... and learned to my horror that she was Capelletti's daughter, that simple challenge to arrange peace between our families became as vital to my survival as the beating of my heart.

After my escape from the Medici ball I approached Papa again for an explanation, demanding to know if he'd sunk Capelletti's cargo, and again was rebuked, this time more harshly than before. Even Mama was shocked by the virulence of his tone with me. It upset her, made her ill for a time. The pain in every joint became unbearable, and she was bedridden.

Her suffering brought Papa instantly to his senses. He cared for her lovingly, allowing no one but himself to feed and dress and bathe her. She recovered under his tender ministrations, and of late a kind of serenity had settled over our household. Only my strange inability to pen a decent verse, even when thoughts of Juliet should have caused my poetry to proliferate, had unnerved me. I wondered if I would ever write again.

This woman, this earthly angel—perhaps "Goddess" suited her more, for an angel is merely sweet and gentle, and Juliet was *fierce*—she inspired me, inflamed my senses, rearranged the thoughts in my mind; she unsettled me so the words, at least in lines of poetry, simply refused to come.

And *she* wrote poetry in her sleep!

The limb, finally sawed through, crashed past living branches and fell to the ground, breaking apart into several pieces. It was then I spotted my father at the end of the orchard standing very still, perhaps surveying this part of his estate, but appearing haunted to my eyes.

I decided in that moment to venture another attempt and descended from the ancient olive. Papa must have seen me approaching, must have sensed my purpose, for he turned and strode away toward the house.

I followed after him.

"Papa!" I called. "Wait for me. I want to talk!"

But he did not stop. My determination strengthened. We would get to the bottom of this story and we would do it today.

"Papa!"

He went in through the back door. Inside I found it cool, and dark after the brightness of the day. But down the long straight hall of the villa I saw him disappearing into the dining room.

I went in after him. Mama sat at the table struggling with some embroidery she was determined to conquer with fingers that refused to cooperate. She was staring perplexed at my father, who stood in a corner with his face to the wall. When she saw me, she shook her head.

I went and stood behind him. Found him trembling.

"Papa," I said gently. "You must tell me what is in your heart."

He shook his head no, and I thought then that if I could see his face, I would find him weeping.

"Please, Papa . . ."

"I am ashamed," he finally whispered. "So ashamed."

I looked at my mother, whose cheeks were wet with tears. *She knew.*

"Husband," she said with more steel in her voice than I'd known she possessed. "He is our only son. He left here as a boy, and perhaps you still see him that way. But Romeo is a grown man. A good man. And he loves you. He will love you even when you reveal your follies. That is what families do, Roberto."

With that, my father turned to me. His face was lined with grief. "Forgive me, Romeo. I have treated you unfairly. Come, sit with me and your mother, and I will tell you everything you want to know."

Chapter Eight

Romeo had not returned to my balcony and neither had Papa allowed me to again attend the symposium, no matter how I pleaded with him. My mind wandered from my chores—sewing, candle and soap making. Nights were the worst. Urgent expectation ruled me. I tossed in my bed and rose a hundred times before dawn, throwing open the balcony door in hopes that Romeo would be standing there in the moonlight, arms outstretched to enfold me.

He did not come.

If he wrote, his letters never reached me. He would not have let my parents know of his missives, and he had no friends among the servants of my father's house through which to secretly pass them.

I suffered dreadfully without even Lucrezia to commiserate.

I wrote to him. Letters baring my soul, sounding out my dreams. All of these I destroyed, fearful of their discovery. I made a ceremony of this before I climbed into my bed each night, lighting a fire in the brazier and dropping in the pages, watching them turn to ash and smoke.

My mind turned from love to worry. Had he forgotten me? Found someone else? Was he plagued with family troubles? Ill? God forbid, dead? I tried with all my might to close off every thought of Romeo, but nothing could be done. He had knocked down the door to my heart with words and moonlight and figs. "I believe in the senses," he'd said. And every night as I lay helpless, twisting in my sheets and longing, longing for his touch, I believed in them, too.

Romeo! I silently cried. *Deny all tradition and be my love!*

He must have heard my call.

Sunday dinner and Jacopo Strozzi was at our table. I found him impossible to bear. Even a touch of those long tapering fingers on my sleeve made the flesh beneath it crawl.

With downcast eyes I picked at my ravioli, worried that this would be the day of announcement—our betrothal. My road to ruin. But Mama was subdued, talking very little—a state she would not have been in if a marriage agreement had been reached.

Papa looked out at the three of us as one maid removed our plates and another set down the meat course. Once they had left, he spoke. His was a portentous tone, laden with anger and suspicion.

"The day after tomorrow I have been summoned to the house of Medici. Don Cosimo has invited . . ." He paused and spoke the name with distaste. ". . . the Monticecco paterfamilias and his son, Romeo, as well."

My breath caught in my throat. I had to force myself to breathe naturally as he went on.

"We will be urged, I understand, to make peace with each other."

"Peace!" Jacopo cried in that nasal whine I had grown to despise. "How can Don Cosimo imagine you can make peace with a family that openly wishes for your ruination? Who has so recently destroyed a valuable cargo? This is outrageous!"

"So it is, Jacopo, so it is."

"You must not go," said the man who would be my father's partner.

I was still as stone, and Mama looked very pale.

"There is no way I can say no to a summons from the Medici," Papa said. "They rule this city. Don Cosimo"—he measured his words carefully—"is the wealthiest man in the world. He is my patron. I am in his debt. The Capelletti are of the Medici Faction, and I must therefore bow to his call."

"How will you bear sitting at the table with such barbarians as the Monticecco?" Jacopo demanded.

A small smile played on my father's lips. "How will *you*?" he asked.

"Me?"

"You will soon be my business partner and . . ." His eyes fell on me. ". . . and a close friend of the family. We will face our enemy together."

"It would be my honor, Capello," he said, eyes downcast.

Jacopo's modesty is false, I thought suddenly. His family's wealth and prestige far exceeded ours. *Why is he playing such a game?*

My father turned to Mama. "Have you anything you have to say or to ask?" he said.

"Is this dangerous?" she wished to know. "For I would not like you to go to this meeting and never come home again."

"Indeed, the Monticecco are murdering thugs," Jacopo interjected, "and they are—"

"Who have they murdered?" I blurted out before I could stop myself.

Everyone turned to stare at the daughter who had spoken without being spoken to first. Jacopo's look was scathing.

Papa answered not to me but to my mother. "No one has been killed, Simonettina." He never used the diminutive in front of those not family, a thought that further sickened me. "Jacopo spoke figuratively. And while the Monticecco are thugs, they dare not raise a finger against me"—now he nodded to me—"or my future partner while we are under Don Cosimo's roof."

Mama smiled at my father, relieved. "May I give you some beef?" she asked in a girlish voice.

"A small portion," he replied.

"Juliet," Mama said, "will you ask Jacopo if you might serve him?"

He turned and smiled at me, yellow teeth and all. I wanted to scream. Instead I lowered my eyes, the dutiful daughter and bride-to-be.

I claimed a sick head for an early excuse to leave the table, and climbed to my room. At the writing table I composed a letter to Lucrezia, begging her indulgence for a favor. Of Romeo she disapproved, I knew, but things were different now, or soon would be.

This is why Romeo has stayed away, I told myself. His peace talks had been taking form. And here I had worried about him and another girl. What a fool I was. Never would I doubt him again.

I slept that night all through, no dreams that I remember, but woke before dawn with a sweet, fruity taste in my mouth.

Romeo had heard my call.

Chapter Nine

*M*y stomach churned as we sat sewing, Lucrezia and I with Contessina de' Medici, in her small salon. This had been the favor I'd asked of my friend—to arrange for my presence in Don Cosimo's house on the day of Romeo's peace works.

The Medici matriarch stitched a row of crosses and cherubim in silver-gilt shot on a priest's chasuble. Lucrezia embroidered a pair of gauntlets for Piero in bright blues and yellows, and I a lawn shirt for cousin Marco's birthday.

My eyes kept wandering to the open door, and I listened for the slightest sound. The time was approaching for the arrival of those summoned for the meet.

"Look how small and even your stitches are," Contessina observed, praising Lucrezia's work. My friend smiled with warmth at the cheerful woman with whom she would soon share the wifely responsibilities of the Palazzo Bardi.

"For whom is the chasuble?" I asked, by way of making polite conversation.

"For Carlo," the older woman answered simply.

I saw an odd look flash for an instant across Lucrezia's face. Contessina, too, had seen it.

"What is it?" I said to my friend, and she became flustered, trying to regain her composure.

"Nothing. Nothing. Not a thing."

"It is all right, my dear," Contessina said, patting her hand. She fixed me in her calm, steady eye. "Our Lucrezia has not yet accustomed herself to the thought of my husband's bastard son."

I forced myself to hold her gaze unfalteringly. "Carlo, the rector of Prato, is not *your* child?" I added.

Contessina resumed her sewing as she spoke. "Three years after our marriage Cosimo went to Rome to manage his branch there. A Circassian slave girl"—a pause as she swallowed was the only sign of emotion revealed—"had been bought by one of his agents, to look after him. She was young, pretty—the Circassians are known for their beauty. She bore him a son."

Lucrezia looked at me. "Mona Contessina raised the boy along with her own children. Made sure he had a fine education."

"How did you bear it?" I asked the older woman.

She closed her eyes, remembering. "I had been chaste and dutiful before marriage. Pious, loyal, and loving as a wife. I gave him pleasure in the bedroom"—her lips bowed into a smile—"and received it, too." She looked at me then. "It was difficult, very difficult when I found out about her. Had Maddalena simply been a nubile young thing who warmed Cosimo's lonely bed, it might have hurt me less. But she was of noble blood, taken as the plunder of war and sold to the highest bidder in the Venice slave market." The next words were painfully spoken. "My husband was very much in love with her."

She could see the looks of outrage on our faces. She spoke gently. "It is the way men are, my dears. Even good men."

"Well," said Lucrezia, "men may stray, but you were not required to take in his illegitimate child."

Contessina considered this. "Had I to do it again," she said, "perhaps I would have refused him. But I've grown to love Carlo as my own. I'm very proud of him. And who am I to complain? Cosimo has given me everything. Great wealth. Children of my own. Respect." Her eyes went soft as she spoke to Lucrezia. "I foresee no such problems with our Piero. He is deeply in love with you."

"And she'll allow no Circassian slave girls in their household," I quipped.

We all laughed at that and went on sewing in silence.

But Contessina's story was jarring.

This is what happens in a marriage of convenience, I told myself. *It would never happen in a marriage for love.*

An hour passed with unnerving slowness. I pricked my finger so many times it made Mona Contessina laugh. Finally, when I thought I could bear the waiting no longer, I heard voices echoing in the hall outside the salon door. My father's was clearly recognizable, as was Jacopo's. I strained to hear Romeo's, but was unrewarded.

Trying to remain calm, I asked permission to go and relieve myself. Contessina instructed Lucrezia to accompany me to her bedroom, but when I said I knew the way, Lucrezia reminded her soon-to-be mother-in-law of my visit before the betrothal ball. I could, indeed, find my own way, she said.

I hurried out and saw that the men had just repaired to the main salon at the end of the corridor. When I approached, I was gratified to see that while the door was closed, it was slightly ajar and voices could clearly be heard. Keeping my eyes peeled for servants, who would not have taken kindly to a girl eavesdropping on their master's business, I stood with my back to the wall near the door. I could not see inside, but I imagined them all having taken places around a table.

"Welcome," I heard Cosimo begin. "It is good that you have come. I think you all know my dear friend Poggio Braccio-lini . . . at least by reputation. He will serve as my *consigliere* in this matter."

How interesting, I thought. Poggio was a famous statesman, author, and orator, but most distinguished for his travels to the ends of the known world for the purpose of finding ancient manuscripts and codices to add to Cosimo's already distin-guished library.

"Capello. Jacopo. Roberto. Romeo." He addressed them all with equal respect. "We are here at the suggestion of your boy, Roberto. Quite an unexpected request, but one that piqued my interest." Cosimo paused before he spoke again. "Let us begin by admitting that wrongdoing has occurred between your houses."

"With all due respect, Don Cosimo," I heard my father say, "I refuse to admit that any of the wrongdoing was mine. Last month some damage was done to my factory on Via San Gallo, and one of my workers was roughed up. More recently a cargo of my silks was destroyed. We have proof that the Monticecco are responsible."

"What say you to that, Roberto?"

"I do not deny it." I heard a deep, melodious voice answer with neither flourish nor regret.

"You see?" Jacopo whined. "He admits his crime."

No one spoke for a space of time, and I wondered what thoughts were whirling just then in Romeo's head.

"What are you not telling us, Roberto?" This was the rich, eloquent voice of Poggio, whom I had heard speak at the Signoria at a public gathering. "Have you an unaired grievance against Capello Capelletti?"

"You may know that my father went to his maker last year," said the Monticecco paterfamilias. He paused, but when he spoke again, his voice trembled with feeling. "On his deathbed he made a confession and last request of me."

"We are sorry for your loss," I heard Cosimo say with sincere compassion. "May he rest in peace." A moment of respectful silence was observed before he went on. "Will you tell us what he said?"

"Very gladly." Roberto's voice grew hard and angry. "Many years ago your father"—I assumed he now spoke to Papa—"seduced my father's youngest daughter." There was more silence. "Do you deny any knowledge of this?"

"Most emphatically!" I heard my father say.

"Well, it is written in our family's records, if not yours."

"Let us, for a moment, assume the truth of this accusation," Cosimo said. "Tell us more."

"I was still a boy, but I remember my sister—pregnant and disgraced. There was never a marriage. She and the child—a boy—died in childbirth."

"Again, we mourn the loss of your sister and nephew," Cosimo said. I heard Papa and Jacopo muttering of their sorrow, too.

"Thank you."

"But, Roberto," Poggio said very gently, "that was many

years ago, and—correct me if I am wrong—no steps were taken then to right the wrong."

"That is so."

"But why?"

"Our family had been weakened by my elder brothers' move to Verona—they had bought a large and prosperous vineyard there. By himself, with only one young son left in the household, my father feared retaliation would lead to annihilation. So he swallowed his pride and did nothing. But on his deathbed his fury—one that been long forgotten by all but him—was renewed. He demanded that I exact revenge for the Capelletti outrage against our family. Should I disregard a dying man's wishes?"

"Of course not," Cosimo replied carefully. "Such promises are sacrosanct."

"But you cannot be suggesting he has a right to ruin me?" said Papa, his voice simmering with anger.

Cosimo did not immediately answer, and I heard a whispering consultation with Poggio. The orator was the next to speak.

"Since the cessation of fighting between the Ghibellines and the Guelfs, and the resolution of Cosimo's 'disagreement' with the Albizzi family, Florence has been a peaceful city. With peace comes prosperity, a condition that benefits all."

"In this case," Cosimo went on, choosing his words carefully, "the good of our city must—respectfully—be weighed against the wishes of one dying man. What I propose is that the Monticecco pay the Capelletti for the full loss of the cargo."

"Fair enough," I heard Jacopo say.

"Please let me finish. You, Capello, should then pay a thousand florins to the Monticecco to settle the 'debt of revenge.' I realize, Roberto, this is not altogether satisfying—no eye is taken for an eye. Nothing brings back the dead, nor a family's lost honor. But I am thinking that perhaps with this monetary solution, my friend Poggio has discovered a new way to settle blood feuds without the spilling of blood."

"With respect," I heard Jacopo say with no trace of that sentiment in his voice, "the repayment for the lost cargo only brings my future partner even. If he then pays the Monticecco for an insult many decades in the past, Capello is suddenly out of pocket. And *he* is the injured party here."

Everyone started talking at once, arguing really. Their voices were growing louder and more bellicose.

"May I speak?" The voice was Romeo's.

My heart fluttered in my chest. I moved closer to the open door, afraid to miss a word he spoke.

"I would suggest this. Let my father pay more for the lost cargo than its worth—a price equal to the 'revenge payment' Signor Capelletti is paying him. That way, each man receives something to satisfy the losses and dishonors done to their families, but neither one ends up the richer."

There was silence as everyone digested the proposal. At that moment I heard a servant's footsteps echoing up the stairway. I darted away and into Contessina's bedroom, took a moment to do my business in her chamber pot, and peeked out the door in time to see the gathering of men emerge from the great salon.

Cosimo stood with arms about the shoulders of Papa and Roberto Monticecco, gently forcing them to embrace. At first it was reluctant, but when they parted, I saw their expressions had softened. Then Jacopo came forth with Poggio behind, speaking quietly in his ear. I could see my soon-to-be betrothed was unconvinced of this unique solution, but now he was confronted by the two enemies, genial and basking in the warm approval of the great man of Florence.

Yet Jacopo's tone and posture were groveling to Poggio. I heard mention of the scholar's famous treatise *On Avarice*, a defense of greed as the emotion that made civilization possible.

"I agree with you, signor," said Strozzi. "It *is* a good sign if a merchant has ink-stained fingers." He held out his hands. "Here are mine."

Poggio laughed, then excused himself to speak to Don Cosimo.

Jacopo hung back at the door and now I saw why. Romeo emerged and Strozzi blocked his full exit. I could see both their faces, Romeo's calm, Jacopo's strangely pleasant.

"I have cause to believe that you and the woman I plan to marry are *simpatico* in ways of the heart," Jacopo began.

Romeo seemed unsurprised, and remained wholly silent.

"Therefore," said Jacopo, "I propose that after a respectable period I will allow you to pay court to her. You may see her in private, share your . . . poetry"—he uttered the word with a distinct sneer. "You may lay your lovesick head upon her knee." He smiled and shook his head condescendingly. "Publicly adore her. Meanwhile, she will live in my mother's house, subservient and groveling. She will obey me and stay cloistered there except to go to confession. She will bear my children, as many as I can get on her. I will, of course, have my mistresses."

Then Jacopo put his face very close to Romeo's and spoke with the most genteel menace. "But if, while you are her courtly lover, you lay your lips or hand on other than Juliet's hand, then you will understand the wrath and power of the Strozzi. I will kill you or, better, perhaps, castrate you and let you live on as a woman."

Then Jacopo smiled almost happily and, with a jaunty tilt of his chin, strode after the other men.

I saw Romeo close his eyes and inhale deeply. It was difficult to discern his emotion. I longed to show myself to him but knew it too dangerous. A moment later he made for the stairs. I waited till all of them were out of hearing before I returned to the sewing room.

"They've made peace!"

"Truly?"

"Truly. I saw Romeo's father and Papa embrace."

Lucrezia was dumbstruck as we sat side by side in the small Palazzo Bardi salon. I'd waited for Contessina to excuse herself before bursting forth with my news.

"When has this ever happened before?" I said.

"I have never known it." She was incredulous. "Once an enemy, forever an enemy. This is how it has always been."

"And Romeo is the first cause of it . . . with Don Cosimo's help of course."

"I was wrong about him," Lucrezia said with quiet certitude. "And I suppose if he can cause peace to break out between two warring Florentine families, then some hope remains that a marriage can be arranged."

"Oh, Lucrezia!" I dropped my embroidery and hugged her fiercely.

"But listen to me," she went on. "I said 'some hope.' We do not know how badly your father's business depends upon Jacopo's partnership. That will always take precedence over a love match between new friends."

It was at that moment I might have told Lucrezia about Jacopo's vicious threats, but I chose to stay silent. "Knowing Romeo, he will find some reason for our marriage to become *vital* to our family's betterment," I said instead.

She smiled indulgently. "It would be wonderful to see you happily wed."

"I *will* be. I feel it in my bones. Ours will be the most glorious marriage in Florence . . . save yours and Piero's," I added with a grin.

She laughed and, picking up the shirt I'd been stitching, handed it back to me. "You'd best get control of yourself before Contessina returns."

"I can't stop smiling."

"She's coming! Bite the inside of your lip."

I did this and was gratified to feel a modicum of restraint returning to me.

"I've brought us a little something to nibble on," said Piero's mother as she entered, carrying a small basket that she placed on the table between us.

"Oh!" I sighed so loudly that both women turned and stared wonderingly at my outburst, one that I could never in a thousand years explain.

It was a basket of figs.

Chapter Ten

"Why on earth would you choose, for a day in the country, to wear all white?" my mother demanded with a disapproving shake of her head.

"She fancies herself Beatrice," said Marco, now being jounced on the carriage seat across from us, next to Papa.

"Beatrice who?" she said, sounding annoyed.

"'Gracious lady dressed in pure white . . . ,'" he recited. "It's Dante. You may not think him an idol, Aunt, but everyone else in Florence does."

This alarmed me, that my choice of costume was transparent even to my cousin. I tried very hard not to frown at him, and give him further grounds to suspect me.

"Don't be silly, Marco," I said lightly. "The dress is Papa's newest gift to me." I blew my father a kiss and smiled. "It's beautiful silk. The white-on-white embroidery is the finest I've ever seen."

But Papa was barely conscious of this meaningless chatter. He was stony-faced and silent, lost in his own thoughts. The invitation by Romeo's father of our family to the Monticecco home for Sunday dinner—though of course I saw Romeo's hand in it—disturbed my father. Ruffled his calm. He could not easily slap away the offered olive branch, knowing Don Cosimo's spies were everywhere.

Mama, on the other hand, had been delighted with the invitation. "I am curious," she'd said, "to see how such people live."

"You're just nosy," I'd teased her.

"Call it what you like. We have no friends among the gentlemen farmers."

"We stay close to our own kind," Papa had snapped, annoyed at this forced visit with a man who—even for reasons that he could now comprehend—had done violence to his business. Even though the agreed-upon moneys had changed hands and the debts had been paid, a brittle crust of resentment yet hardened my father's heart against the Monticecco.

I peered out the carriage window as we crossed the Arno on the Ponte alla Carraia, gazing at the families dotting the shore on the late-summer day. A woman laid cold meat and a round of cheese on a colorful rug. Brothers played ball in the grass. Men in a row sat with bent knees, fishing lazily. A mother called urgently to a small boy toddling toward the river's edge.

We so infrequently crossed the Arno and took to the hills, rolling soft and verdant south of Florence. The uniqueness of the small journey set my mind aflame with its sights. From the sights sprang words. I wished fervently to be clutching an ink-dipped quill in the privacy of my thoughts, and writing them on paper.

Though lately, all I had mused upon was Romeo. I wondered how much of each day he thought about me, for I could not stop myself thinking of him. If I saw a young man of any shape or size, he became Romeo. The sight of my volume of Dante, any balcony, any tree, the moon . . . and figs, of course, drew me back to the object of my desire. This obsession was pleasurable, though, and altogether unalterable. My appetite for all-things-Romeo was insatiable. When I sewed, I sewed for him. When I sang alone in my room, I sang to him. My prayers were for our marriage, my dreams of our children.

Now before me spread a day of infinite opportunity and adventure. I was going in broad daylight to meet my love and his family. The thought made me tingle, like the feel of water rushing over my skin. It would be perfect—a blank canvas upon which two artists—Romeo and Juliet—would paint their future life. A delicious prospect, this day. With every turn of the carriage wheels and the dull clopping of horses' hooves on the hard-packed road, rising higher into the hills, passing farms and villas quiet of workers this Sunday Sabbath, everything shone brighter, and all became unearthly clear in my vision.

When we pulled through the gates of the high stone walls, I saw stretched out on one side a vast vineyard and a small pasture, on the other a deep and wide grove of trees. Before us a hand-some villa gleamed bone white in the noonday sun, its red tiled roof bleached pale pink in its glare. A graceful loggia spanned the second floor, and before the heavy carven double doors a blue and yellow tiled fountain splashed a joyful welcome.

Romeo was first out the door, followed by the man I'd seen at Palazzo Bardi, and a tall, slender woman with a mass of thick brown hair worn loose over her shoulders. She was pretty even before she broke into a smile of greeting. It was Romeo's smile, the pearly teeth, all inherited from his mother.

The three of them helped us down from our carriage, plying us with questions as to the comfort of our journey. Introductions were made all around. Romeo bowed to me. In the commotion, no one noticed that when he took my hand to kiss it, he turned it and laid his lips softly in the middle of my palm. No one knew my knees jellied and a place deep inside my womanly center shuddered with delight.

Once I'd recovered, I saw that Mama and Romeo's mother, whose name was Sophia, were attracted to each other like iron is drawn to a magnet. They'd not been in each other's company a minute before they were chatting like old friends. But Mona Sophia, at closer observation, wore pain as an undergarment—well hidden but existing in the depths of her. I was sure of it.

My father's posture spoke volumes of his discomfort, but I saw at once that Roberto Monticecco, perhaps swayed by his son's insistence, was determined to put Papa at ease.

"Will you let me show you my vineyard?" he asked when he saw his wife leading my mother into the house. "I have some caskets of superb Sangioveto, aged for seven years."

What Italian man could pass up such an offer? I even saw a hint of a smile playing on my father's lips. "I've a brother in Abruzzo who is a vintner," Papa said. "He claims his Brunello to be the finest in Tuscany."

"A challenge!" Roberto cried. "Come along, then. We shall see."

And just like that, Romeo and I were standing alone with Marco, staring silently at the splashing fountain.

"I once heard of a fountain that spouted red wine instead of water," Marco offered, pertaining to nothing.

"Let me guess," Romeo said. "The French court?"

"That is the kind of decadence I would like to see one day," I said.

Both young men turned to me, astonished by my statement.

"Well, cousin Juliet, I had no idea you had such notions. Then you would travel if you could?"

"I would see the world," I answered him. "All of it—Greece, the Holy Land, the places where Marco Polo sailed. Did you know that the last voyage your namesake made for the great Kublai Khan was to deliver the Mongol's princess daughter to her betrothed in Ilkhanate?"

"You surprise me," Romeo said.

"Why surprise?"

"Your boldness. Your erudition."

I wanted to say, "I thought you knew me better." But perhaps Romeo meant only to confuse my cousin of our intimacy.

"A want to travel is bold?" is what I did say.

"For a Florentine lady? What do you think, Marco? Is that not audacious?"

"My cousin showed all of us her mettle at the Dante symposium. After that, nothing surprises."

By now we three faced one another.

"May I show you our olive orchard and its works?" Romeo asked as he untethered the two horses from our carriage.

"I would like that very much," I answered, perhaps too quickly, too eagerly for a proper girl, but perfectly for an audacious one.

"In want of an elder woman," Marco said to me, "I suppose I must become your chaperone."

I smiled gratefully at him.

"Then we're off," Romeo said.

I followed as Romeo led our carriage team to the pretty fenced pasture where other horses grazed. He let them in through a gate and in the next moment made a shrill whistle. From the Monticecco animals a single white horse pricked up its ears and, separating itself from the others, came galloping toward us. At the fence the mare put down her head and demanded Romeo scratch it.

I recognized her as the one on which Romeo had made his escape from the Medici ball. I saw Marco's face. He recognized it, too.

"Fine horse," Marco pointedly said.

"She loves you," I told Romeo, unable to take my eyes from him.

"Blanca." He fixed his gaze on me. "I adore her." He became aware of Marco's stare and, pulling in his horns, spoke to him. "When I returned home from university, my uncles sent her to me as a gift. They wrote and said, 'We understand you are lacking a horse of your own. Every man needs a horse, so we have sent you this fine lady.'" He returned his attentions to me. "Do you ride, Lady Juliet?"

"Truthfully, horses frighten me, though I've read with great interest of the Warrior Nuns of Bologna."

"Can you see her in battle armor?" said Marco, suddenly teasing. He began to pretend one-sided swordplay with me with an invisible weapon. I indulged his antics for several moments before giving him a poke in the ribs. He let out a shriek and fell dramatically to the ground as though mortally wounded.

All of us laughed, and as Marco picked himself up and dusted himself off, Romeo and I started away side by side.

"I would like to ride," I said. "Especially a horse as beautiful as yours."

"In faraway lands?"

"With my lover," I whispered a moment before Marco caught us up.

"In harvest season we knock the olives off the trees with sticks," Romeo told us, "and then they're ground in here for no more than six minutes."

We were in the small millhouse, the two-ton round grinding stone clean and still in its giant granite bowl.

"Then the olive paste is placed between woven mats, these laid atop one another and pressed here." He stood aside so we could see the massive wooden screw press. "The liquid produced is part oil, part water. The oil, of course, settles on top."

I saw Marco rolling his eyes in boredom and gave him a filthy look. Our little performance was not lost on Romeo, who suppressed a smile and went on with his lecture. What else could he do, with my protective and not-a-little suspicious cousin keeping his beady eyes upon the young man he had so recently chased from the Medici ballroom?

"Come, follow me," said Romeo with not a trace of sarcasm in his voice. "The best is yet to come."

And indeed, when we approached the olive grove, there was something wonderful about it—something that calmed even the sharp-tongued Marco.

It was not so much an ordered orchard as a shadowed forest of trees, some of them very ancient. Their thick, gnarled trunks looked like the careworn faces of old men, their million shimmering leaves more gray than green, and the fragrance redolent of another time. Branches with unripened olives, skins purple and white, hung low and heavy near our heads.

Enchantment shone on Romeo's face, and when he smiled at me, it might have been him making introductions to Dante and Beatrice, Boccaccio and Petrarch. *He loves these trees,* I thought. *They are his home, his family.*

"The olive is a miracle of a tree," he murmured, "surviving in the most hostile soil, rocky and dry, and yet it gives forth the blessing of its precious oil. 'Liquid gold,' Homer called it, a divine gift from the gods and nature. If I ever have a daughter, she will be called Olivia." He patted the trunk of one with the flat of his hand. "This cultivar is called 'Frantoio.' Its flavor is more fruity than sweet."

We stopped at the base of a mammoth specimen, forty feet in height and too large if six of us had all joined hands to ring its trunk.

"This one begs to be climbed," Marco announced.

"That is so, my friend," said Romeo, smiling broadly. "I have done it a hundred times. Let me show you the first foothold."

They went to the other side, disappearing, their voices growing faint. Romeo returned alone and in moments Marco called down from a limb above our heads. He looked pleased with himself.

"Don't get lost!" Romeo called.

But Marco had already disappeared, the clutch of jittering leaves the only evidence of his presence a moment before.

Romeo turned to me and held me warm in his gaze. "'*This is no woman,*'" he said, "'*but one of heaven's most beautiful angels.*'"

They were Dante's words, but spoken as if from my lover's own heart.

"I've missed you," I said. "Waited every night for you to come."

"Did you think I'd forgotten you?"

"Sometimes."

His smile was self-satisfied. "Will you ever doubt me again?"

"Never." I turned and faced the tree trunk, scraping a bit of the bark with my fingernail. "I was there, you know."

"Where?"

"The Palazzo Bardi. The day you brought our families together. I heard you speak, bringing our fathers to terms."

"With no small help from Don Cosimo." Then incredulously, "You were *there*?"

"Outside the door. Eavesdropping."

He laughed. "You never fail to amaze me."

"And you were brilliant," I said. "You achieved the impossible."

He placed a hand on my waist. "Then you heard what Jacopo Strozzi said to me."

"About becoming my courtly lover, and the life I can expect as his wife?" I said, looking back over my shoulder at him. "Oh yes."

"He did not come today," Romeo drily observed.

"He called your father's invitation 'cynical,' the gesture of peace a sham. He refused on principle, he said, and it gave my father pause. For a time, Papa considered refusing to come as well." I couldn't help smiling. "But my mother won the day. She pleaded and reminded Papa he could not risk Don Cosimo's displeasure."

"But I wonder at Jacopo," Romeo said with all seriousness.

"He must not believe a chance exists that you and I . . ." He did not finish his thought.

"Would it satisfy you," I asked him carefully, "to merely become my courtly lover?"

Romeo placed his hands on my shoulders and began to answer.

"How do I get down from here?" Marco cried from above. Legs straddling a thick branch, he could clearly see Romeo touching me—possessively—I, soon to be betrothed to another. Marco seemed unperturbed.

"The 'Y' behind you—step through it," Romeo called up to him. "A series of limbs like a stairway will bring you to ten feet from the ground. Hang from the branch by your hands and the distance is halved. Then a graceful, bent-kneed drop, and you're home."

"Thank you. And unhand my cousin or I'll be pilloried for a bad chaperone." He disappeared in a profusion of rustling silver leaves.

Romeo and I parted, taking up a formal stance, one that might now fool all but Marco. But, I thought, if my features betrayed a fraction of what I felt for this man, then I would fool no one, and tempt the Fates with all manner of terrifying outcomes.

Romeo read my thoughts.

"Strength and resolve," he said.

I smiled. "Strength and resolve."

Romeo led us into the villa through a back door and down a hall passing the kitchen, where the cooks were busily preparing our meal. He put a finger to his lips as we came upon the dining room, where our mothers sat side by side at the table with their backs to us. We paused silently, long enough to hear fragments of their conversation, more intimate and rich with compassion than their time together should have allowed.

"My sons to the plague. My daughters in childbirth," murmured Mona Sophia.

Mama nodded her head. "Mine to fever." I saw her clutch Sophia's hand. Romeo's mother turned and smiled with tears in her eyes. "We are tied to life by so slender a thread."

Now we understood how our mothers had come so quickly to tender accord. They had both lost all their children to death— all but Romeo and me.

Romeo beckoned us past the dining room to a small chamber, his father's study by the looks of it. A desk was piled high with ledgers, and some manuscripts, and scrolls tied with leather thongs sat on wooden shelves. But on one wall was displayed an unexpected and astonishing array of weaponry—shields, swords, and daggers.

Marco came immediately alive and went straight to the wall. "May I?" he asked Romeo, and received consent to handle the arms. He took down a stiletto first and touched his finger to its tip. "This is fine workmanship," Marco said, "but very old."

"The Monticecco were not always growers," Romeo said. "For two centuries we were smiths."

Now Romeo pulled a gleaming broadsword down from the wall. I marveled at how easily he held the weighty sword, his arms more sinewy than heavily muscled.

As Marco replaced the stiletto on the wall, Romeo uttered, "Marco, attend me!" and my cousin turned with fine-toned reflex in time to receive the broadsword that Romeo had tossed him.

Marco grinned as Romeo took down from the wall another sword, and they assumed the bent-leg stance of warriors, face-to-face.

I think my mouth had dropped open, though not a sound came out of it, for who was a woman to tell two men they should not fight, even as this was sure to be a mock battle?

Marco, challenge sparkling in his eyes, struck first, but Romeo was quick with his parry and caught the blow with the side of his sword. The sound of metal on metal, so foreign to my ears, made me gasp.

Then Romeo's sword came in a wide arc, but was stopped cold by Marco's own prowess with a weapon—one I had never known he possessed.

Both were afire now, but the room was small. With a series of quick reciprocal blows Marco backed out the study door and Romeo came after. I followed, helpless and unsure whether to be amused or frightened.

Now they were fighting in the long hallway, the clanking swords making a fine racket. Mama and Mona Sophia rushed to the dining room archway and watched, clutching each other with only mild terror, for it was clear from the young men's expressions that they meant each other no harm. Still, an accidental cut, infection . . .

Playful as the fight was, and evenly matched, it was mightily spirited, and with every blow came grievous cries and guttural groans. Then Marco, with one knee bent, lunged deeply, and only Romeo's swift and graceful retreat kept the tip of the blade from meeting his chest.

With a loud, barbaric shout, Romeo swung his sword in a wide circle above his head and with a great crashing sound knocked the blade from Marco's hands. It went clattering down the hall and landed at our mothers' feet.

Marco and Romeo, beaming with manly pleasure, embraced each other like brothers.

Wordlessly, Mama and Mona Sophia retreated back into the dining room.

Marco went to retrieve his weapon. I watched from the study doorway as Romeo returned to the room and replaced his sword on the wall. I said nothing to Marco, panting as he passed me and went in, and moved to place the sword back on its hooks.

Romeo stayed his hand. "It is yours, Marco."

"Mine?"

Romeo smiled, wiping the sweat from his brow with his sleeve. "That was an honorable fight. And you admire the weapon."

"It is too generous," Marco said, serious for once, and I thought deeply moved.

"Do you refuse my gift?"

"No! I accept it with all gratitude, Romeo." Marco placed his first friendly arm around a Monticecco shoulder and beamed with pleasure.

Romeo fixed me in his gaze then, quietly triumphant.

Here, I thought, was a very determined man.

Chapter Eleven

"My parents' marriage was arranged," I said. "Altogether traditional."

Romeo and I were finally, blissfully alone, lying side by side on our backs on a rug beneath an ancient grape arbor. Marco, our less-than-diligent chaperone, delighted with his gift, had taken the broadsword out of our sight to do battle with his shadow.

"She was very pretty, my mother. Simonetta Visconte brought a fine dowry to the Capelletti coffers, one that allowed Papa's business to grow, and his prospects as a Florentine merchant to soar. She provided him with three healthy sons and a daughter. What more reason did they need for their affections to grow?"

Romeo's eyes never left my face as I spoke.

"Then, in the year I was ten, Papa's silks came to the attention of Don Cosimo. Contessina had decided that all the beds in every one of their houses—both city and country—were ancient and musty and needed refurbishing. To his great delight Papa was awarded the commission. He went mad scouring the known world for the finest fabrics that existed—silks, brocades, velvets, damasks—and brought them before the pair of them, laying out the bolts with terrific pride.

"It was a textile spectacle the likes of which even the Medici had never before seen, and Contessina, modest and unassuming as she was, found herself reveling in the beauty of the wares. 'May I have this one for my bed, Cosimo, and that one for Lorenzo's? . . . And the villa at Careggi?' When all were chosen with care for each and every bedstead and canopy, Papa revealed the greatest surprise of all—the yardage was to be a gift, every inch of it. There would be no charge whatsoever. All that he required was the friendship and goodwill of the Medici from that day forward."

Romeo smiled. "A true Florentine businessman, your father. Everyone wishes for Don Cosimo as a patron."

"It was not the only reward," I said, remembering. "The next year Don Cosimo hosted the great Convocation in Florence—popes and emperors from the Eastern Church and from Rome, statesmen, authors, philosophers, scribes. . . ."

"And the Greeks," Romeo added.

"Yes, the Greeks. Of all of them, their influence was most profound. They spoke so lovingly of their great sage, Plato, and his ancient wisdom, that when all the men had gone home and most Florentines had forgotten the debates, Don Cosimo was still afire. That was when he sent his man as a scout who scoured the whole world for the great books lost to the Barbarian invasion. . . ."

"Poggio Bracciolini," Romeo said. "Those adventures made him a famous man."

"They did. He brought back the works of Hermes and Solon and Aristotle. But most of all Plato. Don Cosimo immersed himself in Plato. All his sons, Piero, Lorenzo and Carlo, he had tutored by Greek scholars."

"Where is this story leading?" asked Romeo, amused.

"Be patient," I gently scolded. "It comes to a fine conclusion."

"So," said Romeo, "the Medici sons were tutored by the Greeks."

"Yes. And then the boys were betrothed."

Romeo's brow furrowed.

"Piero to Lucrezia Tornabuoni," I said.

"Aha! And through Don Cosimo's patronage of your father, you and she met?"

"And became friends at once. We loved each other like sisters. But the Fates were not done with us yet. In his study of Plato, Don Cosimo learned that 'the Great Man of the Greeks' believed that highborn women should be provided the same education as men. They could enter the public sphere and even become leaders. They were guardians of children and therefore important in society and family both. If Lucrezia was to be the mother of his grandchildren, then Lucrezia must have the finest of educations."

The ending of my story was dawning on Romeo. He began to smile. "And so she decided that if she was to receive this splendid education, her friend—her sister—must receive it, too."

"Just so!"

Romeo shook his head admiringly. "You are quite a pair,

you and Lucrezia. Plato would have had women like you in mind when he spoke so glowingly of the female gender."

"I have never told that story before," I said. "No one was a bit interested."

"It's just as well." Romeo became uncommonly shy when he said, "I don't want everyone to know you as well as I do."

"No one ever will." I took his hand. "You must tell me something of yourself now."

He shook his head modestly. "There is nothing much to know. At least not of me." He thought for a moment. "The great story of our family is that of my mother's and father's love."

"I want to hear!"

Romeo smiled, remembering, and paused to collect his thoughts for its reciting. Finally he began. "Their marriage, too, was arranged. Like so many couples, they had never met until their wedding day. She worried he'd be a toothless old widower who belched and farted all day long, and he that she would be overpious and frigid. But that was not the case.

"They were both sixteen. Sophia was exquisite, all peaches and cream and filled with a love of life and a soft, sweet nature. Roberto was a handsome, strapping youth owning an appreciation of everything beautiful, and horny as a stallion."

I laughed at that and Romeo, encouraged, went on.

"The moment they clapped eyes on one another they were smitten. Hopelessly and passionately in love, and grateful for their good fortune. But the wedding day was a long, drawn-out affair, with ceremony and contracts, benedictions, dancing, and feasting—endless feasting. The few moments they were allowed near to each other—when the rings were given, or partnering in a dance—their touch was like fire burning the skin. They spoke to each other with their eyes, silently mingling their souls and their minds . . . until they were pulled away to greet a family client, receive a gift, taste a delicacy.

"Finally, *finally* came the procession to my grandfather's house—this villa. They wished so desperately to be alone, but the revelers had followed them into their chamber and put them to bed. Everyone stood expectantly around them waiting, as tradition demanded, for copulation to begin.

"Then suddenly my father, eyes blazing, leapt from the bed and like a whirlwind, swinging his arms and shouting curses at them all, demanded 'privacy' for himself and his bride. Everyone was stunned, scandalized. But he didn't care. He herded them out, slammed the door, and locked it behind them. Mama says she laughed till she cried, unsure whether she had married a hero or a madman. My father went to the bed, gathered her in his arms, and proved to her, he likes to say, that he was both.

"So my parents were blessed with the rarest of all marriages—one of equal parts convenience and unbridled passion. She—like your mother, Juliet—was fertile and provided the Monticecco line with many healthy sons and daughters. And so to my brothers and sisters and me it was proven from the earliest age that there was such a thing as marital bliss. We saw the joy that true love could bring to a man and a woman, and how children—even those of the wildest spirit—could feather the warm nest of family.

"Mama, Papa, and my sisters and brothers were at peace in our home, in our vineyard and orchard. I spent fragrant summers climbing the gnarled silver-leafed old men, beating the olives from their branches with sticks. I learned from my father and grandfather the wisdom of seasons, signs of a coming storm, the cycles of the moon for growing, the smell and feel of Tuscan earth between my fingers."

"What a sweet dream your life was," I said.

"Until the plague struck Florence." Romeo looked away. "It sought many sacrifices from our house. My mother's father. Both my brothers." He sighed. "Mama sickened, but blessedly did not die. Papa, fearing my death more than the loss of his last living son's presence, sent me to live with his brothers at their vineyard outside Verona, where the plague had not come.

"I cried like an infant at the parting, my last sight of Mama. Her skin was still scarred with shadows of the buboes. Papa wept, hugging me to him as though he did not mean to release me. Finally he pretended courage. Promised me I would return to his house, see my mother again. Then he placed me in a cart with a driver and sent us on our way to Verona. My last sight of the olive grove sent me into fits of such weeping that the driver scolded me, telling me to thank God I was alive, as were my parents, and that Florence was not so far from Verona, and that one day I would return.

"But my uncles Vittorio and Vincenzo, they were as kind and loving as the year is long, and were glad for a strong nephew at their vineyard. They doted on me. Treated me like their own son. Had they not taken so seriously my father's admonition to make a man of me, they would have spoiled me. They brought me a tutor who claimed my only passion in learning was for writing, and writing only so I might send letters to my mother. He'd been wrong about that, of course. For I fervently studied the art of growing things, whether vines or crops of beans or wheat, or orchards of pears or olives.

"I railed against the prospect of going to university. A waste of time, I'd complained. In truth it had been more my desire to remain on the land, and misery at separation from my kin once again. I had grown to love my uncles dearly. 'You must become a man of the world,' they insisted. 'You must learn to keep ledgers, for even growing is a business, and what is a Florentine if not a good businessman?'

"So I went to Padua in the end and enjoyed it more than I had believed I would. I discovered poetry, and Dante, whose words were like living things to me, and whose verses of love brought memories of my mother and father, and promise of the woman whom I would one day marry and adore." He turned to face me again. "I feel like I've been talking for an hour."

"Very nearly," I teased, though I truly was in heaven, listening to his voice, the story of his family.

"You now," he said, turning on his side to face me. I found myself bemused. Never had someone attended my words and thoughts so closely.

"Do you remember three years ago, Signor Alberti's poetry competition?" I asked Romeo. Leon Battista Alberti was one of the foremost influential men in all of Italy.

"I was in Padua," Romeo said, "but I heard of it, of course. All contestants were to write in the Tuscan language, not Latin, on the theme of friendship. Am I remembering correctly?"

"You are." I began to blush and smile. "I wrote a poem for it."

"But you were"—Romeo silently calculated—"fifteen years old!"

"And very full of myself. I had just discovered my knack for verse, and I loved my friend Lucrezia very much. So I wrote about her and our friendship."

"But the contest?"

"Well, some famous men had entered their poems—Altabianco, Dati. Of course I could not very well submit my own under my real name or sex. The competition itself was a very grand affair, held at the cathedral. Ten papal secretaries were sent all the way from Rome to judge it."

Romeo's eyes were wide and disbelieving. He shook his head in wonder.

I went on. "The crowd that came to watch the poets read their work out loud was huge and enthusiastic. It was not hard to convince my parents to take me, for all of Florence was there. It was less easy for me to 'get lost in the crowd' for a time before the contest began. I slipped to the front where contestants sat waiting for their turn at the podium and found the kindest-faced man of all, and handed him a folio with my poem and a letter saying that my uncle, 'Giuliano Beatricci,' was too ill to attend, but would someone be so kind as to read his poem with the others.

"So it began with great pomposity, the poets all striving to capture 'the hidden thing' that was friendship. One evoked Prometheus to exemplify higher, purifying love. Another spoke of Circe and Medusa to prove that love, when fixed on the wrong object, can descend into the realm of beasts. I waited and waited, and still my poem was not read ... until finally, when the last contestant had finished, Alberti himself arose and, holding my folio before him, announced that an amateur poet—Beatricci—had been too ill to attend and wished his work to be read. And with my heart beating so loudly I was certain my parents could hear it, I listened to my words spoken aloud to all of Florence."

Romeo laughed delightedly. "You astound me."

I laughed with him. "That day, I confess, I astonished myself."

"But did the judges not, in the end, disappoint Alberti and all the contestants with their decision? I seem to remember . . ."

"You remember well. They refused to award the crown to anyone. Said the modern poets and the Tuscan language fell short of the ancient poets and of Latin."

"What else would you expect of stuffy Roman judges?" he said.

"Well, Signor Alberti was mightily angered, but the poems were copied many times over and sent to princely libraries all over the world."

"So your poem of friendship now resides in princely libraries?"

I smiled a triumphant assertion.

"I, too, was influenced by Alberti," Romeo said. "When I was a boy, I attempted to replicate his most famous physical feat."

"Jumping from a standing start over the head of a man standing next to him?"

"The very one."

"And what happened?"

"I broke my leg."

We laughed again.

"But come, Romeo, there is more of Alberti in you than that."

"Perhaps." He thought for a long moment. "He believed in discipline and self-cultivation, and that any individual could accomplish any feat, however difficult it might be. I was reminded of him at my homecoming, here, last year. I had left as a boy and returned as a man. I was happy to resume my work in the orchard, and I passed the nights by candlelight trying my hand at verse.

"But all was not well. My sisters had died having their babies. Mama had begun suffering in the grip of pain, more and more crippled with arthritis in her hands, and my grandfather's death unearthed a malignant family feud. Now, for the first time, the Monticecco had an enemy. And my once-peaceful father"— Romeo shook his head sadly—"had become a vandal." Romeo thought for a moment. "Maybe Alberti's spirit was in me when I sought peace between our families."

He stroked my cheek with the back of his hand. "And perhaps I learned my love of the senses from the man—though it never occurred to me before this moment. Alberti took great pleasure, he claimed, in seeing things that had 'a certain beauty.' He believed that a jewel or a flower or a lovely landscape could restore a sick man to health." He gazed at me searchingly. "I think if I were dying, the sight of you could bring me back to life."

The thought suddenly chilled me, and I dismissed it offhandedly. "I do not see you dying anytime soon," I said.

"Unless I were to die of love." He leaned down and sweetly pressed his lips against mine, but we were startled at a voice shouting from the end of the vineyard row.

"Juliet! Romeo! They are calling us to dinner!" It was Marco. "Come now," he ordered us, "and look calm and unruffled, or I'll impale you both on my new sword!"

Romeo helped me to my feet and called to Marco, "At your command, Captain!"

Chapter Twelve

*D*inner with the joined families was a delight. A table had been set beneath a broad-limbed walnut, settling dappled light on the white linen cloth we had brought the Monticecco as a gift. Roberto sat at the head with my father at his right hand, Sophia at the other end, my mother at hers. Romeo and I sat side by side across from Marco, who watched us, the jester with a new friend and a juicy secret.

Before the first course was brought out, we all sampled the Sangioveto, which was delicious—earthy, with a hint of spice. There was warm crusty bread that smelled of rosemary, great bowls of ripened olives, and in smaller ones whole heads of garlic baked soft and crushed, swimming in a sea of green oil.

Our mothers were tight as two beans in their pod.

Our fathers, while not yet fast friends, were loosened by wine, much goodwill surrounding them, and the perfection of a warm, leisurely afternoon. *If Don Cosimo could see them now,* I thought. What had begun by his stern orders was gently flowering into sincere camaraderie.

No detail was lost on me. Every smile, every smell, a walnut leaf that fluttered down to the bowl of oil as Romeo reached to dip his bread there. All of it I memorized. All of it would find its way into verse.

I was startled by his hand clutching mine under the table. He spoke, meanwhile, to Marco of a *calcio* match to which he wished to be invited. I realized with a start that his hand was slick with olive oil, and he kneaded my fingers one by one, all slippery and warm, never missing a word, pressing the webs between them, laughing with Marco as men do, and sliding his palm across my palm.

Strength and resolve, I thought. He was testing mine.

"Juliet," my mother said, "tell Mona Sophia of your *brigata*."

"My *brigata*?" She spoke of the female confraternity of which I was a part. "Oh . . . ah . . . the girls have been friends since childhood. . . ." Romeo rubbed his thumb over my knuckles. "I . . . we meet . . ." His fingertips grazed the top of my hand. ". . . on every occasion . . ."

Mama grew impatient with my stammering answer. "They escort one another to confession, gather at banquets, talk of many matters—piety, womanly duties. Did you belong to a *brigata*?" she asked Sophia with sincere interest.

"In Rome, where I grew up, we had no such girl groups, though sometimes friendly women would go on pilgrimages together, meet for ritual purification. . . ."

I saw Papa look up sharply above my head. I turned and to my horror found Jacopo Strozzi towering over me. Romeo quickly and smoothly withdrew his hand from mine, and I prayed the movement had not been observed.

Clearly, Jacopo had had second thoughts about the seriousness of Romeo's and my flirtation.

"*Buon giorno,*" Jacopo said to Roberto. "Forgive my unexpected arrival. My own family gathering has been called off, and
I thought your kind invitation might still stand."

"Of course!" Sophia stood. "I will tell Filippo to set another
place." When she walked away, I noticed that she did move as if
she was in pain.

Roberto looked less pleased than his wife, having only just
learned comfort in my father's presence. Jacopo, coming at this
rude hour, with his grating voice, was most unwelcome, but
hospitality must of course prevail.

Filippo appeared with another bench, and a maid with a
plate, goblet, knife, and spoon. Jacopo took a seat next to Marco,
who actually grimaced at me. The soup course was served.

"Have you heard the rumor," Jacopo began, not looking up
from his minestrone, "that England will now buy the lion's share
of its wine from Spain, not Italy?"

"I had not heard that, no," said Roberto.

Sophia lowered her spoon. She looked distressed. "This is
bad news. Much of the Monticecco wine is exported to King
Henry." She caught her husband's eye.

"Not to worry, *cara*. It is only a rumor." Despite Roberto's
confident words, I saw that the story upset him.

"Even if it is true, Mama," Romeo said in a soothing tone,
"we always have our oil." Then he turned to Jacopo and, while
retaining a pleasant smile, bored into the man with suspicious
eyes. "Where did you hear this gossip, signor?"

Jacopo seemed to be brought up short by the question, but
he quickly answered, "My brother now serves as a *signore.*" He

turned to Mona Sophia. "But of course your husband is correct. It may not be true in the least."

"Well, shall we refrain from gossipmongering, then?" my father said with a sharp edge in his voice. "We are having a pleasant afternoon here."

"At least we were before you arrived," said Romeo to Jacopo.

"Romeo!" Sophia cried. "Mind your manners. Signor Strozzi is our guest."

"Yes, forgive me. I forgot myself." Romeo's voice bore no inflection, thus no real apology.

Jacopo bristled. Papa looked annoyed, though I could not discern with whom he was more perturbed.

Suddenly Romeo stood in his place. "May I say a few words?"

All but Jacopo nodded their approval.

"The Monticecco are delighted by this visit from the Capelletti." He smiled and acknowledged Papa, Mama, and me. "As a gesture of the new friendship between our two houses, I wish, on behalf of our family, to extend the olive branch of peace to yours." He stepped away from the table and moved to a sheet-draped mound. He pulled the cloth away with a flourish to reveal three gray-leafed saplings, their fat root-balls wrapped in jute. "Or should I say the whole tree!"

Beaming, my mother clapped her hands and embraced her new friend Sophia. Even my stern father was moved by the gesture.

"There is one for each of you," Romeo continued, the implication that Jacopo Strozzi was not a member of our family unspoken, but less than subtle. I hardly dared meet Jacopo's eyes.

Instead I stood up and went to Romeo's side. I caressed the slender trunk of one of the trees and smiled at our gathered families.

"On behalf of the Capelletti, I accept your beautiful offering. But we are not tree keepers, so perhaps you might come to our garden and help us plant them. Explain their care."

"It would be my pleasure," he said, and bowed to my father.

My heart leapt as Papa smiled at him.

"There is one thing more," Roberto said, speaking directly to Papa. "I understand that you are having difficulty arranging for transport of your goods ever since . . . the sinking of your cargo."

"That is true," my father said. "Everyone's ships are engaged for the time being."

I noticed Jacopo sitting up straighter in his chair and his jaw beginning to clench.

"I would like to offer you the use of one of the vessels with which I contract to transport my wine to England . . . until you can make other arrangements."

Papa was more than a little surprised, even shocked. "That is a very generous offer, Roberto."

Romeo's father leaned forward and held Papa's eyes. "Let us be frank, Capello. Under the circumstances, it is the least I can do."

Everyone was silent, respecting the honesty and naked humility of the sentiment.

Everyone but Jacopo, who bristled with such frustration that I was forced to bite my lip to keep from smiling. I didn't dare look at Romeo.

At that moment a parade of servants arrived, carrying a display of festive main dishes, which, by their magnificence, capped the sober moment with laughter. A whole roasted pheasant arrayed with some of its prettiest feathers was followed by a crackle-skinned piglet, its jaw clamped around an apple, and a huge dressed mullet that appeared to be leaping out of a sea of greens.

Roberto held his goblet high and Papa did the same. *"Salute!"* they cried in unison.

"To friendship," Mona Sophia said, holding her glass aloft.

Romeo helped me into my seat, his shoulder grazing mine. "To love," he whispered soft, so only I could hear.

To love, I thought, and, though no words were spoken, knew that my Romeo had heard.

The talk was lively. Wine flowed. Marco kept us laughing with his antics and terrible puns. Leaves rustled overhead as the last yellow light of day turned to mauve, deep purple, then black. Servants lit candles and torches, and in the evening chill the men brought wraps for their women. My father had gone to the carriage to fetch one for Mama. Romeo returned from the villa with two shawls of fine gray wool. As I watched him place one around his mother's shoulders, I felt Roberto lay another over mine. I smiled up at him, thinking, *Here is my father-in-law in his first act of kindness to me.* I chanced to see Jacopo across the table, frowning.

"You have a sour look about you, signor," I said very quietly, so no one else could hear. "I hope you are not ill."

He fumed, refusing to answer, so I shrugged my shoulders and welcomed Romeo back to his chair.

Another round of wine was drunk as we nibbled at cheese and olives.

"Well," Papa said after a time, "it pains me to say so, but we must start back to town sooner than later."

There were cries of objection all around.

"Next time, the Monticecco will come to the Capelletti's house," Mama announced, and everyone loudly chimed their approval.

Slowly and reluctantly we began to gather our things. Jacopo had said his good-byes with the barest acceptable show of politeness, and stomped away toward the pasture. But as the two families walked slowly toward our carriage, upon which the three olive saplings had been tied, a figure came raging out of the dark at us.

"My horse has thrown a shoe," Jacopo huffed.

"Oh my dear," Mama said, sincerely concerned.

"Our stable hands are gone on the Sabbath," Roberto said. "I'm afraid I'm not adept at shoeing."

"I am," Marco offered. "It won't take long."

As he and Jacopo headed for the stable, our fathers fell into conversation and our mothers hurried into the villa, happy for the respite and a few more moments of each other's company.

Romeo grasped my hand and walked me quickly into the shadows at the side of the house.

"Was that your doing?" I whispered in the dark. "The thrown shoe?"

"His horse complied nicely," he said.

"And Marco?"

"Our new friend . . ."

Abruptly Romeo turned and pulled me to him.

I gasped, but my arms flew around him. Then his mouth was on mine, his lips and tongue still sweet with wine and warm, gentle but probing. I do not know how I knew to kiss, but my natural hunger drove me till I was lost, drowning. I felt a hand on the smooth skin of my breast. I took that hand and pushed it deep within my bodice, crying out when his fingers found the nipple. His other hand covered my mouth. I bit his palm hard and with a cry of delight he buried his face in my neck, covering it with kisses. Pressed tight as we were, I felt his urgent hardness and ground my hips to his. Now a hand on the flesh of my thigh.

"No!" I whispered.

"No?" he whispered back.

"Yes," I sighed, and his throaty laugh mingled with mine as his fingers found my sweetest spot, now wet and soft and yielding.

Voices and footsteps! Jacopo's. Marco's. They were leading a horse.

We pulled apart, aggrieved at our separation. I pushed down my skirt. Romeo surveyed the moonlit yard beyond the shadows.

"Are you composed?" he asked breathlessly.

"Hardly," I said.

"And I am hard."

I laughed. "What a pair."

"We must make haste or they will suspect. Come, straighten yourself. Out into the moonlight walking side by side. Talking loudly. Arguing."

We did as he said, stepping away from the shadow of the house.

"But that is not his meaning," I said with feigned impatience. "When he says, *'Truly, she grieves so that whoever were to see* her would die of pity,' he does not speak of Beatrice. It is the *other* gracious lady of whom he writes."

We had come into the sight of our parents, Marco, and Jacopo, who now stood at the carriage.

Romeo smiled broadly at my father. "Your daughter's scholarship exceeds mine, signor," he said with mock disdain.

Papa smiled indulgently.

"Too much education ruins a woman," Jacopo insisted, altogether serious, causing everyone to stare at him.

Mama looked alarmed, then said in a kindly voice to Jacopo, "Ruined? Not your Juliet."

This seemed to calm him, that I was still his in my mother's eyes.

"Of course not," he assured her.

Jacopo took up my hand and kissed it. I was forced to smile despite my loathing. He took to his horse and sat waiting for our departure, already impatient.

I was last into the carriage, Romeo helping me in. *My private scent,* I thought, *is on the hand that steadies me now.*

"Good night, Romeo," I said, hoping he heard my love in those simple words.

The passion of his gaze told me he did.

But I was not the only one who had observed that gaze.

Jacopo was staring at us with a look I can describe only as wonder, as though he had grasped an impossibility—that the daughter of a silk merchant and a young man of no standing whatsoever in Florentine society might defy all convention, ignore his pronouncements and vile threats, and dare to love each other.

This made him, I thought with a shudder, a very dangerous man.

Chapter Thirteen

I found myself after that extraordinary Sunday in a state of Limbo, a strange purgatory of obsession and desire for Romeo that churned my senses and left me weak, and of loathing for Jacopo that, strangely, made me strong. But that which gnawed at me most relentlessly was the question I had asked Romeo. The one he had never answered.

Would it satisfy you to merely become my courtly lover?

For all the fine words and passionate intimacies we had shared, I realized with alarm, we had never once spoken of marriage. When Jacopo threatened him with death or castration if he laid more than a chaste lover's hand on me, or a head gently on my knee, Romeo had remained silent. I had wished at the time for him to lash out at the insulting supposition that he and I would be content with that common arrangement. So many of the great ladies of Florence boasted courtly lovers, young men, unashamed of the passion they bore for their beloved—the unattainable personification of womanhood—who publicly and sometimes mawkishly proclaimed that love with verse and song under their ladies' loggias.

Would Romeo be thus content? Why had he never answered my question?

Of course I had provided my own explanations for this compulsive worrying. I believed with all my heart that Romeo loved me, desired me, but that he had thought it unwise to reveal our plans to Jacopo, better to allow him to think our intentions were in no way serious. Romeo's answer to my question had been interrupted by Marco climbing down from the olive tree. And of course Romeo would never had striven so passionately to make peace between our families had he not been intent on marrying me himself.

But truly these arguments did little to satisfy me. I realized that my dream of a marriage for love with Romeo had, to this moment, been nothing but an assumption on my part, and never his promise. His sincere adoration of me could be preserved intact with me as Jacopo Strozzi's wife, and Romeo as my courtly lover. And the truth was that Romeo had desired peace between the Capelletti and Monticecco before he and I had met.

These unsettling ruminations were made infinitely more unbearable by a long silence between us. For three weeks as summer bled into fall, he had made no attempt to see me, either publicly or in the privacy of my garden balcony. Neither did letters arrive with assurances that he was, even now, carving the path to our future.

And for the first time ever, I found myself at a loss for words. The inked quill in my hand was stilled, stymied by the chaos of my thoughts, paralyzed by this crisis of confidence in my lover.

Mama had asked me please to stop at the factory on the way

to confession with Lucrezia and the other girls of my *brigata*, and bring a stew to Papa. I agreed, calling for the litter a bit earlier than planned. I had always enjoyed spending time with my father at the silk works. The men were friendly as I nosed around the weaving and dyeing rooms, and Papa delighted in showing me the newest pieces and letting me choose my favorites to take home for my gowns.

But this day I was in a foul mood, having lain awake half the night, my worries like gnomes crouched around my bed whispering their bedevilments till I thought I would scream.

I went to kiss Mama good-bye, but she was distracted by the problems of the kitchen maid, Viola, just that morning found to be pregnant. My mother handed me the covered iron pot wrapped in a small rug, cautioning me not to burn myself, as though I were a six-year-old, then turned back to the weeping girl, who was terrified at the prospect of losing her place in our household. I knew Mama had too soft a heart for that, though she would surely make the girl suffer some agonies of worry—as the price of her profligacy.

The first nip of autumn chafed my cheeks as I climbed into the litter, glad I had the pot upon which to warm my hands.

At the factory I alighted and the bearer handed me the pot in the rug, now barely warm, but smelling richly of beef and rosemary and beans. Below the old sign proclaiming CAPELLETTI SILKS I saw a trio of Maestro Donatello's artisans sketching out a new one that would surely include Jacopo Strozzi's name.

The arched stone doorway, grand enough for a palace, belied the rough industry of weaving and dyeing behind it. The cavern of a room into which I stepped deafened with its clacking looms and toothed warping machines manned by hard-backed weavers, who all stopped to nod at me and smile. The reek of woad and saffron and weld wafted in from the dyeing chambers beyond, where every man—clean as his person might be—wore a pair of dark-stained hands at the ends of his wrists. In cubicles were throwers, twisters, and winders of the silkworms' thread. Here were clean hands and delicate fingers at work. And out of my sight completely was the warehouse that stored the bulk of Papa's goods.

I headed with his midday meal through my favorite room of all. It was quiet and unmanned, and bolts of finished silks stood upright like soldiers in strict array by color, pattern, and weave. Vermilion, indigo, yellow, green. Figured silks, repeating patterns of rondelles, birds, and trees. Floral designs of pomegranates and artichokes, rich brocades, and velvets with silver-gilt welts.

And on the table upon which the fabric would be spread for viewing lay a pair of scissors nearly two feet long, from tip to handles. I had always, as a little girl, found the shears fascinating. They were far too heavy for me to hold, and I loved to watch my father wield them with easy grace. But now I just wished to be done with my errand and be off to the meeting with my friends, the only true comfort of my life.

Papa's office was ahead, its door open. *There were voices. Two of them. I heard my name spoken aloud.* I stopped where I was, then moved with stealth to one side of the door. I listened . . . eavesdropping again.

"She is eighteen, Capello, more than ripe for marriage." Jacopo Strozzi spoke these words. "Do you deny it?"

"I will not deny it," my father said, but his voice was strained.

"Then let us make this betrothal. The sooner, the better."

"You try me, Jacopo." I heard the soreness in Papa's tone. "We are beset with serious problems in the dyeing chambers, and all you can think of is the marriage bed."

"I have told you why suddenly our vats produce nothing but dull browns and moldy greens. You refuse to believe me."

"I do refuse to believe it is sabotage. Roberto Monticecco would never dare to take such actions now."

"*Now?*" Jacopo said. I could just imagine the sneer on his lips. "Now that you are 'friends'? Do you really believe a man with so deep-seated a grudge has forgiven you the ruination and death of a sister and a nephew?"

My father's silence worried me. *Argue with him, Papa,* I silently cried. *Tell him the breaking of bread and the sharing of wine and good cheer between our families were sincere. Tell him!*

"What if I were to bring you proof?" Jacopo said.

"If you have proof, why have you not brought it forward before?"

"I did not wish to stir the pot. Capello, our partnership papers are not yet signed. . . ." A whine came into Jacopo's voice. "Everything is so fragile. I worry, I worry. . . ."

"No, no. No need to worry. We are strong together. My silk. Your wool. No one will sell more fine cloth than Capelletti and Strozzi."

I heard the sound of a hand clapping a back.

"And our families shall be joined as well," Papa added. "Sooner than later."

"Ah, my friend!" Jacopo exclaimed.

No, not your friend, I silently cried, *and not my husband!*

I knelt and set the pot on the floor outside the door, turned on my heels, and fled through the silk room, into the racket of clacking looms, and out the arched door.

"Take me home," I said to the footman.

I fumed inside the litter amid the cushions, the pace of the bearers suddenly slow and aggravating. My temper flared and I pounded on the floor. "Hurry!" I called. "I am ill!"

I *was* ill. Sick at the thought that Papa would give his blessing to this despicable creature—one who so maligned Romeo's innocent family. One who would happily marry me, imprison me in his wretched mother's house, take mistresses himself, and permit me an impotent courtly lover. Damn Jacopo Strozzi! Damn him to the Eighth Circle of Hell, where, with all other "fraudulent counselors," he would be clothed in flames that charred his flesh.

Damn him!

Chapter Fourteen

Romeo Love,

Something must be done, and done quickly. Jacopo Strozzi presses Papa for my hand, and our betrothal may be soon announced. You and I have never spoken aloud of such things, so I must trust my heart in this matter. Pretend I know yours. Risk humiliation. But your actions to this date have given me reason to believe you feel as I do. With my soul laid bare I await your response.

— Juliet

I folded and sealed the letter with red wax and went slowly down the stairs, wishing to avoid my mother, who sat close by the window embroidering. Brightly lit as it was, she still squinted at the tiny stitches with her weak eyes. I was so stealthy she never looked up from her sewing.

Then I hurried out the courtyard door. Across the small central garden was the kitchen, where Cook—fat and rosy-cheeked and armed with a mallet—was pounding a fillet of beef as though to kill and not soften it. So intent was she, she never looked up. But the one I sought was near the alley door, kneeling with her back to me, scrubbing a kettle.

I went and knelt down beside Viola. She was sixteen and pretty with pale yellow hair and delicate features, now red and swollen from crying. My mother treated her miserably for a servant who was not a slave. Many wealthy Florentines employed them—dark-skinned blackamoors and pale-skinned Circassians from the Russian steppes. Viola was simply a poor Tuscan girl. I found her to be full of common sense and sweetness. And I always believed her features were fine enough that had she been clothed in silks and brocades, her hair prettily dressed, she could easily have passed for a gentlewoman.

"Lady Juliet," she said, and stood.

"Can we speak privately?" I whispered.

She faced me fully with a questioning look.

"Come outside." I slipped out the door. In a moment she followed. Together we stood in the alley, where several chickens and a pig grazed on the offal that rotted in piles where it had been thrown.

"So you are still in my family's employ?" I asked.

She blinked back the tears and nodded.

"Is my mother very angry?"

"I thought she would have my head on a platter, like John the Baptist's."

"Perhaps I can smooth the way for you. Speak to Mama of Christ's forgiveness in such matters."

"You would do that for me?"

I searched her blue eyes, then smiled. "Who is the father?"

Her face lit with the suddenness of the sun emerging from behind a black storm cloud. "It is Massimo. The butcher's son."

"The one who delivers our meat?"

She nodded, smiling fully.

"So you are not unhappy at your predicament?"

"I was fearful of losing my position here, as I give my mother money for our family. And Massimo and I are yet too poor to marry. But how can I be sad when this boy . . ." She stopped, unsure if it was wise to continue.

"When this boy . . ." I urged her to go on.

"When he loves me, and I him. I will have his baby. What a blessing from God that is!"

"It is a blessing, Viola. As is your love."

She looked at me strangely, as though surprised that such words would be uttered by someone like myself. I came closer and leaned in to her ear.

"I wish such a love for myself."

Viola drew back, happily shocked. "Lady Juliet!"

"I urgently need to send a letter to a certain gentleman."

"Not Signor Strozzi?"

"Not Signor Strozzi." I smiled conspiratorially. "Could Massimo be convinced, for a price, to deliver the letter with all secrecy to a villa across the river?"

"I think he could."

"Oh, Viola, you are a good friend." I pulled the letter from my skirt pocket and slipped it into her hand. "No one must know. No one but you and Massimo. Can you promise that?"

"I promise."

Now I slipped a small pouch with some coins into her other hand. "Perhaps this will pay for a wedding."

Viola was beaming now.

"But secret," I said.

"On the life of our child."

I smiled. There could be no more faithful an oath than that.

Massimo proved a swift messenger and Romeo, I was much relieved to know, an eager respondent, for the following morning I was awakened at dawn by loud sounds in the walled garden. I threw on my robe and quietly opened the door to the balcony, there to find my love, in only shirt and breeches, had cleared a patch of thick undergrowth, digging in the earth. The three olive trees his family had given mine stood in a row nearby.

He had not seen me come to the rail, so I leaned upon it watching him work, his broad shoulders narrowing to a taut waist, the muscles of his buttocks rounded and firm. The sight of his shapely thighs rippling made me warm between my own. He stopped to wipe his brow and I said quietly, for just his ears:

"Romeo . . . Romeo . . ."

He stilled and came to attention but did not immediately turn.

I grew bolder. "So you're here fulfilling your promise, are you?"

"A promise once made must never be broken," he said, and came full around to face me.

I was aware of no one listening from where I stood, and by his boldness knew that no one below could have an ear on us either.

"This promise," I said, sweeping my hand at the walled garden, "is of trees planted. What other promise do you make?"

He held my eye as he said, "For love to grow."

For love to grow? I thought. *All well and good. But still no talk of marriage. Have I been made a fool of? Does he really mean to be no more than Jacopo Strozzi's cuckold?*

"Romeo!" It was my father's voice echoing in the garden.

I withdrew with all haste into my bedroom, closing the door

behind me. Once inside, I heard footsteps in the hall outside my door. I leapt into bed and pulled up the covers.

Just in time.

Mama entered, carrying my breakfast tray. She set it down on my marriage chest.

"What is all the racket in the garden?" I asked, pretending to rub sleep from my eyes.

"Our new friend Romeo Monticecco is here to plant those olive trees. He's a nice young man, is he not?"

"Nice enough," I said, still unsettled by Romeo's less-than-perfect answer.

I sat up and threw my legs over the edge of the bed.

Mama handed me the bowl and a spoon, then commenced bustling about, opening the window to the walled garden and peeking out. "I think I should ask him to stay for the midday meal."

I wanted to hug her, but I remained cool and passionless.

"Will you send Viola up with some hot water for my basin?"

"Of course." She seemed distracted, mildly upset. "I haven't finished the nightcap I was embroidering for Mona Sophia. I cannot let Romeo leave empty-handed."

"What about the drawstring bag I've been working on? With just an hour's more work you could finish it, and send that instead."

Mama brightened considerably. "A lovely idea." She went out and closed the door behind her, leaving me alone with my thoughts and the sound of my lover—if not my future husband—digging in the walled garden.

Chapter Fifteen

When Viola came in and I rose to dress, I was suddenly light-of-head, and my heart began to beat wildly. The maid said nothing as she emptied the steaming water into my basin, but she was smiling happily, as though she knew my sweet secret.

"Yes, it is he," I admitted.

"He's very handsome," she said. "And he is kind. When Cook sent me out with some watered wine, he bowed to me—a kitchen maid—and smiled the prettiest smile."

"I like his smile, too," I said. "Can you stay and help me dress?"

"Cook will be cross."

"I'll make your excuses."

So Viola removed my night shift and, once I had washed, pulled a fresh one over my head. Then we stood shoulder to shoulder at my red lacquer cabinet, staring at my gowns—skirts, bodices, and sleeves, a rainbow of silks. With my doting father a merchant of the stuff, I boasted a wardrobe as fine as the wealthiest girl in Florence.

Never an upstairs maid, Viola had dealt in vegetable peelings, plucked chickens, and dirty pots—never lace and brocade and satin. Now her eyes were on stalks. I could see she wished to reach out and touch them.

"You decide for me," I said.

"I?" When I nodded, the girl let out a deep sigh and reached in for a shimmering skirt of a color that bled between green and peacock blue.

"Don't forget," I said as a gentle reminder, "this is the midday meal, not a Medici ball."

With great thoughtfulness she took out a rich yellow bodice embroidered with peach thread. Pleased with her choice, she found the matching sleeves. I plucked the skirt from its hook and together we laid the outfit on the bed and stared down at it.

"This will do nicely," I said. "A good choice."

"Sit down and I'll fix your hair," she said, assuming a sisterly tone.

I obeyed her, enjoying her pleasure. Viola proved deft with her hands, weaving four small braids that lay close to my head but left much of my thick hair curling down at my shoulders.

I was more than satisfied with her efforts. I would speak to Mama of Viola—it was time I had a lady's maid.

Then she helped me on with the yellow dress, seeming to take delight in every sleeve lace tied, every button fixed, every skirt fold fluffed.

"You are beautiful, my lady," Viola whispered, starry-eyed.

Then she became stern. "Now bite your lips. Pinch your cheeks."

I did as I was told, and she held the mirror for me again. In the wavy glass I tried to see what Romeo would see. *Am I pretty? I must be,* I thought, *for all girls in love are pretty.* Well, enough of that. I must go down.

Before she let me go, Viola dusted my neck and shoulders with a delicate rose-scented powder and, with puckered lips, blew the extra off.

"He is a lucky man," she said, her features suffused with hope and joy, for herself as well as for me, I thought.

As I hurried out, she called after me, "You'll speak to Cook?"

"No worries, Viola!" I called back.

Then I was on the stairs and at once I heard my mother's voice and Romeo's at the table. I had tarried too long with my hair and clothes and girlish chatter.

I was late.

Then I heard his laugh, deep and rich in his throat, and my knees all at once turned to jelly. I slumped on the stair. *Was it fear I felt? Too keen an anticipation? Or was it memory? Groping breathless in the shadows. His fingers on my thigh, my—*

"Juuu-li-et!" It was my mother's merry call. "Is that you on the stair? Come down. Our guest is waiting!"

Mama is the key, I thought. Through skillful scheming I must make her an accomplice—no, *the mastermind* of my joining with Romeo. She must believe it her own idea, and then use her wiles on Papa to convince him thusly.

"Coming!" I called back.

When I came round the arch to the dining room, I received a further shock. I had known Papa would be absent—he ate most midday meals at the factory. But the sight of my beloved alone with my mother at our table, and in such a state of easy grace, took my breath away.

She was chatting as she was wont to do, of small things, with the deepest earnestness. But where my father would merely tolerate such banalities, attend with only half an ear—Jacopo's boredom was barely hidden—here Romeo was facing Mama full, nodding in agreement, his eyes alight with interest. Was he sincere, I wondered, or was he playing her, charming her with false concern? If he was, I could not fault him, for moments ago I had harbored a scheme of my own to play my mother. But no. I recognized the look on his face. I'd seen it before—when he'd attended his own mother, his beloved mother.

And I'd seen it when he'd looked at me.

He was *listening*. A man listening earnestly to a woman speaking. It shook me to the core. And another thought: as the men of Greece and ancient Rome were said to hold in highest esteem the love of other men and beautiful boys, here was a man who appeared to love the whole of womankind. I guessed he might have borne affection for grandmothers and little girls as well.

Then he looked up and saw me. He jumped to his feet. "Lady Juliet."

"There she is," my mother cried as though a long-lost cousin had appeared. I took my seat and turned to Romeo. "I could hear you working from my bed. What a racket you made."

"That garden is strewn with rocks."

"Will the olives grow there?"

"Not as large as the fig near the balcony," he said, holding my eye. "That is a beautiful tree."

I found it hard to keep a straight face.

"Capello tells me it is the oldest in all of Florence," my mother said. "Juliet, you must pick a basket of figs and send them home to Mona Sophia."

Romeo turned back to my mother. "How kind of you, signora. She adores that fruit, and we have none of it on our farm." He placed his hand on hers and his voice softened. "You made her so happy with your visit. She smiled for days afterwards. Spoke of her new 'lady friend.'"

My mother's eyes glittered with joyful tears, and she clutched Romeo's hands in hers. "I felt the same . . . although I called her 'sister.'" Now Mama's warm gaze fell on me. "The ladies of my *brigata* have all gone their separate ways, and I have longed for such a friend."

"Well, it seems you've found her," I said, then turned to Romeo. "You should bring your parents here. Let us entertain you. Maybe on John the Baptist's Day."

"We could go to Mass together," Mama suggested, alive with ideas. "View the procession. Then come home for a meal."

"A feast," I corrected, happy at the turn this talk was taking.

"We will bring the Monticecco wine," Romeo said, with mock solemnity.

"Cook can make her pigeon tart," my mother added, clapping her hands delightedly.

"And one of her famous confections," I said, smiling gently at my mother. "What a lovely day it will be."

Cheerful as the midday meal was, I claimed the need to rest

in the afternoon, thus avoiding a sewing session with Mama. She would need her concentration for finishing the drawstring bag in time for Romeo's departure, I suggested, and she readily agreed.

He went back to work in the walled garden, I to my room. Speaking with him alone from my balcony—even after our cordial dinner—would be thought untoward. I was still, after all, promised—if not yet betrothed—to another man. My hopes of Mama's help in bringing our family and Romeo's together were for this moment just that—simply hope.

But the sound of Romeo's labors so close with no sight of him was torture. A way must be found to waste none of his precious presence. Then I saw it—the means to my salvation. I went to my writing table where it had always stood, on the wall near the door, and made to move it. Small as it was, the wood was stout, and even the smallest repositioning scraped loudly on the floor. Mama would hear.

Lift I must.

This was no task for a gentlewoman, but a burly man, and as I wrapped my arms round its corners, bent my knees, and with a grunt felt it lift off the ground, I had to laugh at myself. What a sight I must be! But a demon had seized me and I *would* have that desk in sight of Romeo.

A few inches was all I could manage at once without a great crashing down at the end. And so in increments I lugged the thing all across the room, thinking that at such a rate Romeo would have finished and gone home before I had seen success.

Finally I settled it at the garden window with a sigh of satisfaction. The chair was easy after that. I sat quite ungracefully, warm from my exertions.

There he was, right in view—my Romeo. I marveled at how excellent were all his parts. How his manner was so lively, yet devoid of arrogance or, like my cousin Marco's, overmuch levity. When he spoke, he was dignified, maintaining intelligent thought, though lacking pretension. But what I found most marvelous was that, by a single word or gesture, he full understood the mind of another . . . and cared to dwell on those thoughts. And though he could not pass the test of constancy—for our time had been so short as yet—I believed him without duplicity or craftiness. Women were forbidden gambling, but if I could, I would stake my life on this man's faithful nature.

Now as he wiped his brow, he looked up at my room, boldly stared with a gaze that anyone could see was a longing one. When he finally looked away, I found I had not breathed for the full length of his stare. I gasped in air.

Good Jesus, this man has bound my heart in a thousand knots and I have no wish to untie them. I am a willing captive, helpless as a slave girl.

Then, like a revelation, I saw the paper there before me, and the quill. I took up the feather in hand and sought the inkpot with uncommon trepidation. Slowly I set my eyes on Romeo in the garden below. This time the sight unloosed the words, and like the Arno at flood tide, they came pouring forth.

My love, you've made a Temple of a fig tree,
and there before it praying are three new olives.
Architect of nature's passion, you dig and plant,
entice the fair sun to play on their branches,
water their roots, for the rain is delayed.
Your shoulders are broad and beneath your shirt

I see them, hard and strong, with arms that have held me,
hands that have found me, fingers that have touched me.
These shoulders, arms, hands, fingers, built the Temple of Love,
lit my heart's fire, plumbed my soul's well,
plucked the sweet Fig of Desire, and placed it on my tongue.

As hours passed, I watched as one by one, with gentle care, he set his charges in the ground, judging the shade that would fall upon them, pruning a wayward branch. But there he did not stop. With amazing industry he set to work cleaning the long-overgrown path that wound through the garden so that a person could again walk there. And lying on his back under the fountain, he brought it to life again, so that water came splashing merrily from the spigot.

I nearly wept when he pulled on his doublet and gathered his tools to go. All his excuses to stay in my view, in my garden, had run their course.

One last time he raised his eyes to my room.

Feverish, I went to my basin and splashed cool water on my face, my neck. I smoothed my skirts. Went out of my room. Descended the stair.

At the door Mama was saying good-bye, handing Romeo a wrapped package that would be the embroidered bag.

"There you are, Juliet," she said. "I was going to call you." But I wondered if she would have. She seemed distracted, her eyes soft with affection.

"Lady Juliet," said Romeo in the humblest tone, "your good mother tells me this embroidery is your work. Mama will be grateful. Her fingers are sore and getting twisted. She can no longer sew." He turned back to my mother. "But you knew that,

Mona Simonetta. I am grateful for your kindness to her. And now I'll take my leave." He smiled warmly at the two of us. "My reluctant leave."

He took Mama's hand and kissed it. Then took mine. Under such close scrutiny he dared only graze it with his lips, and never even met my eye.

Then he was gone.

Mama and I stood unmoving near the door, silent and stunned by the loss of Romeo's light.

"I am fond of that young man," she said in a quiet voice. "So fond . . ." Then, never meeting my gaze, she turned and left me.

Slowly I climbed the stairs, hope rising with every step. *Mama loved him. Loved Romeo like a son. Perhaps a son-in-law. She wished him for me. I was sure she did.*

"Juliet!" Mama called from below. She'd come back to the stairs.

I peered down to see her looking up with consternation. "The figs," she said. "You forgot to give him the figs."

Once in my room I hurried to the balcony door and threw it wide. I stood at the rail staring ruefully down at the prettily restored garden, the silver green leaves of the new olives glittering in the afternoon sun. Yet without my love's presence it was empty, cold.

I wished to recall the verse I had written of him and turned back to my room, to my writing desk. That was when I saw it.

A cloth package on the balcony ledge below the fig tree's stout limb.

I walked slowly across the stone as if to my destiny. A foot square, the thing was wrapped in clean jute and tied with thin cord. I touched it. It was soft. I took it in my arms and went inside. Then I locked my bedroom door.

The knot was easy to untie. I laid aside the cloth wrap and found my gift from Romeo. Carefully folded—a long white shirt, a gray doublet, breeches, a pair of men's shoes, a flat cap. Beneath the hat a note.

"Midnight," it read.

Chapter Sixteen

The household was long asleep when I rose from my bed and lit a single lamp. The wait had been interminable, my mind afire with excitement and worry. I listened for Mama and Papa to fall into silence in their room, the servants to close and bolt the front door.

Feeling quite the outlaw, I donned the clothing Romeo had left me, first the lawn shirt that smelled of soap and lavender, then the breeches. Before I pulled the fustian doublet on, I thought, *These must be his clothes.* I brought the garment to my face, inhaling the faint manly scent that was certainly his, one that I would in future years better come to know.

The slippers were large on my feet, but not so much that lacing them tighter could not make them do. I had loosely braided my hair and found that the large cap covered it all. Taking the candle, I walked—as a man—across my bedroom floor, feeling strange and vaguely silly. I opened the balcony door and peered into the dark.

What was Romeo thinking, having me dress as a boy? And at this hour? But of course there was only one meaning. He was coming for me, and he meant to take me out in the streets of Florence. But why? This would put me in danger, and if he loved me . . .

My restless heart began its hard pumping again. My nerves were so frayed that when the campanile bell tolled the first of its twelve chimes, I came nearly out of my skin.

Then I heard a faint rustle at the garden wall. A low thud. All was in shadow but the sounds grew nearer. The crack of a twig. The soft scrape of shoe leather on bark. Creaking wood. I stood at the balcony door certain that crossing this threshold at midnight would alter the course of my life.

Altogether.

Irrevocably.

In the instant I stepped through, down from the overhung branch dropped my outlaw partner, landing light on his feet, then rising to his full height before me.

"Romeo," I whispered, but he put a quieting finger to my lips. *Don't speak*, he mouthed silently. He went into my room, returning with the lamp. He held it before him and took in the sight of me from head to toe. He smiled, less amused than approving.

He took my hand and led me to the balcony ledge. I shook my head—I could not climb the fig; of that I was sure—but he bade me look down with the lamp's light and I saw that there, firmly propped, was a garden ladder. I looked back at him. His face was alive with adventure. His eyes urged me to trust him.

I nodded my agreement.

He grinned and slowly—so to demonstrate what I must

soon do—threw one leg over the wall. He beckoned to me and, holding the lamp, had me watch how his foot had been placed on the ladder's first rung. Then he swung his other leg over, moving down, making room for me above him.

Fearful as I was—for I had never moved my body so—I did not tarry and lifted my leg, twisting and clutching the balcony wall. I felt a hand on my ankle helping me place my foot on the rung. Then with a leap of faith I swiveled and threw my leg to follow the other. That, too, was guided by Romeo's hand and suddenly I stood, both feet on a ladder rung outside my bedroom balcony.

The feeling was heady.

I heard Romeo lowering below me, rung by rung. I reached down with my toe and found the step. Brought one foot to meet the other and that way descended to the garden floor.

He took my hand then, guiding me around the newly cleared path—it had all been part of his plan!—past the olives to the wall that separated the garden from the street.

"Wait here," he whispered, disappearing back into shadow.

A moment later he returned, the ladder under his arm. He placed it against the wall, careful to make no sound at all, then swiftly climbed to the top and called me to join him.

Suddenly I felt bold. I gripped a rung above my head and ascended. Moments later, there I was at the top.

"Remember what you did on the balcony?" he said in low tones. "It is the very same here. One leg first. Swivel. Then the other. I will be waiting to guide your feet." Then he was gone over the wall.

I took a breath of the night air. It filled me with courage, and barely thinking, I made my move. Another ladder and the promised help were there, and in moments we were both on the ground.

I turned to Romeo. Triumph lit his face. He set the lamp down, dousing it, and stood and kissed me full and heartily.

Was I dreaming? Was this real? Here I was outside my garden wall just past midnight garbed in male clothing pressed hard against my lover.

Romeo pulled from the embrace, donned a full cloak that had been lying near the ladder on the ground, then placed an arm about my shoulder.

"We are two friends carousing," he said as he walked us into the street. "Don't leave my side."

"Never," I said as we headed for the corner.

Dante was right, I thought. *Love is insane.*

Chapter Seventeen

*H*ow shocking it was to see that the streets were so alive amid the curfew in the dead of night. Massive lanterns on the corners where fine houses and palazzi stood threw wide collars of light around them diminishing into shadows, where could be seen small groups of figures loitering, others squatting in door-ways. As we strode past, keeping our heads together, I could see that the lion's share were gambling—dice. Frowned upon by the church and moral authorities, the game was beloved by all men, played with reckless abandon causing some to lose fortunes or, if violence ensued, even their lives. Few of these Florentines looked up from their candlelit pleasures at two young men passing.

Then it struck me. Romeo and I were meant to be seen as two male lovers.

"Are we disguised as *Florenzers*?" I whispered. This was the German word that described such men. So many were known to reside in Florence that the city's name now connoted the condition.

"You may speak normally, 'Giuliano,' " said Romeo with a sly grin. "No one is listening. And yes, we will be seen as a pair of sodomites out for a night's stroll."

A loud cry echoing from a darkened alley as we passed it stopped me cold.

"Romeo!" I said, clutching his arm. "Someone is being hurt. We must—"

"No one is being hurt, my love. Look closer." He guided me a yard into the alley, and now I could make out the shape of a man pressing a woman against the stone wall. Her skirts were hitched high, her legs wrapped around his hips.

Carefully protected as I had been my whole life, I rarely had occasion to lay eyes on a prostitute, no less one vigorously engaged in her profession. But the posture of the woman and her patron was not so far removed from Romeo's and mine at his villa wall, and I thanked the darkness for hiding my hot red cheeks.

Coming toward us now was a small but raucous *brigata*— young men all centered around one of their own, leaning in and teasing him with leering, drunken epithets.

"How many times were you able?" one rejoined.

"Four," the lucky lover replied, sounding very proud.

"Right," another man cried, poking the braggart in the chest, "and I've got four balls!"

"And your *cazzo*'s four inches long, fully erect," a fourth man insisted.

As we passed them arm in arm, their eyes fell on us briefly. I thought I saw in the gaze of several of them a certain hunger for two pretty young men, but we moved on without incident.

Now as we headed toward the cathedral piazza, I heard

Romeo whisper urgently, "Separate, Giuliano," and he pushed me aside. We continued walking, but ambling several feet apart from each other. A moment later I saw the reason for it.

A roving patrol of *polizia*, large and tough, carrying lanterns and armed with nightsticks, was hustling all the loiterers, gamblers, and whores from every alleyway and loggia. They would not look kindly on a pair of Florenzers, I thought.

The patrol had stopped to harass a clutch of dice players in the doorway of the cathedral. Angry shouts and the crack of nightsticks on flesh and bone were alarming. Romeo deftly steered me out of sight onto a side street. He shielded my body with his own.

"Why have you done this?" I whispered. "I am mystified that you've chosen to put me in danger."

"It was necessary. You'll see." He peered around the corner, then pulled back quickly, flattening us both against the wall.

A moment later the patrol, with bludgeons raised threateningly, was herding the grumbling gamblers before them, past us on the street.

When all was clear, we emerged, crossing the piazza to the cathedral doors, which were now deserted.

Once again I marveled at the sight, both familiar and foreign. Countless times I had come to worship or make confession under the dome of the most celebrated church in the world, yet I had seen it only by the light of the sun, and never in moonlight. And certainly I had never crossed its threshold in the sacrilegious garb of a man. Joan of Arc had been burned at the stake for such a blasphemy, I thought with a shudder.

But Romeo was holding one of the great doors ajar. The church was always open with no fear of vandalism or violation.

Everyone knew that the consequences of such a sin would be paid for more dearly in the next life than in this one.

"Come quickly," said Romeo.

I followed him in. Devoid of worshippers, students of Dante, penitents, and priests, the Duomo by candlelight was terrifying in its size and echoing emptiness. The massive dome above us was a great, looming starless sky.

He walked boldly up the center of the cross-shaped nave, I a few steps behind him. But at the main altar there was no need for instruction. We both fell to our knees and crossed ourselves. I heard Romeo quickly and quietly murmuring a novena.

"Good Saint Anne, mother of her who is our life, our sweetness, and our hope, pray to her for us and obtain our request."

I wondered for what request he might be praying, but a moment later he was on his feet, making for the altar containing votive candles. Putting a coin in the box, he took two tapers and lit them, then returned to my side and, grabbing my other hand, pushed me through a door I had never noticed before.

"Where are we going?" I said, realizing too late that my voice was magnified many times over in what appeared to be a narrow, low-ceilinged passage.

"Just follow, Giuliano," he said as softly as he was able, yet his voice was easily heard. "Step up now. We will be climbing."

"Climbing?"

"Yes. Stairs. Many stairs."

My heart—that necessary organ that pounded as frantically in fear or exertion as in love—now began a wild thumping.

Indeed, we were climbing.

Except for the light of two candles, we ascended in the airless pitch-black, both spiral stairs of stone and others steep and straight. The shadowy lines of Romeo's cloak swaying rhythmically before me held me spellbound, making the careful placing of my feet on the steps even more difficult. But for Romeo's presence, the upward passage was altogether terrifying.

We emerged suddenly onto a narrow railed ledge that had us looking down from a great height onto the Duomo floor, a vast expanse of marble, now bathed in a patchwork of candlelight. Above us Brunelleschi's egg-shaped cupola hovered in fantastic emptiness, its lower edge spaced evenly with circular windows.

I turned to Romeo. "You've been here before?"

"Several times." He peered up into the darkness. "They say one day the whole of the dome will be painted by the great masters. Even now, plain and whitewashed, it is breathtaking."

I was yet bewildered by Romeo's actions this night, and his motives. He confused me, this wild and gentle man. He appeared unabashed, wholly confident. I could not fathom the questions to be asked. *Have we arrived at our destination? Why have we come here?*

"Are you ready?" he finally said.

"Ready? Is there more?"

"Oh yes. We climb more stairs." His eyes glittered by the light of the candles we held between us.

"You look like a naughty boy who's made off with Cook's warm pie," I said.

He grabbed my hand, abruptly turned, and pulled me around the whole ledge's perimeter and in through another door. Suddenly we were climbing again, within what must have been an inner wall of the dome itself! These stairs were long stretches straight and steep, with occasional turns and several moonlit windows as we rose to the ever-narrowing egg's end.

"Four hundred and sixty-three steps," Romeo whispered breathlessly and pushed open a metal-studded door.

The cool air blasted fresh against my face as we emerged into the world of night as I had never seen it. The sky was vast—a black crystal bowl enclosing a full circle of horizons, and the stars pricks of white fire moving and alive, seeming only inches beyond my fingertips.

From such a height my familiar city was a foreign landscape. The bell tower next door looked immense, and in moonlight the expanse of red roofs was an undulating sea, the Arno in the south a glimmering silver ribbon.

Romeo led me to the cupola's rail. He took my hands and placed them on it, far apart, as if to steady me. Then he came and stood behind me, draping his arms around my shoulders to enfold me. He leaned down to speak and I felt his warm breath on my neck.

Now he pointed to the western sky. "There is the constellation under which I was born—Taurus, the bull. See the V shape there? It is the bull's face. I was born in May and the great astronomer Paolo Toscanelli—who my father hired to cast my horoscope—said that I was 'imbued with earth elements, exemplifying the fecundity of nature.' As for my future, I would have 'great successes in life, and many strong children.' "

"Strong children?" I said teasingly. "That conjures terrible visions of a broad-faced, wide-hipped wife to bear them."

Romeo laughed at that. "Toscanelli also predicted—and my father always reminded me—that I would find 'a lover of great fortitude.' " He gazed at me deeply but said nothing. Then suddenly a gust of wind knocked the cap from my head and we both lunged for it. It escaped us, and we watched it flutter down and down till it came to rest on a pale rib at the cupola's widest curve. My hair had unloosed from its braid.

Romeo pressed himself against my back and hugged me tighter, his arms a protective cocoon as we stood against the buffeting breeze.

"Do you know your stars?" he asked. "The house you were born in?"

"Pisces, the fishes," I said, "but my horoscope has not been drawn. Don Cosimo had Lucrezia's done, but in fact, it is generally thought unimportant for girls."

Romeo turned me to him and his eyes went soft gazing at me. "Have you any idea how beautiful you look in the moonlight?" He traced his fingers along the ridges of my cheeks and chin as he recited:

> *A halo of bright stars is your crown*
> *The moonlight in your hair unbound . . .*

"That's good," I said. "Go on."

But he shook his head slowly no, his eyes steady on mine, then kissed me, hard and soft at once. There was no more strength in my doughlike legs, but my arms were steely, pulling him to me, *into* me if I'd been able. I was past embarrassment of my sudden, greedy hunger.

His hands were on my breasts, searching beneath the doublet for flesh. Mine found the hardness between his legs. I groaned at the shock of it. I loved the taste of Romeo's mouth, smoky sweet and warm, and by his soundings knew he found my devouring an equal pleasure.

We sank to our knees and in a single motion he unfurled

his cloak and laid us down upon it. The stone beneath us was unforgiving, so he pulled me atop him. In breeches it was easy to straddle him, and while perhaps a shameless posture, it was altogether natural and altogether pleasurable. He laced his fingers through my hair and with it drew me down to kiss him again.

Oh, what a heavenly mattress was this man!

The thought came that the cathedral dome would be lit by our fire like a great torch, for all of Florence to see.

"Tell me what you're thinking," Romeo demanded suddenly.

"What I'm thinking?" I whispered, pulling back, catching my breath.

"Yes. Right now. You have a certain look when your mind is working."

I told him my vision of a brightly illuminated Duomo apex.

He moved his hips under me with a wicked smile. It made me gasp.

"An explosion of light?" he said, and moved again.

I laid my hands on his chest and found the two tiny buds of his nipples beneath his thin shirt. I brushed them gently with my fingertips.

"What are *you* thinking?" I said.

"What a strangely beautiful bride you will be."

I strove to remain calm. It was the first that he'd spoken of marriage. "Why strange?" I asked.

"A bride in men's clothing."

"What do you mean, love?"

"We must marry tonight. Here. Now."

I shook my head no, but found myself speechless at the thought.

"There is no other way, Juliet." He sat up, suddenly sober, and gently helped me off him. We sat side by side, our backs to the rail.

"What about our parents' blessings?" I demanded.

"We have mine, but we shall never have yours."

"But my mother loves you. She would speak to my father. . . ."

"Your father will not agree. He is more tightly bound to Jacopo Strozzi than it seems."

"How do you know this?"

"I have made it my business to know." Romeo took my hand and held it to his lips, then brushed his cheek along its back. "His silk business was foundering even before my father's saboteurs sank his cargo. The Strozzi wealth and Jacopo's partnership are necessary to keep the silk works solvent. The promise of your hand in marriage was your father's way of sweetening the contract, keeping his new partner happy in the early days of their dealings.

"And Jacopo is a determined man. He is a third son with brothers who have healthy male heirs. The bulk of the Strozzi wealth will never be his. This has made him bitter. He realized a need to partner in a well-established concern, for his money is limited. What he did have to invest in Capelletti Silks was just enough. He and your father are a perfect fit. That is why when he learned of my father's sabotage on yours, he grew so angry. It threatened Jacopo's own interests, for if Capelletti Silks foundered, so, too, did all of Jacopo's best-laid plans. The humiliation before his mother's eyes would have been unspeakable."

I felt my face begin to burn. "Then how can you and I possibly marry?"

"Without anyone's knowledge or permission. While it will certainly infuriate Jacopo, he will not feel betrayed by his business partner. At worst it can only be seen as an appalling act of rebelliousness by his daughter, who is, after all, only a brainless woman. Jacopo can thereby save face—a necessity. Of course we will have to endure your parents' wrath."

"Papa will never forgive me."

Romeo took my face in both his hands. "The scandal is sure to rock Florence. We will be shunned, unwelcome in the best homes." A smile cracked his features. "But we will be *married*, Juliet. We'll always have a place with my parents. We'll make a very happy foursome."

"Until our 'many strong children' come?" I said. Jest though it was, I must have looked unconvinced.

"Oh, love, how can we not be together?" Romeo cried. "Without the sight of you every day, the smell, the taste of you, I would wither away. My blood would turn to powder in my veins. And you? Have you not found in me a mirror for your soul? When you look at me, when we speak, touch, do you not see who you really are? I dare you to deny that in my presence you love yourself better. I *know* this is true, for I love myself better in yours."

Worry still creased my face.

"Juliet, do you trust me?"

"I should not—this is such a lunatic scheme. But I do, Romeo. With all my heart." I kissed his hand. "But how shall we be married here and now?"

He stood and offered me his arms and pulled me up. "By a priest . . . and a friend of Dante's."

Chapter Eighteen

*J*ust moments from the cathedral up the Via Ricasoli was the Monastery of San Marco. I had passed it countless times in my life, never giving it a second thought. The Dominican friars who lived within were known to live calm and tranquil lives.

Now having traversed the arched cloisters overhung with elegant frescoes, up a flight of stairs and down the dim inner hallway lit only by feeble flickering candlelight, we stood still as statues and hardly breathing, outside the plainest of wooden doors, waiting for it to be opened. My long hair, without the cap to hide it, we had tucked inside my collar.

"Knock again," I whispered. "Perhaps he didn't hear. Or forgot we were coming. Might he have forgotten?"

Romeo shook his head, but his worried eyes were fixed on the door. Finally, with a creaking loud enough to echo alarmingly down the tomb-silent hall, it opened. There before us, a bit bleary-eyed and still straightening his brown robe, was Friar

Bartolomo. He peered out, looking both ways, and quickly ushered us in, muttering, "Pray God you were not seen. Pray God, pray God."

"Have no fear, Father," said Romeo in hushed tones. "We were very careful."

The cell was bare stone on all but one wall, upon which was painted a most fabulous fresco in jewel-toned colors, of Saint Dominic in the act of reading. I had heard rumors that Don Cosimo, claiming San Marco as his spiritual home, a place to which he retreated regularly to pray, had had frescoes painted by Fra Angelico in all the public rooms, and in every one of the monks' tiny cells.

The cot and desk and chair, I saw, were of the rudest materials and design, and the crucifix on the wall no more than two unadorned pieces of crossed iron. A few volumes of Dante's works were piled one upon the other on the desk. Dried flowers hung heads-down from the ceiling, and a long shelf crammed with bottles and vials of potions, and parchment envelopes I assumed to be medicinal powders, were, save the frescoes, the room's only luxury. On a hook hung a simple white robe of nubby linen, perhaps for sleeping.

"Let me look at you both," the friar said, his voice urgent.

Romeo turned to me then and with gentle hands pulled the hair from under my doublet's neck, settling it over my shoulders. It seemed such an odd thing to do and was yet so natural, as if I were already his, and so intimate an act his right. This made me smile. I tried to stifle it, and found Friar Bartolomo amused by our little performance.

Finally Romeo stepped to my side as if presenting me.

"Ah, I remember this lady," said the monk. "A student of the Poet, and overly bold for a woman."

"She is a poet herself, Father. You should hear her verse. It's very good."

His eyebrows rose in two round arches.

"You are a poet, too, Romeo," I said. "You began a pretty one on the Duomo roof."

"You took her to the top?" The friar looked scandalized.

Romeo smiled proudly. "That is where I proposed marriage."

Friar Bartolomo was staring at me, a look of dismay creasing his features. "I cannot marry you like this," he said.

"What?" Romeo was aghast. "But you told me . . ."

"The male garb. It is a sacrilege, my son. Blasphemy."

"But you must. As I told you, this is the only chance for us to wed."

The monk was sadly shaking his head.

"Is all that I need a skirt?" I asked.

"Well, ah . . . a skirt. Yes."

I was trembling as I said to the priest, "Will you lend me your robe? That one there." I lifted a finger to the white garment on its hook.

"*Ach . . .*" He was quite at a loss for words. A strange woman asking to don his personal apparel.

"Yes, *please*, Father." Romeo had assumed the tone of a penitent, as if pleading for God's mercy. I worried that he might fall to his knees, and perhaps so did Friar Bartolomo, for all at once the monk turned and snatched the linen robe from its hook and thrust it at me.

"What we do for love," he whispered, and pushed Romeo from the room, pulling the door closed behind them.

There I was, all alone and needing to make myself a bride. I stripped quickly and stood there shivering in my nakedness, nipples so hard they were painful. I threw the robe over my head, happy that the friar was a short man and the garment clean, smelling of starch and lavender. I took up the doublet again and slipped it on over the linen dress, pulling the laces tight, approximating a lady's bodice. I stepped back into the shoes, which, with the outfit, looked comically large. I tried to arrange my hair prettily, but without a mirror I was stymied.

All at once I thought, *Here I stand in the moments before I become a bride—all alone.* I had always envisioned Lucrezia dressing me for that occasion, as I would do for her, the feel of Papa's precious silk against my skin, studded with a thousand seed pearls, fresh flowers woven into my hair. . . .

Well, it was not to be so. This was different. Romantic and unique. Something we would someday tell our children. *Your mama wore a priest's nightgown and floppy shoes to her wedding.* The thought made me chuckle.

It was then I spied a dried nosegay hanging on a string. I could not make out the particular flowers in their desiccated condition, but they would do. Carefully, so as not to crush them, I separated a half dozen from the bouquet and wove them through my hair.

With a single fortifying breath, I opened the door. Romeo was all smiles at the sight of me. The friar was bemused. But he wasted no time.

"Hurry," he said. "Follow quietly after me, and pray God we

meet no one. Wait!" He rushed back into his cell and collected two books.

Then with Romeo's arm about my waist we made haste behind the friar and presently found ourselves in the Chapel of San Marco under Fra Angelico's altarpiece of the Virgin Mary and Christ among the saints. When Friar Bartolomo turned to face us, we fell quickly to our knees and made the sign of the holy cross on our bodies.

Suddenly I felt all apprehensions lift from the priest's mien. He placed one hand on my head, one on Romeo's. Though my eyes were lowered, I was sure he was smiling.

"Dante and his Beatrice," he murmured. "In a perfect world she would not have died and the two would have married."

Friar Bartolomo read passages from the Bible, all in the Latin tongue, and several benedictions.

"Romeo Monticecco," he said. "Do you wish to marry this woman?"

"I do," Romeo answered, smiling broadly.

"Juliet Capelletti, do you wish to marry this man?"

"Yes!"

When the friar paused then, I thought the ceremony over and sought my husband's eyes. But they were impish, as though he and Bartolomo possessed a secret. When Bartolomo began to speak, again in Italian, the secret was revealed.

"*'She is a creature come from Heaven to earth, a miracle manifest in reality.'*" He was quoting Dante! "*'Ever since you were a boy you have belonged to her.'*"

Now Romeo quoted, passion thickening his voice. "*'This is no woman, but rather one of heaven's most beautiful angels. A lady, refined and sensitive in love.'*"

I groped for only a moment before I responded, speaking Dante's words with quiet reverence. "*'Now my bliss has appeared. I am clothed in happiness.'*"

Romeo clutched my hands and tears sprang to his eyes. "*'As this battle of love rages within me, I am more humble than my words can tell, for here is a God stronger than I, who shall come to rule over me.'*"

I found myself speechless, at a loss for all but emotion.

"*'Love governs your souls,'*" the friar intoned, again quoting the poet.

"I will cherish and adore you," Romeo said. "I will have no other."

These words were not Dante's. They were Romeo's own vows.

"I will cherish and adore you," I repeated. "I will have no other," and added, "For all days and all eternity. For you are my lover and my friend."

He took my face in his hands and kissed me then, with a passion perhaps unseemly for the Chapel of San Marco. We were utterly lost in the kiss, that sweet collision of flesh and mingled breath—so that when the friar spoke, we were startled.

"Have you the rings, my son?"

"Yes, yes," said Romeo, and produced three of them—pretty bands of braided gold.

Bartolomo signaled that they should be given and with shaking hands, as custom demanded, he placed two on my fingers and one on his own.

"Romeo. Juliet. You are married, my children. In the eyes of the Father, the Son, and the Holy Ghost"—the friar flushed—"and blessed by the spirit of Dante!"

I took Bartolomo's hand and kissed it with gratitude.

"You should go now," he whispered with terrible urgency.

"I'll have your robe returned to you," I told him as Romeo helped me to my feet.

"No need," he said, smiling. "I will get another. That is your wedding dress."

Romeo pulled him into an impulsive hug. "I will never forget this!" Then taking my hand, he led me from the chapel.

I cannot say I remember making our way back to my father's house. It was dark, and Romeo, holding me close by him, hid my eccentric wedding gown under his cloak. It was a dangerous walk, but I felt nothing that could not be likened to joy. I was a married woman, married to a man I loved.

My dream had come true.

I came to my senses as I climbed over the wall to my balcony.

"Dawn is breaking," Romeo said. "Into your bed."

"Our bed," I teased. "When will you come to it and make me a complete wife?"

Romeo graced me with a slow smile. "I'll surprise you." Then he grew more serious. "And when we've bedded, we'll tell the world of our marriage."

"Let it be soon, my love. My husband." I liked the sound of the word on my tongue.

There were noises at my bedroom door. "Go!" I said.

He kissed me quickly and descended the ladder. I watched his shadowy form in the last dark moments before first light, and then throwing off his doublet and shoes and the friar's robe, I leapt naked into bed, pulling the covers up to my neck. There would be no sleep for me now, only repetition in my mind of the great adventure of the night past. Some trembling thoughts of my angry father and an outraged Jacopo. My mother, despite her words, would be happy in her secret soul for me. I was sure of it.

But most of all there were visions of my love as husband, father of my children, sweet companion of my life, for all my life.

O Romeo . . .

Chapter Nineteen

With the harvest upon the countryside he did not come to me. A week, two, passed since our marriage with nary a letter, but my heart was calm. He was mine, I was his, embraced by the God of Love and sanctified by the church. It had grieved me to remove my wedding rings and, placing them in a tiny satin pouch, hide them in a hole I had torn in my mattress. But our secrecy would not be long-lived. As soon as Romeo and I had bedded, we would promptly announce our joining to the world.

The days grew chilly, the stone floor beneath my feet damp and drafty, but I walked in the sweet warmth of perpetual spring. Mama grew suspicious of my unnatural mood and when at the table Papa mentioned a generous gift of wine sent to us by his "friend" Roberto Monticecco, I was forced to stifle my urge to cry out, "Your *family* now!"

It was a great relief when Lucrezia and her mother invited me to go with them to Maestro Donatello's bottega, where much of the work of her wedding was taking place, for I'd had no time for private conversation with my friend since the night of my own marriage.

The place was a hive of artistic industry with a dozen apprentices working, as was done at all such artists' workshops, on everything from splendid frescoes and marble statuary to silverwork, death masks, and festive costumes.

Mona Elena Tornabuoni, a pretty-faced but spectacularly obese woman, was held in thrall by the maestro's explanation of the craft involved in the filigreed gold salt cellars she was considering for purchase. Lucrezia and I had hung back out of her hearing so that I could admit to my marriage to Romeo and the rare events that had brought me to that moment.

By the time I'd finished, her features had slackened, the pretty mouth falling open in an O, the green eyes growing suddenly unfocused.

"You look as though I've told you of a murder," I said, dashed with disappointment. "Lucrezia, I thought you would be happy for your friend. I have made a marriage for love."

With thumb and fingers she squeezed her forehead. "You put on men's clothes, tramped about in the street with gamblers and prostitutes and Florenzers, climbed"—she shook her head disbelievingly—"four hundred and sixty-three steps to the top of the Duomo, then put on a monk's robes. . . ." Lucrezia seemed unable to go on with her recitation, and I was growing more and more angry.

I finished for her. "So I put on a monk's robes, but do not forget I used Romeo's doublet for an odd bodice, and some dried herbs as flowers in my hair, and I snuck down the hall of the monastery with a rogue friar and a half-crazed lover, and blasphemed before God by taking my vows of marriage!"

"I did not say that!"

"But you thought it. You did, Lucrezia. Do you deny it?"

"No," she said quietly.

"Lucrezia, Juliet," Mona Elena called without looking back at us. "I want you to see these bowls and tell me what you think."

"We'll be right there, Mama. We're deciding on some gilded fruit decorations for the tables."

Lucrezia turned back to me. She was near tears, but then so was I.

"So only *you* are allowed a happy marriage?" I accused her.

"Of course not. But why could you have not waited? Your families had become friends. Romeo was near to making it possible in an open way. A legal way."

"I told you he said it was not possible! I told you what he learned about Jacopo and Papa's business."

"That is what he told you."

"And that is what I believe! Why would he lie?"

Lucrezia forced herself to hold my angry eyes. "Your Romeo is a good man. A peace-loving man. He's proven that. But he is impulsive, Juliet. Willful. Wild. I think he loves danger too much. Taking you out in the streets at night dressed as a man? Don't you see? Danger sweetens the brew. Makes it more delicious."

"No."

She took on a stubborn expression. "I know you too well. You may be a romantic, but do you swear to me you did not question his mad adventure? Why he would put the woman he loved in harm's way?"

"Of course such things occurred to me, Lucrezia," I finally said. "And yes, Romeo courts danger, but it is well measured."

The image returned of my cap being blown from my head and landing on the red arch of the Duomo's roof.

"This is what I love about him, don't you see? He is gentle. But not too gentle. He is thoughtful and scholarly, but at times his mind soars to far and exotic places. Places where I would like to be. He adores me, but he does not grovel or whine like a sick dog. When he holds me, when he touches me, I *know* that I have been held and touched." I was blushing now, but it did not matter. I could see that Lucrezia's expression was still unaccepting.

"Romeo is my husband, and I have done well marrying him. One day, you and my parents and all of Florence will understand that, and if you do not"—my voice was stronger and prouder than I thought possible—"then to hell with you all."

A terrible and angry quiet fell like a wall between us.

"Lucrezia, I need you right now!" Mona Elena called. Hurt beyond measure, my friend turned away and joined her mother.

The painful silence between us continued for the rest of the afternoon, though Mona Elena was too busy chatting about wedding preparations to notice. Night had fallen as the Tornabuoni litter approached my house.

"So I think we are settled on the dinnerware," she droned on, "though the ornaments may be too expensive. What they charge for goldwork these days . . ."

I was relieved when we came to a halt.

"Thank you, Mona Elena, for bringing me with you to the maestro's bottega."

"But of course, my dear. You are so much a part of our

family"—she gazed fondly at her daughter—"and this wedding."

I gave Lucrezia a kiss, but she remained cool and rigid.

As I descended from the vehicle, the front door of my house
suddenly flew open and Papa burst through it, followed by two
agitated men. As they raced away on foot, my mother, pulling on
a cloak, came to the door, a look of terror on her face.

"Mama, what is it? What is happening?"

"There is a fire at the factory!"

Our litter appeared now, next to the Tornabuoni's. I saw Lucrezia and Mona Elena staring out, bewildered.

"Your father does not want us there," Mama said as she
climbed into our litter, me following her in.

So my mother does have a backbone, I found myself thinking.

Then I began to pray.

We rode in silence, both of us shivering as much with
fear as the bitter night. The grunts of our bearers were loud in
the otherwise quiet streets. Soon, though, we began hearing a
commotion—shouting, clanging, and a crackling roar that I had
never before heard, but knew must be the voice of fire.

Mama and I from one litter and Lucrezia and Mona Elena
from another emerged, wide-eyed and gasping, into a Dantean
circle of hell. The office end of the factory was ablaze, the windows of all three stories belching flames. Along the outside of
the weaving chambers and warehouse there was a long line of
men—many of them our factory workers—heaving bucket after
bucket to the front, where Papa and Jacopo tossed water onto
the extravagant orange inferno. The hissing steam, the black roil-
ing smoke, and the licking fingers of fire that darted out at will

were so terrifying a sight that I felt Mama's knees buckle almost at once.

Lucrezia and I, on either side, propped her up again and moved her back to our litter. There she sat with her feet on the ground—Mona Elena patting her hand—refusing to go inside and calm herself.

"He will burn to death!" she kept crying.

"No, Mama, he is well back from it, though I fear the office and showroom are lost."

We watched as Jacopo, soot-covered and looking very much in command, moved down the bucket brigade and began shouting at a young man I now recognized as my cousin Marco, and several of our factory men, to direct their loads to the divide between the showroom and the weaving and dyeing chambers, the latter still miraculously untouched.

"See how brave your future husband is," Mama whispered, recovering her wits, but grating on mine. "And clever. Should fire reach the dyeing vats, there could be a great explosion."

Suddenly the thought of what she had just proposed caused Mama to shrink back into the litter. It was well that she did, so she could not see my abject expression. But Lucrezia saw, and turned her face away, for we had left on bitter terms the subject of my "husband."

And then as though by the magic of thinking of that person, Romeo appeared before my eyes, racing round the corner at the head of a band of men! I could see they were his father's workers, but they were dressed, not for their labors in the vineyard or orchard, but for some celebration. Now Roberto Monticecco brought up the rear, shaking his head disbelievingly at the terrible conflagration.

At Romeo's shouted orders they joined the bucket brigade, relieving some of the factory men, who fell to the ground limp and exhausted and mightily grateful. Roberto and Romeo went to my father and wordlessly took up the effort by his side.

Heartsick and frantic as Papa was, he nodded thanks to the Monticecco men, and my heart soared to see it.

The fresh manpower behind the water brigade finally turned the fiery tide. Soon there was more smoke than flame, and then no more left of the blaze than a facade of blackened stone and charred window frames. The fire out, the night became dark again, with only a few street lanterns flickering on the faces of the dazed and exhausted men.

I followed Mama as she threw herself sobbing into Papa's arms. He appeared too tired to be angry at the foolish women who had disobeyed his command and followed him to the disaster.

Marco, greatly relieved, embraced his aunt and uncle.

Silently I sought Romeo's eyes. His face was racked with divergent emotion: waning passion from the fight, pride in his men's bravery, but sorrow, too, for my father's loss, and, if I was not mistaken, joy at seeing me again—his love, his wife.

Jacopo strode up to the clutch of us then, and I thought— with a flicker of apprehension—that I saw a darkness there, one beyond his oily, soot-smeared face. In the next moment, and to my horror, I knew I had not misjudged.

He gave Romeo's shoulder a vicious shove.

Roberto was the first to spring defensively forward. He placed his body full between his son's and Jacopo Strozzi's. In the next instant Papa pushed Mama from the center of the clutch and confronted the face-off.

"How do you dare disrespect my son?" Roberto demanded of Jacopo. "He and my men just helped save this factory."

Jacopo spit on the ground at Roberto's feet. Everyone within sight gasped at the appalling insult.

My father put a hand on Jacopo's arm. I could see he was trying in vain for calm, and to find the right words in question.

"Jacopo, my friend. What has been the offense here? As Roberto says, Romeo and his men risked their lives to save our property."

"Thank God we were nearby," said Romeo, still bristling.

"We'd come into town this afternoon," Roberto explained, forcing evenness in his voice. "We all went to the cathedral to give thanks for our successful harvest."

Jacopo seethed. "More like successful sabotage."

With that, Romeo surged past his father and clutched Jacopo round the neck with viselike fingers. I startled at the fury I saw in his usually gentle expression.

"You accuse us of sabotage!" he cried.

Papa pushed the men apart. His features were twisted with confusion. To Jacopo he growled, "Explain yourself."

"I was walking home from Arentino's and thought that I should go to the factory and check the manifest for tomorrow's shipment. As I rounded the corner, I could see smoke pouring from a lower window. And then I saw a man running away." His eyes passed over the faces of all the workmen who had gathered in abject silence to hear the accusation. They fell on Filippo, a man I recognized as the Monticecco's house servant. "That man," Jacopo declared.

"That is impossible," Roberto cried. "Filippo has never left my side. First at the cathedral. Then at the inn where we celebrated. But more than that, he would have no reason to set your factory afire." Roberto turned to Papa with baffled eyes. "We are friends, Capello."

"How easy it is to claim friendship." Jacopo's mouth set in a stubborn line. "I know what I saw."

"You're lying," Romeo said. Everyone quieted and the unnatural silence simmered dangerously. "Why are you lying?"

With lightning speed Jacopo's fist arced through the air, landing a sharp blow to the back of Romeo's head.

Instantly the workmen were alive with anger, as though the blow had been made to a hive of bees. Now they were ready to fly at one another.

But Roberto called out, "Everyone! Quiet yourselves! Stand down!"

Papa sought my mother's eyes. "Take Juliet home. At once!" His eyes flashed angrily. "You should never have come." Then without hesitation he turned from us and pushed his way back into the throng.

Mama turned to me, panic in her eyes. I could see she did not wish to leave her husband in harm's way. Neither did I wish to leave mine. But there was no choice.

We joined Lucrezia and Mona Elena, who had stayed behind at the litters. I saw worry on Lucrezia's face, for she knew that my circumstances—complicated and untenable before—had just become dangerous in the extreme. But I saw no recrimination in her eyes, none of the anger or outrage with which she had punished me at the bottega not two hours before. Perhaps I only wished it was so, but I felt Lucrezia's compassion—the sisterhood that binds all women in love.

With a whispered word of caution, Lucrezia and her mother went their way. Mama and I were taken home.

Chapter Twenty

*W*e sat for a time at the dining table, clutching hands, silent in our misery and worry.

"They're all right, Mama," I said. I knew she believed I meant Papa and Jacopo. "If anything had happened to either of them, we would have heard by now."

"At least your father and Roberto were keeping cool heads." The words she spoke were true, but her furrowed brow belied her calm.

I brought us cups of warm wine and we sipped them, hardly meeting each other's eyes. I could see Mama's lids beginning to droop, but I did not dare suggest she go to bed.

Finally the front door opened and Papa was in our midst, all smoky and black-faced and strangely jolly.

"Everything is well," he said wearily. "Well as it can be, having lost the office and the showroom. But the factory and warehouse were untouched, praise Jesus. And truth be told, the parts that burned were old and falling down. We shall rebuild. No worries."

"But what of Jacopo and Romeo?" I said with perhaps too telling an urgency. "They were at each other's throats."

"They have forgiven each other for their insults."

"And the accusation of the Monticecco's fire setting?"

"Withdrawn," said Papa with a wry grin. "A bit reluctantly, but withdrawn all the same. Those two will never love one another, but even now they are working side by side to clean up the mess."

I felt a jab in my chest at those last words, for the thought was jarring and the image it provoked was false, for Jacopo hated Romeo. Jacopo knew of our love. *But could he know of our marriage?*

I gasped at the thought.

"What is it, sweet girl?" my mother asked, concern darkening her features. "Are you ill?"

"No. It's nothing."

"We should go to bed," my father announced. "Come, Simonetta." He took Mama's hand. "We are all very tired."

"And relieved!" my mother said, smiling up at her husband.

We climbed the stairs together and they watched me into my room. I shut the door behind me.

I was anything but relieved.

I paced and paced, the space of my room and out to the balcony and back. Finally I relented and put on my nightdress and climbed beneath the covers. But I was full awake, as though it were bright dawn after a good night's sleep.

Agitated, I rose from the bed and lit a candle at my desk. Sight of the flame brought memories of the factory fire. I picked up the quill.

Conflagration.
The fires of Hell do I see,
beneath the orange flames
fight my love and my enemy.

Inferno.
Blessed for the sight of my husband adored
brings our fathers pain
and bittersweet accord.

Devil's fire.
Set by him in jealousy's wake
finally vanquished by Good
and by Love's sake.

I was grateful for the time that passed like a sweet spell in the writing. And then like a gift of more magic, I heard a crunching on the balcony floor. I rose and swung open the door, flinging open my arms, knowing it was Romeo.

Knowing this would be my wedding night.

And there he stood, moonlight and shadows. The shoulders broad, waist narrow. Feet set wide apart. Muscular legs strong. His beautiful hair was wild, his eyes shining bright. But he lacked a smile.

And he was covered neck to groin in blood.

The sound I made he stifled with his hand as he plunged into my room and pushed closed the door.

"What has happened? Where are you hurt?"

"I am unhurt." He moved like a cat to the bedroom door and locked it. "This is not my blood." When he turned to me again, the pain was so vivid on his face that I scarce believed him.

"Whose blood?" I said, growing fearful for the answer.

Romeo began to pace from corner to corner, as I had done earlier. He wrung his hands, then raked them through his hair. Yet he would not speak, name the victim.

"Whose blood!" I cried.

His lips were trembling. He plucked absently at the gory doublet. He seemed deranged. "Marco's."

"My cousin?"

He nodded. Then his face crumbled and he fell to his knees. "I killed him. He died on the end of my dagger."

My arms, which had been welcoming, then beseeching, fell limp at my sides. Words escaped me. But there sitting on his heels before me was my poor desolate husband, now beginning to weep. I went to him and came down gently before him, unsure how to touch him, but wishing desperately to comfort him.

I lifted his chin. Tears were brimming, his cheeks a shallow pond.

"Tell me what happened."

He closed his eyes and his mouth worked silently. I could see him remembering, though the words came slowly and hard.

"The fire was out. You and your mother were sent home. My father and yours"—his lips contorted in a pained smile—"refused to believe Jacopo's lie."

I was biting my lip hard. I took Romeo's hands in mine, horribly aware that the blood that had dried upon them was of my own family.

"So we set to work. Inside. Throwing out in the street what remained of furniture and bolts of silk. The company books were somehow spared, and there was much rejoicing for that." It seemed too hard for Romeo to continue, but I urged him.

"Go on."

"I told my father to go home. That Mama would be worried. The men and I would stay till all was finished. Jacopo"—Romeo's face twisted again—"suggested the same to your father. So there we worked, side by side—silkmen, orchardmen, vineyard men—sorry for the loss, but with goodwill and grateful for no injury to anyone."

He stopped and opened his eyes, looking deep into my own. I saw confusion there, as though he sought but could not find the single moment when things had turned for the worse.

"I was out in the street. Most of the men had come out. We were neatening the piles of rubble, burned beams. What remained of your father's desk. Then Jacopo spoke up. Said to Filippo, 'You started the fire. No one can tell me different.' Everyone stopped still where they stood. Filippo said, 'Take that back, or I will break your face.' And our vintner, a gruff man to be sure, he said quite loudly, 'Strozzi pig.'

"All at once the goodwill vanished and everyone was trembling with anger, looking for a fight. I went toe-to-toe with Jacopo and said he should curb his foolish tongue, for Capelletti and Monticecco had made peace, not once, but twice, and I would not allow him to rupture it. Marco was at his side, agreeing with me. Urging Jacopo to stand down."

Romeo's breathing grew ragged and his face pulled into a grimace. "Then I heard sounds behind me. A thud. A cry. Sickening. I turned to see Benvolio down. His head . . . crushed. One of the silkmen was standing over him, his eyes mad, a burned beam still clutched in his hands. That was all it took.

"All hell broke loose. Men shoving men. Punches thrown. Knives drawn. I went to Benvolio, knelt at his side. He was moaning, bleeding from the ears. Then someone kicked me in the back. Hard. My hand flew to my dagger and I came to my feet, ready to fight. But it was Marco standing there, pushing away the man who had kicked me. His hands were outstretched like this"—Romeo opened his hands in supplication—"as if to say 'I'm sorry, my friend.' And suddenly he was *lunging* at me." Romeo drove his fist into his palm. "Just like that! It happened so fast. He was pressed up against me, chest to chest, and I saw, behind him, Jacopo. Grinning."

Romeo sobbed. "Then I heard Marco moan and I knew, I knew, oh Juliet, I knew he was on the tip of my dagger! But before I could move to release him, Jacopo came crashing into his back. His arms went around us both and he *crushed* Marco into me. Crushed him further onto my blade. *Uugh!*"

Romeo covered his face with his hands. "There came his warm blood seeping. . . . I smelled Jacopo's stinking breath on my cheek and he whispered, 'I set the fire.' And then we both felt Marco—oh God, forgive me—we felt the life go out of his limbs. Jacopo pulled away and cried out loud for everyone to hear, 'Murder! Look, here is murder!'

"All scuffles ceased. All eyes turned. Marco was dead at my feet. The knife was still in my hand." Romeo turned away, ashamed to meet my eye, but I pulled him back.

"Yes, there was murder, my love. But you were not its cause."

"Prove it!"

I was speechless.

"Prove it to anyone. Just try." Romeo came to his feet, pulling me with him. "Everyone will swear to be a witness to the murder of Marco by Romeo. Even my own men were fooled."

"It's another of Jacopo's lies. We will tell our fathers. Explain."

"No." He laughed miserably. "There is no explaining it, Juliet. There is only a dead Capelletti at the hands of a Monticecco. That is all anyone will wish to know."

"How did you come here? Why did they let you go?"

"My men closed ranks around me. I bless them for their loyalty. They wanted me to run, but still I could hear them whispering, 'Murder, murder.' I did kill Marco. How could I explain it was not my intention? They held off your father's men and pushed me, pushed me from the street near the factory. As I went, I heard Jacopo Strozzi shouting, 'Let him go. He will not get far, for all of Florence will know of his deed!'"

Finally Romeo was dry-eyed. "So I came here. Where no one would expect to find me. To my wife." He looked at me beseechingly. "Can you forgive me?"

"Romeo, love, you have done nothing that needs forgiving." But the words caught in my throat, and Romeo heard.

"You see?" he said grimly.

"I see nothing but the sad death of our friend and good cousin Marco!" I cried. "He was your kin, too, when he died. So let me offer my condolences to you."

I took Romeo to myself, and he clutched me with hard, sinewy arms.

"Is it not an unkind cut that the one soul who succored our love is gone?" he said.

"Monstrously so," I agreed.

There we stood, trembling with silent grief, for how long I cannot say.

"Let me take your clothes from you," I finally said with all gentleness.

He stepped back and I pulled apart the blood-soaked leather laces of his doublet. He pushed it from his shoulders and it fell like a dead thing on the floor. The arms of his white shirt were dark brown with gore, and this he let me pull over his head. I went to toss it away, and turned back, regaining sight of him.

There he stood, my own husband, Romeo, in naught but his stockings and bare-chested. Despite his pain-racked face he was so beautiful to my eyes that I went and embraced him again, laying my cheek against the soft warmth of his breast.

"I am death, Juliet," he rasped softly. "A young Reaper."

"No. I hear your heart beating. You are life. You are my life." I looked up at him. "Romeo. Husband. This is our wedding night."

He tried to smile, but even such words as I spoke were weak medicine for what ailed him.

Thought of consequences for Marco's killing, murder or not, pressed in on me, heavy, a suffocating cloak. I sought to throw it off with brave words.

"Soon you'll go. Your uncles in Verona will shelter you. And meanwhile, together, we will set this right."

I saw a flutter of a smile, the pain ebbing from his features like an outgoing tide. "Our wedding night," he murmured ruefully.

I took him by the arm to my basin and bade him wash his hands and face in the frigid water. I dried them for him with a scented towel, then took his fingers and placed them on my face. I heard the rush of breath, his relieved sigh.

"Your hands are cold. You should warm them," I said, and pulled open my robe to reveal the thin, fluttering night shift.

He let go a small gasp and could not help but smile. A moment later his expression flattened in remorse.

"It's all right, my love. I promise you. We must take some joy before you go." I reached for his hands and put them at my waist.

That was all was needed.

He pulled me hard against him, laying his warm mouth against my neck. A shock, like lightning, went through me. I moaned and clung to him, as if only he could preserve my life. We kissed and kissed again. I heard, as if from a distance, our short gasping breaths and small wet cries.

Then I was airborne, lifted effortlessly from my feet, and laid with less gentleness than urgency on my bed. He grappled with his hose and I with my robe. I saw him straddled above me, fully naked and steely hard. I laid my arms above my head and he accepted the invitation it was to remove my gown.

With more restraint than I believed either of us possessed in that moment, he found the hem and slowly, very slowly, untangled it from my thighs. The breath suddenly caught in my throat with the thought of my undressing.

My complete nakedness before a man's eyes.

But far from mortifying me, the thought sent a rush of pleasure to that part about to be unveiled and so surprised me I barked a laugh, startling Romeo from a passionate grimace to a grin. He finished my disrobing with a single upward sweep and we came together in a kiss of pure joy and celebration. Our limbs twining, the flesh moved like silk on silk. His hands, warm now, grasped my knees and pulled them high against his sides. I was open, exposed to his center, and now when he put his mouth on my breast and suckled, I was wild with wanting him in me.

Deep, O Romeo, plunge deep!

Whether my cry was aloud or inside my head I cannot say, but he did hear me and complied.

Complied, oh yes . . .

Filled, I was, with his strength and sweet pain. Rocking with a rhythm I did not know I owned. Then he slowed, halted. The look on his face was desperate.

"What, love? Speak to me," I whispered.

"Oh, Juliet, I want this not to end. I want to stay like this with you forever."

I laughed and kissed him. "Can we start again?" Teasing, I moved my hips.

He moaned happily and answered with a great thrust.

"Husband!" I cried with mock dismay, but feeling a thrill in all parts of me.

"So I will start again, good wife, but very slowly." He moved as he'd promised, and the sweetness was so great I thought I would die of it.

"Don't stop. Don't stop," I said.

He did not stop but moved ever more slowly, ever more deeply.

"Oh. What is this? Is there a name?" My breath was jagged.

He put his mouth to my ear and flicked a tongue inside for reply.

"Oh no, no," I begged him.

"I'll go faster now, Juliet. Faster." The man was good at his word.

"No, Romeo . . . oh, Romeo . . . oh . . . oh . . ."

"I'm coming to you, my love," he whispered. "You must come to me. Come to me!"

With all of my being and all of my soul . . . I obeyed my husband.

We lay there side by side, nothing touching save our fingers entwined. The room's chill was creeping up our still-warm, damp bodies. Romeo reached down and brought the coverlet over us. He lay on one elbow over me and tucked the sheet around one shoulder, kissing the other, pushing his nose behind my ear and tasting it with his tongue.

"You are more salty than sweet," he observed.

I turned and licked his cheek. "You are more sweet than salty."

"There is a poem in that, I think."

I looked to my desk and thought of the verse I had written not so very long before, of the fire. Now it seemed a lifetime had passed. Still, I was startled to see a shade of dawn in the window.

"You have to go," I said.

He lay very quietly.

I sat up. "You must go. Now." I rose from the bed and, throwing on my nightgown, went to my clothing chest. I withdrew a shift and from beneath a pile of linen removed Romeo's doublet and Friar Bartolomo's white robe—that which I had worn as my wedding dress. I placed them all in front of Romeo, who had wrenched himself to sitting. Then I found his hose tangled in the bedsheets.

"First hose and nightshirt," I said in the voice of a housewife. "The doublet next. Over that the friar's robe. I'll find a rope for your belt. It will be a good disguise. They'll be looking for Romeo, not a young monk."

He began dressing with desultory slowness.

"Faster," I said, watching the sky lighten the window.

He grew slower yet.

"Romeo!"

Anger flashed in his eyes. "I'll never see you again."

"You will. I promise you will. We have not come this far to be torn from each other forever. We are meant to be together! Romeo and Juliet. Even the Fates cannot part us."

He could not help but smile at my ravings.

"But you must hurry. Leave the city before sunrise. Can you steal a horse?"

"Better a mule if I am to be a friar." He was lacing up his doublet. "First a murderer. Now a thief. Some husband." I helped him on with the robe. "I'll go to the Monastery San Marco," he said. "The stable there."

I pulled the coiled silk tie from my bed curtain and wrapped it round Romeo's waist.

"Your hair," I said. "There is far too much of it."

"Cut it off," he ordered me.

There was a blade under my bed. I took it and with no hesitation began to chop. It was a ragged job but far better than it had been. With the robe's hood on his head he looked a proper novice. The sight of him in his disguise made me smile unaccountably.

"Will I make a good escape in this?" he asked.

"Only God will know this 'servant' was inside his wife last night."

"Juliet!" Romeo laughed at my outrageousness and hugged me to him. But then the embrace grew desperate. I had to push him away.

"Go, Romeo. Now. You dare no longer stay."

"And I *will* see you again? Hold you in my arms?"

"Yes. Yes!"

When the balcony door opened, we both startled at how light it already was. With a final glance he leapt over the wall and scrambled down the fig tree's trunk. I watched my lover-monk run the garden's curved path and, tucking his skirts in his rope belt, scale the garden wall.

Then he was gone. All sight of him. The melody of his voice.

That he was with me still, there was no doubt. His seed. His scent. The taste of him in my mouth.

Despite my cheerful words of our future meetings, the hollowness of his absence overwhelmed me at once. I pulled closed the balcony door, but as it shut and my eyes fell on the pile of his shorn hair, I felt panic rise, as though that door, with Romeo outside it, had closed forever.

"No," I said aloud, scolding myself. I straightened my back. He was my husband. I was his wife—well wed and well bedded. Romeo would find refuge with his uncles while somehow we found justice for him. There could be no question of it.

For the God of Love was merciful, and presided over all.

Chapter Twenty-one

The gloom of Florentine autumn could not have settled more heavily than it did the day we bore Marco to the Capelletti graveyard. The mourning party, one that for our small family should have been modest, began to swell from the moment we left our home. Citizens, having eschewed their peacock silks, had this day donned their dusty black and their grimmest countenances.

Marco's body was borne upon an open bier covered only with a sheer linen gauze by eight men, his friends and family on foot following behind. The cortege moved slowly, but in no way silently. All around me I heard the muttered curses upon Romeo's name. "Monticecco murderer," they said. "Fire starter." "Slayer of the new Florentine peace." "Vile butcher of the city's beloved son."

Oh, how I longed to shout, "You are mistaken! He is innocent! His family are peaceful people. Friends. It is Jacopo Strozzi you should so revile, not Romeo!"

But there I was, trapped beneath my black veil, trapped in the prison of Jacopo's lies, mistruths that the good people of Florence, so unused to peace between our warring families, were all too eager to embrace.

Several families shared the graveyard, their tombs small marble edifices above the ground, these leading to subterranean chambers and tunnels. I was no stranger to this charnel house, for many of my people had died and here been laid to rest. We were taught, even as children, to turn a steely face to the Reaper.

The tomb door—a heavy stone that pivoted on a creaking mechanism—was pushed open by two strong factory workers. Men with torches went in first, ducking their heads, as the doorway was unnaturally low. Priests with their somber chants and swinging incense balls were next.

The family followed, I on my mother's arm. She had been long past tears on the way across the city, but as we entered the tomb, I heard her sob once, then sniff sharply as if to regain her composure. As we accompanied the corpse down the long aisle, we were not spared the sight of our loved ones in every horrible stage of decay. On either side of us on their marble slabs lay Papa's ancient ancestors in long collapsing piles of bone. Then my uncles, great-uncles, their wives and children. The smell was quite unspeakable—sweet, sickening dust, so fine that it felt we were breathing in the dead. Mama clutched my hand tighter as we glided ghostlike deeper into the catacombs, for here reposed the sons and daughters she had borne, in more recent stages of moldering death.

A small commotion and the sound of scraping stone up ahead signaled that Marco had been lifted onto his place of final rest. The priests grew feverish in their prayers and finally Mama broke, weeping loudly, her cries echoing within the arched ceiling of the tomb.

I forced myself to look upon Marco's face under the gauze. I somehow thought he would look different in death, for he had been so animated in life. But there he was, recognizable after all as my dear cousin, always ready with a smile, a sly jest to make me laugh.

A pain stabbed through my chest with the knowledge that Marco had died on the point of Romeo's dagger. Whether by purpose or pushed there, that was the fact of it. Had Romeo and I not loved each other, my cousin would not be lying here dead.

Now it was I who sobbed aloud. I felt a hand on my shoulder and turned to see that Jacopo Strozzi was my comforter. It took all my strength not to cringe away from those bony fingers, fingers that had clutched Romeo and Marco to him in a death grip.

It was unbearable. I feigned an even louder cry and doubled over in a semblance of pain, but it was meant to unhand me from Marco's murderer—and succeeded.

Thankfully the priests' droning had finished, and they turned away from the bier. Others were only too glad to follow them from the tunnel, and none too soon we were back in the dismal but welcome light of day.

The crowd outside the tomb had grown somber. I saw for the first time that day Lucrezia, looking, I thought, as alarmed as she was sad. She was flanked by her husband-to-be and Piero's father, Don Cosimo.

Everyone closed ranks round the clergymen, who would now speak of God's mercy for our beloved brother, and my fa-

ther, who would offer Marco's eulogy. The priests were mer-
cifully brief and stepped back into the crowd that had grown
utterly silent.

My father, grief and the gray light of day having aged him,
began to speak.

"My eldest brother's only son was named after his father.
The Two Marcos, we called them, for the two were alike in
more than name. Some men—I think perhaps I am one—see
more shadow than light in the world. To this father and son,
all was illuminated with boundless hope and unaccountable
joy. My brother's death was a sad thing, but he had lived out
his life. My nephew, whom I had taken to my heart like my
own child . . ."

Papa was unable to go on, but all understood the unspoken words—a man dying too young. There was a furious hush,
seething with indignation and rage.

Then the unexpected happened. The impossible. The
outrageous.

The crowd parted and into the void walked Roberto Monticecco, spine straight and expression mournful. He might have
been a leper, the way people backed from the sight of him. Others seemed poised to attack.

Jacopo moved to my mother's side and placed a steadying
arm around her shoulders. I dared look at my father, whose
mouth had fallen open in shock and dismay. Holding Papa's eyes,
Roberto opened his palms helplessly and shook his head.

"Stop," Papa said. "Stop there."

"Capello, let me speak."

"Speak? What will that accomplish?"

"I've come to offer my condolences."

"I do not want them."

"You know this death was an accident."

"I know no such thing."

"Why would my son wish to harm his friend?"

"They were not friends," Jacopo offered in an offended tone.

"They were," I said, almost before I knew I had spoken.

All eyes fell on me, and I thought Jacopo's glare so sharp it might slice off pieces of flesh.

"Do you *defend* Romeo?" my father demanded indignantly of me. "Were you there?" A place under his eye had begun to twitch. "What does a silly woman know of such things?" His cruelty was unexpected.

I was frightened and humiliated, but I had to finish what I had started.

"Of course I was not witness to the stabbing." I winced as I said the word, remembering the first sight of Romeo at my door, covered in Marco's blood. "But Marco told me how he thought Romeo the best of men."

"Sadly, it was one-sided, this sentiment," Jacopo insisted, growing visibly angry at me.

"No," Roberto said. "My son told me several times of his love for Marco."

"Why should we believe him?" Jacopo persisted. "Why should we believe you?" he said, glaring at Roberto. "You have offended this poor, suffering family by your presence here. Capello is too polite to tell you to leave, but I am not."

Roberto looked pleadingly at my father and at Mama. I could see she was moved by their new friend's words. She wanted so to believe him. Certainly she was thinking this moment of Mona Sophia. I saw her trembling hand begin to rise. Papa stayed it with his own.

"You should leave now," he said to Roberto. "Otherwise I cannot promise your safety."

Roberto stood his ground for a moment more, pleading with his eyes.

Then a rock was thrown, connecting squarely with his jaw. He cried out and clutched his face. Mama and I gasped in unison, but the sight of Roberto's blood dripping between his fingers seemed an instant incitation. The sea of mourners that had parted to admit him now drew closer around him.

Blades were unsheathed.

I saw Jacopo among those who crowded in, clearly pleased at the turn of events. "Papa, do something," I said, not bothering to lower my voice.

He did nothing, and panic rose in me. In moments, Romeo's father could be torn to pieces.

"Stop." The single word, uttered low, was firm and commanding. "Stand down."

I recognized the voice at once, and the mourners—turned surging mob—had known it as well. They stood in place as though a heavenly hand had blocked their way.

Cosimo de' Medici, the most reasonable and respected of men, had spoken.

"Roberto Monticecco," he went on, as though he were addressing a gentleman at one of his balls, "we understand your desire to offer your sympathy and to defend the honor of your son, but perhaps it was unwise for you to come. I suggest you go home. And for the time being, if I were you, I would lock my doors and gates . . . for the safety of your wife and your workers."

The crowd grumbled their assent, pleased at Don Cosimo's warning.

I saw Papa out the corner of my eye. He seemed relieved.

A path opened and Roberto, stiff with dignity, walked through. Once he had disappeared, the space filled with mourners.

Don Cosimo spoke again. "Capello, my friend, you have not finished your eulogy of Marco. Will you continue?"

Chapter Twenty-two

The funeral concluded, members of our family, friends, neighbors, and Papa's clients walked home to our house. It was a truly dismal procession, for it had begun to rain, but all were quietly alert, as Don Cosimo and his son had come, on foot, as well.

Still at Mama's arm, I felt her nervousness. The greatest man in Florence had never graced us with a visit before. Marco, for all that we loved him, was neither a rich nor a prominent man. Don Cosimo's coming, therefore, was a sign of the profoundest respect toward my father, and Papa's civic stature—by this simple act—was greatly enhanced.

He sat at the head of the dining room table. Don Cosimo was given a seat at his right hand, Jacopo at his left. Men of rank filled the other chairs. Everyone else crowded around behind them. The room was overflowing, thick with the smell of wet wool.

Papa had nodded his permission for Mama and me to stay

and listen to this council, but we stood well back, and Mama whispered to me that I must not, under any circumstances, speak. My defense of Romeo at the graveyard had been unconscionable, and no other outbursts would be tolerated.

When everyone quieted, my father spoke.

"Thank you for coming, beloved friends. We have been drawn, against our will, into a serious and dangerous circumstance. The hard-won peace of Florence has been broken with a violence that can only remind us of the warring Guelf and Ghibelline factions. Perhaps it should come as no surprise that if the Monticecco and the Medici"—he turned to acknowledge Cosimo—"and their *amici* were to align themselves accordingly today, Roberto and Romeo Monticecco would claim themselves Ghibellines—rural farmers—and I and my patron, Don Cosimo, would be city-bred Guelfs."

"Are you saying this murder signals the resurgence of that ancient blood feud?" our neighbor asked, unable to mask the worry in his voice.

"Yes," came the answer with calm assurance. But it was not Papa speaking.

Jacopo Strozzi continued. "Not two months ago we learned the true reason that Roberto Monticecco sank Capello's cargo of silk. It was a case of the deepest family hatred, and pure revenge."

There was outraged whispering among the listeners.

"To be fair, Jacopo," my father said quietly, "it was Romeo who sought peace between our families. Roberto admitted the secret scandal that had pitted our families one against the other. And they did pay us reparations."

"And you were forced to pay *equal* reparations," Jacopo insisted with the voice of indignity.

"That is true," Papa said.

"I tell you that it was a false peace, one that the Monticecco never meant to keep. Roberto's sister was dishonored and disgraced, and no amount of money paid would ever make that right."

"This is true," the head silk weaver solemnly offered. "There is nothing worse than the loss of a family's honor. Such a thing seethes inside a person till they die."

My father was listening hard to everything said. I thought I saw more argument on the tip of his tongue—that there had arisen true warmth between the members of our family and the Monticecco. He could not have forgotten how well Mama loved Mona Sophia, and Roberto had sent generous, unexpected gifts and offered every goodwill.

But Papa said nothing.

"It is beyond all reason that Romeo goes unpunished for the killing," Jacopo continued. "We know where he has gone. His uncles in Verona are harboring a violent murderer. I say we go there and wrest him away from that unholy sanctuary. Then we see justice served."

"I will go," the head silk weaver said.

"Let me come, too." This was one of Papa's merchant friends.

Others offered themselves up for the terrible journey to Verona. Jacopo could barely suppress his glee, but with every new volunteer, Papa looked more and more alarmed. I did not dare face my mother.

"We will leave in the morning," Jacopo announced. "Arm yourselves well, as we have no idea how strongly the Monti- cecco uncles will defend their feckless nephew."

"Just let them try," a factory worker warned.

"If they take up arms, they might just find themselves with- out them," another joked, and pretended slashing off his hand.

Everyone laughed.

"That is enough."

The men startled at the sound of judicial authority. Then all eyes turned to attend Don Cosimo, whose face was a grim and threatening mask.

The listeners, including my father and Jacopo Strozzi, seemed to shrink back, as if they had been confronted by a coiled viper.

"What is this talk of revenge?" he demanded, his voice quavering with passion. "Do you propose to go, as a mob, to the city of Verona, drag a young man from his uncles' house, and, without trial, put him to the sword?" He looked around for an answer, but everyone was silent. "A crime has been committed—we know that. But is it not a more heinous crime to plunge Florence back into that dreadful cauldron of ven- geance from which it has so recently emerged? Do you think the violence would end with the death of Romeo? I, for one, cannot see it *ever* ending."

He gazed around the room with apparent mildness and said in the softest tone imaginable, "I am neither a prince nor your king, so I have no say in what you choose to do. Do what you please. What your conscience dictates." But when he sat back in his chair, I could see fear in the eyes of every man there.

Thus was the sway of the Medici, whose disavowal of influence was more powerful than a threat.

"What should we do, then, Don Cosimo?" Papa asked, as a child would ask a father. "Surely you do not mean for Romeo to go altogether unpunished?"

Don Cosimo placed his fingertips together and bowed his head. "Let the Signoria write a Decree of Banishment," he answered.

My heart began pounding in my throat. That word evoked thoughts of Dante Alighieri, who had, himself, been unjustly banished from Florence and who'd died exiled from his beloved home.

Was that now to be Romeo's fate?

"For a Florentine," Don Cosimo went on in a provoking tone, "is banishment not the same thing as death?"

Several men muttered their agreement with the sentiment. My father nodded thoughtfully.

Then Jacopo spoke. "With due respect, Don Cosimo, a cold-blooded murder has been committed. Who knows if Romeo might not steal back into the city and wreak more havoc than he has already done?"

The Medici patron considered this question with closed eyes and tight lips that worked and twisted. In the awful silence I cursed Jacopo Strozzi to high heaven. I had for some time thought him contemptible, but now I saw that he was an evil man, one who had accomplished great harm to the innocent, with no apparent twinge of conscience. I saw that if Don Cosimo's mind could be further swayed against Romeo, he was a dead man.

And I would be a widow.

Don Cosimo opened his eyes. "I have had several opportunities to speak to the young Monticecco, and it is my considered opinion that he will be of no further harm to any of us."

I saw my father's shoulders sink with relief. Jacopo bristled, but did not dare contradict the most powerful man in Italy.

"I beg you to consider our fine city," Don Cosimo continued, "one that has become renowned the world over for its cathedral dome and Baptistery doors, its works of art, and its rich heritage of commerce. We are a people who dare stand toe-to-toe with the pope and to welcome through our gates the great philosophers of the East. Should we allow ourselves to sink so low as to revenge a single killing, no matter how tragic, and throw our populace back into the turmoil of violence that we have finally put in our past?" He looked around at the faces of his fellow Florentines, defying them with his quiet authority. "So, are we decided?" Don Cosimo asked, a touch of levity having crept into his voice.

There was muttered assent all around. Several men at the table rose to their feet.

My mother sighed so audibly that she quickly shrank back with mortification.

My own knees went weak and I braced myself against the wall, forcing an emotionless expression.

Then Jacopo stood in his place. A thrill of unnamed fear clutched at my throat. And when the man smiled that long-toothed yellow smile, every sense in me cried out, "Run! Leave your father's house, for disaster is at hand!" But then he placed his spidery fingers on Papa's shoulder and began to speak. His nasal drone had never sounded more repulsive to my ear.

"While our decision does not please me, it was properly made and I, a loyal citizen of the Republic, shall abide by it. But as my own interests have been diminished by the foul murder of my future partner's nephew—a young man who would have, in the course of time, become my partner as well, and a pillar of Capelletti and Strozzi Silks and Wool—I seek a closer tie to this illustrious family."

Then to my horror, Jacopo's eyes found me where I stood trembling. Though I looked straight ahead, I could feel Mama's eyes boring into me.

"There has been for some months," he went on, "talk with Capello of a betrothal between myself and his daughter, the Lady Juliet."

Contented and congratulatory sounds suddenly replaced the dark grumbling, and a slow smile began lifting Papa's features.

"I therefore propose that our betrothal be announced here and now. . . ."

Mama clutched my arm and whispered, "Joy is born amidst sorrow! Oh, Juliet, you are to be a bride!"

I am a bride, I thought miserably. *This is not possible.*

Papa made to stand, but Jacopo again stayed him with a hand on his shoulder.

"If I may beg one thing more of the girl's father . . . ," he said, addressing the crowd. Now he looked straight at me, holding my eyes with unabashed possessiveness. "I wish that the betrothal be short and that the banns of marriage be spoken with all good haste. In a week or two, perhaps. Once that is done, the partnership papers should be signed and our business arrangements formalized."

I could not withhold my groan of desperation, but it was

masked by noises of approbation, some of which were so enthusiastic as to sound lewd to my ear.

Papa was nodding and smiling at Jacopo.

Then the final blow.

Don Cosimo stood in place and, looking out across the room, found me and fixed me in his gaze.

"You are a dear girl, Juliet, one who is held in the deepest affection by my son's wife-to-be. This has proven to be a painful day for us all . . . except for this proposal of marriage."

Mama stepped up close to me, hoping, I thought, to be seen by Don Cosimo. "Therefore I wish to bestow my full blessing on this happy coupling . . ."

No, I thought, *I do not want your blessing on this marriage!*

" . . . one that will restore the peace to Florence. So with my son's permission, I suggest a double wedding—Piero and Lucrezia, Jacopo and Juliet!"

Piero de' Medici nodded his enthusiastic approval of the plan, and the place exploded with celebration and cheering.

I burst into tears.

Mama laughed and clapped me to her, believing, as all but Jacopo Strozzi must have believed, that mine were tears of joy. What girl, after all, would not feel fortunate in the extreme to be marrying into one of the wealthiest families in Florence, and so beloved by the Medici that they would share with her the wedding day of its heir?

Mama wiped my tearful face with her sleeve and led me through the congregation of men to the head of the table. A numbness had crept over me, and though I knew my legs were carrying me, it was dreamlike, very dark. I felt as though I was walking to my doom.

Papa, Don Cosimo, and Jacopo were beaming. As though preordained, my father nodded at his patron, and in the next moment, Don Cosimo took up my hand and Jacopo's and, placing one on top of the other, held them clasped between his own.

"I do hereby announce the betrothal of Jacopo Strozzi and Juliet Capelletti," he said, smiling. "May God bless your happy union."

The deed was done. The nightmare real.

I was to be the wife of two men.

Romeo

H *ow could it have come to this?* I thought. *I, Romeo of the proud house of Monticecco, slinking out of Florence into exile in a monk's disguise on the back of a broken-down beast of burden.*

Stolen, at that.

My manhood had been stripped from me as I trembled before Juliet in her room, she cutting off my hair to make me safe from capture. She consoling me with promises that we'd meet again. Then tearful and disgraced, I had abandoned her, left her standing on the balcony—the same stones upon which I had first wooed her so tenderly that I'd wholly won her heart—and accepted my banishment.

On this plodding journey, the most terrible of my life, I mourned my losses—my mother and father, whom I treasured and adored. The olive orchard that was my blessed childhood and would have been—but for the jealousy of one vile man— my bright future with Juliet and our brood. And I cursed the loss of Florence, the greatest city in the world, my home.

I had on that dreary ride a hundred times tried to console myself with the belief that Marco, delightful clown and faithful friend, had felt the first shove from behind. Had known it was Jacopo's death embrace pushing him farther onto the shaft of my dagger. Had heard, in the moments before he passed out of life, Strozzi's confession, "I set the fire."

If no one else believed me, I thought, at least Marco had.

It was all the solace I'd allowed myself. That, and my scheme for righting all the wrongs that had been perpetrated against me and my wife—my beautiful, heaven-sent Juliet.

But here, bumping along the exile's road toward Verona, I knew my "scheme" to be no more than a seedling, one that had yet to break through its thin shell to reach damp earth and push up and up, seeking sunlight and fruition. My mind was yet muddled with anger and sadness and mad scenes of revenge. How could a man keep a cool head and plan a clean and measured rescue of his wife from her father's home in a city that had banished him, on pain of death, for his return?

Time would be my friend, I told myself. In the coming days, ensconced in my uncles' safe and tranquil villa, I would cool the fires in my brain, compose my wild thoughts into some coherent design. Yet time, I knew even then, was my enemy. Jacopo Strozzi was capable of anything. I had to work quickly, cleverly ... or all would be lost.

I arrived under cover of darkness at the Monticecco Vineyard outside Verona. As I had always remembered it, the gates of the high stone wall surrounding it were lit by four large lanterns, attended by a gatekeeper. But I, cowering under my white friar's cowl, was unrecognized by this man, one I had well known in my growing up here.

Ahead I saw my uncles' two-story villa, a place they had always insisted on keeping lit up like a palace, never short of oil for their lamps, provided by their dear brother, Roberto.

"A man of God," I was let into the house at once, only to be mistaken again for a monk by a house servant who must have been hired after my departure to Padua. He showed me into the first-floor salon, one my uncles had transformed into their vineyard office, the business being the center of their lives.

Sight of my uncles Vittorio and Vincenzo poring over their ledgers, their two favorite hounds at their feet, cheered me immeasurably. They looked up in surprise as the servant ushered in this unexpected visitor.

"Thank you, Francesco," Uncle Vincenzo said, and the man went out, shutting the door behind him. At once and with the greatest relief I threw off my hood.

"Romeo?" Vittorio said to me. Then he looked at his brother. "Good Jesus, he's become a priest!"

A moment later they were on their feet showering me with hearty kisses and embraces, and I quickly disabused them of my clerical affiliation. They called for food and wine to be brought in and locked the office door.

I commenced to tell my story. Then I blurted my frantic and confused plans for returning to Florence to liberate my bride and find a life with her elsewhere.

There was a long silence when I had finished. My uncle Vittorio—rotund, ruddy-faced, and perpetually jolly—spoke up. "Well, at least you are in good company. Your idol, Dante, was himself banished from Florence." He threw his dog a tidbit. "And they *begged* for his return."

"After he was dead," I murmured miserably. "I tell you, I

cannot wait to be invited back. I have to go and take Juliet from her father's house."

"You mean abduct her," Vincenzo said. He was the more serious of my two uncles, slender and handsome like my father was.

"She is my wife!" I cried.

"A return to Florence under these circumstances is death," Vincenzo finally said. "Certain death."

"Did anyone see you arrive here?" Vittorio demanded to know.

I thought not.

Still, the brothers shared a worried look.

"We must get you to safety. The Strozzi will know where you've come. They cannot be allowed to find you here."

That they would pursue me was a thought, in my distracted state, I had not considered.

"Forgive my stupidity, Uncles," I said. "I never meant to place you in harm's way."

"No bother," said Vincenzo. "We will ferret you away where no one will find you."

"Even us," Vittorio added with the joviality I had always loved.

"There is a small house in the Torricelle woods we have just acquired," said Vincenzo. "The owner died. We have never been there, but they say the path is marked well enough if you know the way."

"But he *doesn't* know his way," Vittorio said.

"He will learn."

Uncle Vittorio hugged me to him. "He is a clever fellow, eh?" He smiled. "Our Romeo, come home to us."

"We've missed you," Vincenzo said.

"I've missed you, too."

"But now we must prepare. Vittorio, you see to the mule. Remove the saddle and bridle and bags, and bring them inside. Don't tie him up. In the morning if the stable hands find him, we will say he wandered here." Uncle Vincenzo turned to me. "Go up and lock yourself in your room. Stay very quiet. Even the servants must not know of your arrival. Meanwhile I will procure the map to our new property. And then, tomorrow night, when everyone is dead to the world, you'll take the map and torch and you will go."

In my old room I wrote to Juliet, assuring her of my love and making apologies for my weakness at our parting. I swore that a scheme was taking shape for my rescue of her, and pleaded that she take heart and wait for further word from me.

This I gave to my uncles with instructions for its delivery to my friendly friar at San Marco. Bartolomo would pass it to Massimo, the butcher's son and husband to Juliet's maid. He had once delivered me a message from my love. It was circuitous, this route, but perhaps safer for its winding path.

The next night I stood staring at the edge of the woods where my uncles had taken me, hidden under rugs in the bed of their grape cart. The head of the narrow footpath had been marked with a rugged outcropping of stone, but the trail itself was so overgrown it appeared I might set the trees afire with the flame of my torch as I walked it.

"Be careful!" Uncle Vittorio warned me.

"He'll be careful," Vincenzo said. "Give him the food."

"The food, the food . . ." Vittorio went to the cart and brought me a cloth sack. "They say a clear spring is a hundred paces from the back of the house."

"God protect you from evil spirits," I heard Vittorio say as I plunged into the undergrowth.

"What evil spirits?" I said, turning back. My uncles' faces flickered in the torch's glow.

"There are none," said Vincenzo unconvincingly. "It was the house of an old woman. Some say a witch. But we do not believe in witches, do we, Vittorio?"

"Better a woman's house than a man's," I said as I turned to go. "It will probably be clean."

And so it was. Clean and tidy and, while quite small, hung liberally with shelves and cabinets containing every sort of herb and potion that a witch, or more likely a country apothecary, would ever need. There were scrubbed pots hung above the hearth, and the place was well stocked with candles—a great boon for a man alone at night in a dark wood. As promised, a small stream ran clear over its rocky bed just a stone's throw from the house.

It seemed a place of great comfort for the concocting of my plan.

I began to write at once.

The scheme itself was more than formidable. To be considered was the choice of conveyance and my stealing back into Florence unrecognized. There was Juliet's liberation from her father's house, though I had great faith in this part, remembering her intrepid adventuring on our wedding night. But even if we should escape undetected from Florence, where would we go from there? How would we live? My skills would be useful in anyone's orchard, but without a small fortune we would be no more than servants of another man. Did I dare ask Juliet to relinquish the privileged life she had known? Juliet, a lady's maid? A laundress?

I believed that my father would gladly sell a portion of his land to stake us, but the thought sickened me. And even if our fortunes saw us in comfortable circumstances, would we—my bride and I—be forced in our exile from home and family to relinquish our good names so as not to be found, and myself branded as a criminal?

I fell into the crone's bed, my head spinning, and slept fitfully. I awoke to a pouring rain that continued all that day, rendering the narrow path out too muddy to traverse. The forest was so sodden and lonely and gray that in quiet moments all manner of demon memories descended upon me. The senses that had cheered me so, now haunted and depressed me. Sight of the fiery inferno at Capelletti Silks. The feel of my clothing soaked through with Marco's blood. Jacopo's stinking breath. His evil whispers.

Acts of the blackest revenge festered and grew in my heart. It pained me to know I had come full circle from seeker of peace to purveyor of vengeance. I wondered if these were the same that my grandfather had felt for Juliet's family, causing him to push my father into the violence that had brought down so much misery on both our houses.

Worse still, my heroic plans of rescue seemed ever less coherent.

All that was clear were my thoughts of Juliet, a vision of her lovely face, and the feel of her warm, yielding flesh as real as though I was holding her naked in my arms. Verse began to come in fits and starts—phrases and odd stanzas.

Here in exile, expelled from her sight,
all thoughts of my Juliet, faithful and light.

Not in flesh but in spirit she is here,
in a house in the wood, now my refuge, my lair.

She is all that divides me from grief and despair,
the taste of her, sound of her, scent of her hair.

Insubstantial as they were, the words were my salvation. Without them, without thoughts of my love, I would have gone mad. At times I believed I already had.

Chapter Twenty-three

Wedding plans were immediately begun.

Papa went to meet with Lucrezia's father at the Palazzo Tornabuoni to join in with plans for the marriage. When he left, he took with him a small casket of gold florins, announcing for the hundredth time how proud he was of this privileged wedding celebration. He kissed me on the brow and reminded me of the honor I was bringing to our family.

My mother, frantic with happiness, took me to Papa's warehouse, which had, miraculously, been spared damage from the fire. Workers were gutting the burned office and showroom, and huge carts were arriving with loads of wood to rebuild the inner walls and floors.

I tried but could not avert my eyes from the place in the street where Marco had fallen on Romeo's blade, and words flew unbidden into my head.

> *Bloody cobble where they stood, dazed,*
> *two friends in death's arms embraced.*

What a dark poem about friendship that would have made for Alberti's competition, I thought.

Mama pulled me away, tut-tutting that I mustn't be morbid on such a happy occasion. Inside, the head warehouseman had laid out on broad tables Papa's finest wares in every shade of virgin's white. From stark snow to rich ivory. From thick-cut pile velvet and gold brocade to gauzy Chinese silk.

Strangely, the giant scissors from the showroom had survived the fire, and now cleaned and polished, they seemed a proud symbol of the continuity of Papa's business.

With the sound of gay laughter three silkwomen fluttered in, carrying large cases in each hand. They were Florence's finest seamstresses, and I recognized that two of them had been called to work on Lucrezia's gown.

Silenced by my misery, I stood back as Mama took charge. Opening their bags, the women laid out amid the choicest silks their buttons, ribbons, frills, and lace. One opened a wooden box filled with thousands of tiny seed pearls, another with sparkling gems of every color, made of paste.

"I like the pearls," Mama told them. "But we will provide our own jewels. Real ones. Come to the house when we are finished here and you can take them."

A stout older silkwoman looked around. "Where is our bride?" She found me hanging back and fixed me in her sight, appraising me closely. "She is quite tall and slender," she said, "but has a nice flare at the hips and a pretty bosom."

Mama smiled proudly.

The woman took my hands and drew me to her. "Come here. Let me measure you." As she wound the tape around my waist, she gazed deep into my eyes for an overlong moment. "What is this?" she said suspiciously.

"What do you mean?" I whispered.

She looked at Mama. "This girl is unhappy," the silkwoman fearlessly announced. And then to me, "You don't want to get married, do you?"

I thought I would die on the spot.

"Nonsense!" my mother cried. "She is the luckiest girl in the world. Imagine the honor. Sharing her wedding day with the Medici."

I was caught in the woman's honest stare as Mama blathered on about my marriage into the Strozzi clan, and the joy it would bring our family in a time of sorrow.

I wondered if my pain was so clear on my face, or if Mama was so terribly blind. But thankfully the silkwoman, who must have known my plight was irrevocable, took pity on me and plastered on a broad grin.

"You're right, Signora Capelletti. I think your daughter's only problem is a touch of gas."

Everyone laughed at that, and I forced myself to smile. I had never felt so helpless, so muddled.

"I'm going to see Lucrezia," I blurted suddenly.

"But we haven't chosen the silk for your—"

"You choose, Mama. You have a better eye for it than me. And I like the pearls, too. Lots of them."

Meeting no one's eye, I fled the warehouse. The litter bearers silently obeyed my orders to take me to Lucrezia's house and leave me there, returning to the factory to carry Mama home.

. . .

I found Lucrezia, who sat with her overblown mother and little Contessina de' Medici at the table, poring over plans for the wedding. I think I surprised Lucrezia as much with my unannounced visit as with the desperate look in my eye.

She said to me in a voice of soothing calm, "Come, sit down with us, Juliet. There is still so much to decide."

Elena Tornabuoni gave me a wary look. She liked me, but her daughter's day in the sun would now be partially eclipsed by a second bride. There was nothing to be done about it. Whatever ire might have been provoked, it was well hidden by efficiency and a veneer of good nature.

"The negotiations between your father and the Strozzi have been concluded, I assume," she said to me, more a statement than a question.

"Yes."

"And have you and Jacopo signed your marriage contract?" This was Contessina in a kindly tone. She spoke of a man's and woman's mutual pledge of marriage to each other, a paper that was crucial to the legality of the event.

"Not yet," I answered. I hoped they could not hear the dread in my voice.

"What are you waiting for?" Elena asked quite jovially.

The earth to open up and swallow me, I thought, but said instead, "I think it will be tomorrow."

"Sit," insisted Lucrezia's mother, patting a chair next to hers. "We think we have come up with a graceful plan to mingle the two weddings, yet allow for each to bring great honor to the individual families."

I took a seat and tried to look pleased. I did not dare meet Lucrezia's eye.

"In most cases, as you know, the exchange of rings takes place in private," Contessina said, "but in this special circumstance, with so many who wish to celebrate—besides our families, friends, and guests, Florentines by the thousands will want to be there—we have decided to place this ceremony in the cathedral, under the eyes of the new archbishop of Florence."

I was thrown into silent but utter confusion. All I could see before me were visions of Friar Bartolomo in the modest chapel of San Marco at midnight. The rough weave of my gown, a doublet for my bodice, and the sweet eyes of Romeo as we married with the simplest words, the blessings of the church . . . and of Dante.

Now the archbishop of Florence!

Now a magnificent wedding ceremony under the cathedral dome.

A pearl-encrusted gown.

Thousand of onlookers.

"The archbishop is a young man, and still a little wet behind the ears," Elena said, "but such an occasion calls for a high church presence, don't you think, Juliet?"

"Oh. Yes. Very high."

"Of course there will be a notary there at the church. . . ."

"Did we not decide on two," Elena said, "one for each couple?"

"Ah yes," Contessina agreed. "So that our sons can deliver a receipt for your dowries to them, and hear the mutual consent of bride and groom." Another legality.

"We were just saying that you and Lucrezia should go to him together," Elena went on, "and take confession. A little note to him . . . he will be delighted. We understand he is quite enamored by the wealth and importance of the Medici."

Always modest, Contessina blushed and lowered her eyes. But she, too, was consumed by these wedding plans for her son. "We thought that when the exchange of rings is finished—"

"Do you know whether Jacopo plans three rings or four?" Elena interrupted.

I shook my head. I had no idea, nor did I want to know.

Contessina, unperturbed by her in-law-to-be, continued. "—then we will proceed with the *ductio ad maritum*—"

"The initiation of cohabitation," Elena added, as though we two idiot girls did not understand the Latin. But of course every girl who ever dreamed of marrying knew what the words meant.

"—everyone escorting the two couples back to the groom's home. In this case we shall all go to the Palazzo Bardi."

Contessina looked pleased. "To my Piero's home, and here our two families' guests will celebrate with a great feast."

"That is the next order of business," Elena added, looking at me. "Your mother and Allessandra Strozzi will be paying for that."

I was squirming in my chair by now, thinking this could get no worse.

"When the festivities are over," Contessina went on, taking my eye and holding it, "Juliet, you, your family, friends, and your father's clients will leave for the Palazzo Strozzi. . . ."

"And hope that not too many raucous youths will be out

to taunt your cortege with their obscene noises and songs . . . ," Elena added playfully.

Even Contessina smiled at that. "Your wedding gifts will be awaiting you there, and then you and your new husband will be put to bed." She looked at her soon-to-be daughter-in-law. "Lucrezia and Piero have requested that the guests be ejected before their first coupling." Then she looked at me with kind eyes. "Is that your desire, too, Juliet?"

All that emerged from my mouth was a croaking sound.

Lucrezia stood suddenly. "I think Juliet and I should go to my room and write the archbishop."

"A splendid idea," Elena agreed.

Lucrezia took me by the hand and led me up the stairs. Several times my knees threatened to collapse under me. We went to her sleeping chamber, now crowded with marriage chests, open and overbrimming with gifts of linens and tapestries, gold plate, and Venetian glassware. The door closed behind us and I stood quaking in a cold sweat. Whispering like a criminal, I told her the truth. How Romeo had come to my balcony door on the night of the fire set by Jacopo. Romeo's account of Marco's murder. The true killer. Finally I spoke of our wedding bed and the joy—despite the horrors surrounding us—that we had given and received in each other's arms.

Lucrezia listened with rapt attentiveness, nodding and making small sounds of encouragement that helped me go on. By the time I had finished, all judgment had drained away as infection recedes from an angry, suppurating wound, and she was, again, my dear and loyal friend.

"So you believe me when I say that Romeo did not murder my cousin?"

"I believe that Jacopo hated Romeo. That jealousy festers in his heart. And I do believe him capable of such an act."

"And Romeo *not?*"

Lucrezia smiled. "And Romeo not. For all his impetuousness and willfulness and love of danger, he is not a murderer." She took up both my hands in hers. "And he loves you so deeply. I wish . . ." She paused and her eyes filled suddenly with tears. "I wish that Piero loved me as much."

"Oh Lucrezia, he will! Once you are husband and wife and you share a life together"—I felt myself blushing—"and a bed, he will adore you. It may be a marriage of convenience now, but it will become a marriage of love. I'm sure of it."

"You cannot marry Jacopo," she said in the soberest tone.

"No, I cannot."

"It would be bigamy, and a sin against God."

A sin against the God of Love, I thought, then said, "But what can I do? Romeo is exiled. He would be killed on sight if he returned here."

"Juliet." Lucrezia squeezed my hands tightly. "You cannot wait another day. You must tell your parents the truth."

"The truth? What truth? That Jacopo is a fire starter and a murderer? That I ran off in men's clothing and married Romeo? That we lay together making love under their roof? My father will never believe a single awful thing about his future partner. Not from a silly, love-struck girl. But he will believe I married Romeo, and that I sacrificed my virginity to him. *That* he will believe. And it will be the end of any chance of having a life with Romeo—the avowed enemy of our family, the despised exile."

"Would he send you to a nunnery?"

"Never. The benefit to our family would be too slight." My

voice cracked as I spoke the next. "Papa would tell Jacopo all and he would, reluctantly, submit to marrying a sullied woman. But he would wait. Insist on locking me away for long enough to be sure that I was not carrying Romeo's child."

Lucrezia nodded with understanding. "The Strozzi bloodline must remain pure."

"Then together they'd seek an annulment to my marriage," I finished.

My friend had begun to look as desperate as I felt.

"Jacopo would have good reason to disrespect me," I said. "Loathe me. Beat me."

"Married life would be death."

The thought silenced us both, but I could see Lucrezia was thinking hard.

"There is something that can be done," she said.

"Tell me!"

"Don Cosimo would never allow you to commit bigamy in the cathedral at the same altar as his son and me."

"Oh, Lucrezia! Will you speak to him?"

She sighed with frustration. "He is gone to Rome to meet with the pope's bankers. He won't return for a fortnight, just before the wedding, bringing a whole phalanx of cardinals with him."

"But I need him now," I moaned. "He would believe me. Believe Romeo. He would see justice done!"

"You will have to wait, my friend. The moment he is home, I will go to him. Get an audience for you with him. He will see you. I know he will."

"But in the meantime . . . ?"

"In the meantime you must be strong. Play the happy bride-to-be, delighted with your gifts. You will be kind to Jacopo, joyful with your mother, simpering to your father. The moment Don Cosimo learns the truth, he will stop your wedding to Jacopo. And in the meantime we will be thinking of how you can go and be with Romeo." A furrowed forehead belied her hopeful words. "This will so anger your father."

"Disgrace him," I agreed. "I think he will disown me."

"Could you bear that? Bear losing your family?"

"To live my life with Romeo? Gladly. More than gladly. Oh, Lucrezia!" I hugged her fiercely, hope rising in me like a strong tide. "I will be Jacopo's perfect bride-to-be."

Then a thought struck me like a hammer blow.

"I cannot in the meantime sign the contract with him. We'll be as good as married."

Lucrezia was thinking hard.

I was trying to think, too, but my mind was a welter of confusion.

Then my friend looked at me and smiled.

"I have an idea," she said.

Chapter Twenty-four

I was strangely calm as we entered the great church. The massive dome dwarfed all those who stood in small clutches, or knelt at the various altars and prayed, and a muted cacophony of echoes swirled around us.

Lucrezia and I were arm in arm, but it was she pulling me forward, bracing me with her firm intent.

"There he is," she said. "He must indeed be enamored of the Medici. He could only have gotten my note moments ago, yet here he comes, looking like a horny husband to his bride. . . . Ah, Father, you do honor us with your prompt attention," she said, waiting for the archbishop of Florence to extend his hand to be kissed.

He was youthful, with an unlined face, and had a scent of perfume about him. His red silken dress trimmed with gold rivaled the gowns of the greatest ladies here. Yet he looked flustered in a way I had never seen a high clergyman be.

"Signorina Tornabuoni," he crooned in the most honeyed

tones. "It is I who is honored." *Your father-in-law and husband will be making huge donations to the church,* I believed him to be thinking, *paying for great frescoes and rich altarpieces.*

"Meet my friend Juliet Capelletti, who will be married to Jacopo Strozzi alongside Piero and myself."

"Ah, signorina," he said, forcing himself to attend me. "The Strozzi . . . such a fine family . . ." *A fabulously wealthy family, though not as powerful as the Medici,* I could hear him silently saying.

"We would very much like to take confession with you today," Lucrezia said. She was, as we had planned, about to offer me first into the confessional, but before she could, the archbishop dropped my hand and took up hers.

"I will hear you at once," he said very loudly.

A group of a dozen worshippers walking by us took great interest in his words. Here was a juicy piece of gossip to be shared later over dinner or at the baths.

"Look, there is an open confessional," the priest went on so they could hear. "I shall listen to the Medici bride-to-be first"— he smiled broadly at Lucrezia, then turned to me—"and then the Strozzi!"

He led Lucrezia away to the row of carved wooden cubicles, leaving me standing there, the onlookers staring with blatant, even prurient interest at the scene the archbishop had created. It was then, to my abject horror, that I saw standing among them another man of God, this one gaping at me with shocked indignation.

Friar Bartolomo.

"Father," I said weakly. "May I speak with you?"

He shook his head no, then swiveled under his brown robe and strode away toward the main altar.

I did not wish to make a commotion, but I could not let him go with such thoughts as he must be thinking. I followed after him and by lengthening my stride managed to walk beside him.

"Please," I whispered. "You do not understand."

"Are you marrying again?" he demanded, his voice taut with anger.

"No!" I was nearly shouting. I lowered my voice, but dared to take his arm and slow his pace. "This wedding will not take place."

He stared at me unconvinced. "Your true husband is exiled in Verona, and accused of a terrible killing. Yet you are here"—he raised his hands helplessly to heaven—"*pretending* to be marrying another man? Whatever his crime"—he leaned in and whispered fiercely in my ear—"your place is with Romeo."

"I know. I *know*."

"I cannot believe him a murderer," Friar Bartolomo said, his voice impassioned. "And of your cousin . . ." He looked me in the eye, then shook his head. "Impossible."

Joy and relief flooded me. "Oh, Father, he is innocent of murder."

The friar considered this and said with a perverse smile, "Though not of thievery. He stole our mule." He grew serious again. "What is your plan, Juliet? How will you avoid this marriage?"

I looked around us desperately. The cathedral was no place to talk. And now I could see Lucrezia exiting the confessional, looking around the cavernous church for sight of me. She waved when she saw me, and beckoned.

"I have to go," I said.

"Honor your marriage at any cost," the monk said with terrible gravity.

"Have no doubt that I will."

Then he left me and with a single fortifying breath, I went to meet Lucrezia.

Chapter Twenty-five

"Father forgive me, for I have sinned."

"What are these sins?" the archbishop of Florence asked me, sounding bored, supposing that a wellborn virginal girl would have nothing much to confess.

I was trembling, though, for I walked a thin line between truth and lying in God's house. I leaned close to the grate and whispered the one thing that I knew to be true.

"I have impure thoughts about my husband."

There was silence as my unexpected words were understood. It took a moment before the priest spoke.

"You will soon be married." His tone was stern. "But even married women must never dwell in the carnal realm. There is real danger, even to the pious, of reveling in the depravity of the marriage bed."

These last words I perceived he uttered with something akin to lasciviousness.

"Tell me what you mean, Father," I said with feigned innocence.

But the archbishop was keen to elaborate. "Certainly you are aware of the days and times that the marriage rights may not be exercised."

"Lent," I answered quickly. Everyone knew that.

"And days of penitence," he added.

"Of course."

"And you know it is a mortal sin of the most serious kind to indulge in . . . sodomy."

"No sodomy, Father. Never sodomy."

He cleared his throat. "And you shall engage in no unusual positions, or God will punish you severely."

I bit my lip hard and made a sound of agreement.

"A woman must make her bedchamber a sacred refuge of piety and solitary devotion. A crucifix or an icon of the Virgin should be hung. A small altar erected. There you will find a center for your spiritual exercise."

"Yes, Father."

He was silent again. Then, "Tell me more about these impure thoughts." His voice had grown thick and husky.

"Oh!" I uttered, as though mortified. "I cannot. . . . I should not. . . . Oh, Father, I'm so ashamed!" I remembered Romeo pulling my knees high to encircle his waist. Was this an "unusual position"? And what on earth was sodomy between a man and a woman?

"There is no need, no need for embarrassment," the archbishop insisted. "Just tell me. . . . Let God be your witness."

In that moment, blasphemous as it was, I invoked blessings from the God of Love, closed my eyes, and allowed myself to gracelessly slump to the floor.

"The lady swoons!" I heard Lucrezia shout. "Bring help!"

Chapter Twenty-six

$\mathcal{M}$y sins were piling high. Now I pretended unconsciousness to my parents.

> *I am a liar, lying in my bed*
> *Faithless daughter, all hopes of honor shed.*

Dear Lucrezia had seen me home, fluttering about her limp, pale friend with stories of my aching head and blurred vision before the collapse. We had quietly argued about what symptoms I should display. What illness I would be feigning and for what effect. We had decided that at all costs I must be prevented from signing the contract with Jacopo, for it was binding. We would, under the law, be as good as married, all the rest of the ceremony mere artifice.

Some couples in lower orders of society went to bed after signing, and before the giving of the rings, as if to seal the bargain and prove their mutual consent. People of the merchant class, like our family, preferred as much gaudy pomp and ritual and feasting as could be afforded.

So here the liar lay in deathlike stillness, all manner of men and women coming and going from my room—Mama, Papa, Cook, Lucrezia, and the much-feared *materfamilia*s of my betrothed's family, Allessandra Strozzi. If my maid, Viola, came, I was unaware. I did not hear her speak a word, and I did not dare open my eyes to find her.

Several doctors were called for their opinions and treatment. There was endless checking of pulses—arms, ankles, neck, and groin. My eyelids were pulled open; my mouth was examined for signs of choking, sores, or a swollen tongue. They listened to my shallow breathing and tapped my breastbone, to which I replied with a faint moan and a furrowed brow. There were many spirited arguments about my mysterious condition. A flux or an ague. As there was no fever or swellings, it could not be the plague. No yellowing of the skin or eye whites, so it was not my liver.

Two doctors leaned over my bed whispering. They kept their voices low, for Mama was in the room, and their conjecture of a tumor in my head might alarm her. A third physician, who smelled of camphor, kept raising my arm and letting it fall limp to my side, till I wanted to shriek at him. But my resolve was strong.

Indeed, resolve was never more needed than for my bleeding, for this was the time-tested treatment for many ills, both known and unknown. I refrained from clenching my jaw to receive the cut, as the gesture might be observed. The knife they used on my forearm was dull, for it dug deep in the flesh before it poked through, and the pain was hot and vivid. Then I lay helpless as the blood dripped freely down my arm and plinked into a metal bowl they'd placed on the floor below it.

I had no relief as night fell, as Mama insisted on staying by my side. I worried that if I slept, I would lose control of my movements and might give myself away as perfectly healthy, and a malingerer of the worst order.

But the day planned for the signing of the marriage contract came and went with no mention of it, and that was worth the world.

By the next morning I was aching from the forced stillness, racked by a gnawing hunger, and much relieved when Lucrezia returned for her turn at the vigil over her sick friend.

I heard her telling my mother as she sent her off to her bed that she would be reading to me, and not to be alarmed if voices were heard.

"There is no talk of the contract," Lucrezia said very softly, moments after the door closed behind Mama, "though Signora Strozzi seems suspicious. She heard the physicians saying they could find nothing wrong with you, though one believed your skin was rather too pink for poor health. And I do not think she believed your father when he assured her that all would go according to plan on our wedding day."

"We don't know what Jacopo has told his mother," I said in low tones, grateful to have the freedom of speech once again. "She may be a villainess, as her son is. Do you think the doctors will return today?"

Lucrezia held out bits of cheese and bread for me, which I hungrily consumed. "You can be sure of it. Prepare yourself to give up more of your blood."

"What of Viola?" I asked with even more urgency. The young servant and her new husband, Massimo, were together the key to our plan, though they were as yet unaware of it. While the girl had taken up some duties as my lady's maid, she could not be spared from the kitchen altogether, and Lucrezia must find a way to be private with her to explain things and acquire her consent.

Our scheme required that Massimo, for a generous price, ride out of Florence to Verona, two days on a fast horse, carrying a letter to Romeo, and return quickly with a reply. We had considered a messenger hired by Lucrezia, but she had done no such thing in her life, and she, like all the wellborn girls of Florence, was watched and regulated her every waking moment. Too, we believed we could count better on Viola's loyalty and goodwill than a courier.

After all, I had made her own marriage possible.

"I will see if your mother will allow Viola to come up and bathe you," said my friend. "Then I can give her the letter."

"Oh, Lucrezia, I so wanted to write him in my own hand."

"Not possible," she said, then, hearing voices outside in the hall, went to my desk and picked up Dante's *Inferno* and brought it back to my bedside. She sat next to me. "My letter is simply put. And the spirit is all yours. 'Come and take me from this place. I am waiting.' Certainly it will require Romeo's cunning and not a little bravery to return to the city and take you away, but I have no more fear than you that he will."

"And did you write . . . ?"

"Juliet, I wish you could see your face. Of course I wrote that you loved him faithfully. And I begged for a swift reply." Lucrezia smiled. "Now let me read to you for a while. It will make the time pass more quickly."

She opened the book and gravely read: "Canto nine, flight of the demons. The Sixth Circle of Hell."

Chapter Twenty-seven

To our immense frustration, Viola was not allowed to come bathe me, and Lucrezia's note to Romeo could not be passed.

I suffered another day of bleeding at the baffled doctors' hands, so that now I truly did feel weak and ill. I had to endure more of their poking and prodding, requiring my supreme effort to appear stuporous. Later, an apothecary came and applied a malodorous mustard poultice to my stomach.

Allessandra Strozzi looked in on me again. I could hear in her voice more irritation this day than sympathy. She repeatedly demanded to know what she was supposed to do with the wedding preparations. Papa used confident words that all would go as planned, but in the fabric of his assurances there were threads of panic.

Without this marriage, he believed, all would be lost.

But I remembered Romeo's logic. If I eloped without my father's permission, certainly a furor would ensue, but there remained in that scenario ways for he and Jacopo both to save face, and the partnership would, in the future, survive.

So far, however, the only reward for my pretended coma was another day gone by without having signed my marriage contract.

That night Cook was sent to sit up with me, but she fell to sleep almost instantly, allowing me the freedom to stretch my limbs and take in deep, soothing lungfuls of air. I even sat up at the side of my bed, wishing that the shutters had been open and the chamber not so tomblike. I wished to gaze up at the stars of Romeo's birth, secure in the knowledge that in Verona he would be gazing at the same sky, thinking of mine.

I admit that in the darkest hours I allowed doubt to inhabit my mind. I remembered the last moments before my husband had left this room, and his uncertainty that we would ever meet again. Truth be told, it had been *I* that had taken the convincing tone, promising we would meet again in this life. Should it not have been Romeo who showed strength and surety of our future together? And why had I heard nothing from him since that night? He should have moved mountains to let me know he cared!

I was shaking by the time I lay back down, and it was some time before my common sense returned. Like a stern tutor, it lectured me about my ridiculousness. Romeo *had* moved mountains . . . to court and marry me. On that last night—the one on which I now judged him so harshly—a friend had died in his arms. Yes, he had wept and trembled at the thought of his sins, yet he had recovered his masculine pride sufficiently to prove himself a perfect lover in this bed.

If I had not had a letter from Romeo, I decided, then its passage from Verona to Florence was certainly impossible.

My self-soothing thoughts, exhaustion, and the snoring cook put me to sleep. I thankfully woke before her at dawn and, steeling myself, returned to my deathlike pose.

The morning brought a most unwelcome visitor.

Why they had allowed Jacopo Strozzi a private audience with my helpless self I will never know. Perhaps he convinced Papa that words of encouragement from my husband-to-be would rouse me from my unnatural sleep.

In any event, I could feel Jacopo's odious presence as he stood above me, smell his musty scent. He kept his voice low, but he bent to my ear, making sure that I heard every sinister word.

"I know what you are doing, Juliet." The way he spoke my name made the hair on my neck rise and stiffen. "I see now how far you would go to avoid marrying me. Clever. You have managed to fool everyone but myself . . . and my mother. She is angry. Very angry. She never liked you. She believed I could do better for myself. Find a wealthier girl. I do not like to think how it will be for you living in her house now. But you *will* live in her house. You will give up this nonsense and rouse yourself. For one way or the other you will marry me. You may choose the planned wedding—that would be pleasant. Or, if you continue this pathetic ruse, I will come in here again with our marriage contract in hand, lock the door, and after I have signed your name next to mine"—he came in close and nipped the lobe of my ear with his teeth—"I will take my marital rights, here in this bed. *That* will wake you up, hmm?"

I lay frozen, struggling for even breath.

"It is your choice, Juliet. Your choice entirely."

When I felt his rough tongue on my face, the bile rose in my throat, threatening my composure, but thankfully he pulled back. A moment later the door opened. Clicked shut.

I choked back my revulsion and tried to steady myself, for the door was opening again. I heard the rustle of skirts and went boneless with relief to inhale the sweet and familiar fragrance of Lucrezia.

I opened my eyes and propped myself on my elbows as she swung the shutters wide, then snatched Dante's *Inferno* from my writing desk before coming to my bedside. She wore a decidedly happy expression, one so hopeful that I withheld the telling of the meeting with Jacopo and allowed her to speak first.

She sat down and finally looked at me. "Juliet, what has happened? You look ill. Has the bleeding . . . ?"

"No. Just tell me your news. I can see that you have some."

"I found Viola alone in the kitchen."

"And?"

Lucrezia smiled triumphantly. "She took the letter and accepted payment for her husband's courier services. He will leave today. They are indebted to you, Juliet. She would do anything to help you."

"Thank God!" I sat up and grabbed Lucrezia's hand. "Is Jacopo gone?"

"I passed him on the stairs as I came up. I think I heard the front door close." She looked hard at me. "*Tell me.* What is wrong?"

Trembling with fury, I told her of Jacopo's threat of ravishment if I ignored his demands to rouse myself, and the appalling picture he painted of my married life under Allessandra Strozzi's roof.

"I have no choice, Lucrezia. I must appear to recover entirely."

She was still smiling. "But look at our accomplishments. Three days gone and you have yet to sign the contract. And Romeo will have our letter in two days. In another two you will have his answer—a happy plot to rescue you and begin your life together."

I shook my head, worried. "How much longer can I delay signing the contract? Time is growing short before our wedding day."

Lucrezia took my hand. "What has happened to your faith in Romeo? Your beloved is exceedingly clever and bold. He would change the very course of the Arno for you."

She made me smile. "He would indeed," I said, ashamed of my momentary doubt. "Change the color of the fishes, too."

"And raise Lazarus from the dead," she teased.

"Wait," I said, leaning over the side of my bed. I probed the hole I had made in the mattress and found the satin pouch I'd hidden there. I placed the two braided gold bands on my fingers and proudly held out my hand to Lucrezia. "No one else has seen them."

Lucrezia admired the rings for a moment, then took me into a warm embrace and held me there. "May God bless your marriage," she said.

Suddenly there were voices close at the door.

We froze, knowing we had come to a critical moment.

"Hide the rings," she ordered.

I put them back into the pouch and stuffed it back into the mattress.

A look of determination hardening her features, Lucrezia dropped Dante's book loudly on the floor and began to shout.

"Oh, oh, Juliet!! Someone, come quickly!" She gave me one last desperate look and whispered, "Lie down."

The door flew open and my parents rushed in.

"She moved and tried to speak!" Lucrezia cried. "God in heaven, I think she is back with us!"

I opened my lids very slowly, in time to see Lucrezia stand away from the bed so that Mama and Papa could hover close.

"Capello . . . ," my mother said, her face awash with emotion.

"Juliet, can you hear me?" my father demanded.

"Oh, husband . . . ," Mama moaned.

"I hear you," I said in my weakest voice, "but I am so tired. So weak. I feel as if all the blood has been drained out of me."

"I told you we should never have allowed them—"

"Hush, woman. Juliet, listen to me. Move your foot."

I did as I was told, using the smallest twitching of my toe.

"Now lift your hand," he ordered me.

I clenched my fist weakly and lifted it off the covers.

With that, my mother fell on me with clutching embraces and copious tears.

Over her shoulder I saw Papa heave a deeply relieved sigh. The wedding could go on as planned. His partnership was intact.

Lucrezia was smiling as she quietly made her way from my room.

Our letter was on the way to Romeo.

Romeo

The day dawned clear, though I waited for the night's cover to see me back to my uncles' house. They were both cheered, but worried to see me so soon. I told them the germ of my plan and gave them another letter for Juliet—brief, but reprising the promise of my love, asking that she procure men's clothing and wait in good faith for her husband. I would return for her.

My uncles were worrying their chins, their brows furrowed.

"This plan of yours . . . ," Vittorio began.

"It is still imperfect, I know."

"We have been talking of it," Vincenzo continued. "Romeo, in any form it cannot be allowed to happen."

"What are you saying? Juliet is my lawful wife."

"And you are the last male Monticecco of your generation. How in good conscience can you risk dying? Nothing can be allowed to happen to you. The family line. Our blood."

"Nothing will happen, save me rescuing her."

"Think of your father, your mother," Vincenzo pleaded.

"I have! Had it been they thus obstructed, Papa would have turned the world inside out to have her. He would expect no less of me."

My uncles remained unconvinced.

"Tell me, how can I think of my parents before Juliet?" I asked them. "She was promised, yet altogether unexpected. So much more than I had had reason to hope for. More than a beauty in face and form. More, even, than a tenderhearted girl, a virtuous lady. I tell you she is *remarkable*. Unique as a woman. Strong of mind. Almost manly in her courage. I have found in this soul a very goddess, though one intolerant of my simpering adoration. And she loves me! Right from the first she fearlessly, wholeheartedly loved me."

I could see my words moved my uncles, though I was sure they had not felt the emotions of which I spoke.

"Never once did I falter in my campaign to win her," I continued. "It was as though I had for my tutor the God of Love himself. I brought her to dance on the pages of *Vita Nuova*. I wooed her with every one of the senses on her bedroom balcony. When our families warred, I made peace. When Jacopo Strozzi urged a hasty wedding, I married her. Uncles, I tell you she is the woman my stars have foretold, and I will settle for nothing less!"

I searched their troubled faces. Clearly, they still had their doubts.

"I have been falsely accused of murder, and exiled from Florence!" I cried. "Where is the honor in letting that stand?"

"There is no honor," Vittorio relented.

I sensed Vincenzo was unmoved.

"Go back to the woods and stay there for now," Vittorio said. "Refine your plan of rescue and revenge. We will think of something."

"Thank you!" I hugged them both, and made my way back to the forest.

Now in the long nights I wrote to my father and mother asking their assistance in whatever way they could afford. It pained me to think of Papa selling either the orchard or the vineyard, and in the end I tore up the letter and put it in the fire.

I tried writing another poem, but all that came was a single line:

The stream, hearing her laughter, races faster.

I cursed the Muses, at the same time praying they had not deserted me forever, and found solace in writing to my wife.

Beloved,

In order to survive my days without sight of you, I have taken to reclaiming the crone's garden, one that in its day must have been magnificent to behold. She grew her herbs and medicines and more than enough food for one old woman to consume. I've taken my hand to parts of this cottage that need repair, for more and more do I see us here together, hiding away from the world. It is humble, I know, but I often picture you framed in the door in a simple gown, your hair about your shoulders. I see you lying asleep in the large bed I have begun to build us, with morning sun falling in dappled light upon your cheeks.

I am not much of a carpenter but have determined that

this bed must be built inside, for never will it fit through the doorway. It will fill half the space of the cottage, maybe more. Would you mind that? Remembering our wedding night, I think not. A garden, a stream of clear water, a writing desk for each of us, and a great bed. What more could we wish for in a paradise?

I'm ashamed to say I smashed my finger while pounding the headboard and searched the crone's shelves for a remedy among her potions and salves and poultices. There I found barks and bat wings, moles' tongues, and finch beaks, grotesqueries that would cause even a man who eschewed superstition some pause. Many plants I recognized by their sight and smell as those any good housewife would keep in her larder. Some I will use to season my food, spice my wine. Others were marked with a black symbol—an oval overlaid with two crossed bones. Poison, I think. Though I did refrain from tasting them, my nose and my instincts recoiled. Better left untouched, I thought.

Enough for now, my love. In truth, I have written more for my own entertainment than for yours, as I believe with all my heart that you will lay eyes on me before you do this letter. I remain your humble servant, love, and husband,

⁓ Romeo

Chapter Twenty-eight

I was never so happy to see my maid, nor she me, as when Viola came to give me a bath. She took confident charge, ordering the male servants to bring up the copper tub, and pail after pail of steaming water. She sprinkled the chamomile and lavender she had chosen with care onto the surface and stirred them in, humming a mindless tune. Only once I was covered to my neck in the fragrant water and Viola was scrubbing my back with a rough cloth did she speak to me in a low, conspiratorial tone.

"My husband is gone to Verona. With your letter. We were all so worried about you, my lady. But you were pretending!" Viola laughed, and the sound echoed across the surface of the water. "Shhh!" she scolded herself.

I had to smile. This serving girl had become a faithful friend. I took her wrist. "Viola, thank you. I would have no hope at all of escaping this dreadful marriage without you and Massimo."

"I would like something in return," she said, lowering her eyes shyly.

"Anything."

"When you and Signor Monticecco have found a home and settled there, you must send for Massimo and me, and we will come serve you. Otherwise, this good deed that we've done will take you from me forever." She handed me the cloth so I could scrub the soles of my feet. "Is that awfully selfish?"

"A bit." I saw her smile collapse. "But it's a wonderful idea. Two marriages for love under one roof."

The smile returned. "I did overhear your parents talking to Jacopo Strozzi."

"And?"

"They intend to keep you here in this house until your wedding day."

This was unhappy news.

"But why?"

"Signor Strozzi has convinced them that it was his visit that brought you around, how he spoke to you of the happiness of your future life together. The many children you would have. So they listen very carefully to his advice now. 'Heaven knows what befell poor Juliet when she was out in the world the other day . . . with Lucrezia Tornabuoni,' I heard him say."

"Does he speak ill of her to my parents?"

"How can he? She is marrying a Medici." Viola thought before she said, "It is more what he does *not* say about her. And the look on his face when he mentions her name. I think if you did marry that man, you would see very little of your friend."

"Well, never fear, Viola. I am not marrying 'that man.' "

"No, you are not. Now tip your head back into the water. I'm going to wash your hair."

Viola had been right. I was altogether prohibited from leaving my father's house. Indeed, I was hardly allowed out of my room. The days would have gone slowly waiting for Romeo's return letter if not for the constant flurry of wedding plans that were carried out in my private chamber.

Mama buzzed in and out a hundred times a day like a bee at the hive. All manner of decisions were at hand—whether to serve eel cooked in bay leaves, or cuttlefish in their ink, as a third course at the feast. Whether we should add to the wine that the Strozzi were supplying, so that wine flowed like water. Whether our gold and silver platters were grand enough, or she should urge Papa to buy new and more extravagant ones. After all, we were celebrating at the Medici palazzo. We could not afford to look stingy.

Allessandra Strozzi came to see my "miraculous recovery" with her own eyes. Her smile was brittle and her voice sharp when she told me how very relieved she was that I had regained my senses. The thought that she knew of my deception made the skin on my arms crawl, and it was only knowledge that I would never spend one day as a daughter-in-law in her prison of a house that allowed me to smile sweetly at her and pretend innocence. That smile enraged her even more, and this was very pleasing to me.

The silkwomen came with my wedding gown, which they had created in less than a week. It was a splendid design of thick white-on-white velvet cutwork, one that lifted my bosom high and fell in grand flares from just under my breasts. The sleeves were silk damask embroidered in membrane gold with birds and palmettes.

As it was fitted on me, tight as a glove, the older seamstress who had questioned me at Papa's factory remained silent as she worked. If she was still suspicious of my cheerful patter—that most appropriate for a happy bride—she did not say. But once, as she held my hand to help me turn, she squeezed my fingers tight, in a secret signal, I was sure of it.

Once Mama had given her approval, the gown was taken off. In the next week the women would work night and day sewing the pearls and gems in place. They warned me proudly that so many jewels would decorate this dress that its weight would multiply ten times. I would be lucky to make it down the cathedral aisle, one said with a laugh. There would be no way to dance.

"She does not have to dance," Mama said, all smiles. "Let the other girls dance. She is the bride."

"Is Lucrezia's gown finished?" I asked, hoping for any news of my friend, and learned it was, and quite a masterpiece at that. In fact, Jacopo's "advice" had curtailed any meetings with her. Once again, I had bowed without argument to his mean-spirited wishes, knowing that my own plans were taking shape from a distance, and his influence in my life would be short-lived.

I schemed with Viola, who was, thankfully, allowed frequent visits to my room. Under a pile of clean linen she secreted in a set of her husband's clothing and a pair of strapped slippers that fit me. In this way I could be dressed and ready in male disguise when Romeo came over the garden wall to collect me.

I must admit I felt pangs of guilt when I enlisted my mother's help in my plot to escape her house. Claiming I needed to see the gems that I would wear at my throat and ears and in my hair, I urged her to bring the family jewel box to my room so we could decide together.

Then I made a great show of interest in each piece, putting it on and discussing its merits and demerits, and whether it would match the dress or detract from it. All the while I was counting the pieces' value, for several of the necklaces, earrings, and tiaras would be taken with me when I absconded with Romeo. I would leave the lion's share behind, but I could not imagine going to my husband with no dowry at all.

And in the nights, endless strings of words flowed into my head. Poems, and I could not tell if they were worthy, or simply Love's garbled messages to a girl on the verge of a joyful life.

For now I was certain that Romeo would come. All doubt had taken flight like the falcons who catch a circular wind on a warm day, rising up and away so far and so high that they can be seen only as dark specks against the blue sky.

He would come.

It was the fourth day since Massimo had gone to Verona. Any moment Viola would come flying through my door all smiles, a letter from Romeo clutched in her hand. It would present his plan—brilliant and dangerous of course—but brimming with confidence in its execution. I prepared myself for a lack of flowery sentiment, a restatement of his love. After all, just his act of abducting me would be proof enough of his feelings.

He would come.

Chapter Twenty-nine

*E*vening arrived with no sign of Massimo's return. When I went to the kitchen looking for Viola, Cook said she had gone to her mother's. This simple statement rocked me. There had been more than enough time for Massimo to have ridden to Verona, delivered his letter, and brought me back Romeo's reply.

In my room I fretted, and snapped at my mother when she pestered me about the choice of confections she wished to serve at the wedding. Cook was insisting on making a luxury bread of almonds and candied fruit, but Mama preferred a sweet wine-flavored custard.

"Just have both," I said, gritting my teeth.

"But the number of eggs for the zabaglione . . . oh, the number of eggs!"

I wished she would disappear.

That night there was no sleep for me, and the hours passed in agony. All manner of fears presented themselves to me—from Massimo's sudden illness on the road, to worry that Romeo had never taken refuge with his uncles at all, but had instead gone off adventuring to far-flung parts of the world. Everyone had just assumed he had gone to Verona. But wasn't my husband known for his wild audacity? Anything was possible with Romeo.

I was bleary-eyed in the morning, yet taut as a rope strung tight between two posts. When I cornered Viola after breakfast, she looked bewildered and said Massimo had not come home. Why he was delayed was anyone's guess, but she, too, had begun to worry. Though neither of us said so, we both knew that the passage between the two towns was famous for its bandits. With nothing of value for the thieves to steal from Massimo, they might have become angered. Even now he could be lying injured or dead along the side of the road.

Another day passed, though this was filled with final plans for the wedding. My gown was brought again to be fitted, this time laden with pearls and gems. The seamstresses had been right. The garment, while breathtaking, was a deadweight upon my body, and even the short time I was forced to wear it depressed my spirits and brought me to tears.

Mama convinced herself once again that I was crying for joy at my upcoming marriage, and the thought that my own mother was so self-deceived as to misconstrue her daughter's heart so entirely made me weep even harder.

I saw the older silkwoman observe me with pity, for she alone knew my suffering. When she lifted the gown from my shoulders, she leaned in and whispered low, "God will protect you, my lady."

I wished to shout back, "I do not need God's protection, for Romeo is coming to take me away!" Instead, I quietly murmured my thanks.

But another night passed, and my surety weakened with every passing hour until I fell into exhausted sleep, sprawled across my bed fully clothed.

I woke to Viola leaning over me, a look of myriad emotions twisting her face. It was barely dawn.

"He's come home," she said.

I bolted upright. "Is he here?"

She nodded.

I jumped up and hurried down the stairs, heedless of my impropriety. Cook was absent from our kitchen, certainly at the Palazzo Bardi overseeing the feast preparations. I saw Massimo outside the window and went to meet him.

He wore the same strange expression as Viola had. My heart fluttered, then began to pound. It was hard to keep my voice even.

"Welcome back, Massimo."

"I'm so glad to see you well again, signorina."

"I was never ill. I was sure you knew that."

"Right. I'd forgotten." The young man was nervous, unsmiling.

"May I have the letter, please?"

"Letter? I gave . . ." He swallowed hard. "I gave your letter—Signorina Tornabuoni's letter—to Romeo. In Verona."

"Yes, of course you did. And he must have given you one back . . . for me."

"No."

"No?"

Massimo looked like a cornered animal. The skin under his nose had begun to perspire.

"Romeo read my letter and did not reply?"

The butcher's son shrugged and averted his gaze from mine.

"That is not possible," I said.

I turned to see Viola standing in the doorway looking stunned.

"I tell you there is no letter!" Massimo shouted unexpectedly. He was desperate now. His face crumbled. "There is no letter." This was said quietly with an air of defeat.

"Did you even see my husband in Verona?"

"No."

I looked at Viola, whose face was a mask of horror and fury. She went to Massimo and beat both fists on his chest. "What have you done!" she cried. "Where is the letter we put into your keeping?"

Massimo looked down at his feet. "He paid me triple."

"Who?" Viola demanded, and pummeled him again.

"Jacopo Strozzi," I answered for him. "Isn't that right, Massimo?"

He nodded miserably.

"No!" Viola moaned, then turned to me. "Oh, my lady, forgive me. Forgive us!"

I could not speak. Not a single word. Instead I turned, leaving Massimo to his wife's wrath, and walked like a haunted spirit through my father's house. I must have climbed the stairs, though I cannot remember the act. Next I knew I was at my balcony rail, staring blindly out at the walled garden.

Two days were left till the wedding. Romeo was in Verona. Don Cosimo had not yet returned from Rome. I had been a fool, putting my whole trust in Massimo. Perhaps I deserved this fate. A fool's fate. Bitterness rose in me like a fouled spring, catching in my throat. Choking me.

I am wholly abandoned, I thought in self-pity, *by God in heaven, by the God of Love . . . and Romeo.*

All that was left was for me to face my dismal future.

Later that day, Jacopo Strozzi came. Mama herself brought me down the stairs, where he waited with Papa, the marriage contract in hand. Silently I signed it, feeling the sin in my heart.

I was a bigamist.

By Jacopo's request my parents happily removed themselves, arm in arm, leaving me alone with my new husband. I turned to face him and managed somehow to hold his eye. He did not smile evilly as I thought he might. Indeed, his eyes were filled with loathing for me. No one knew of my attempted betrayal, or his triumph over me. No one except, perhaps, his mother. Yet in his even stare I saw humiliation.

For the rest of our lives together he must endure the truth of my revulsion for him as a man, and I his crime of murdering my cousin.

Perhaps, I thought, I should write an additional canto for Dante's *Inferno*—"The Tenth Circle of Hell." Still I could not find the words to speak to Jacopo. My only satisfaction was that this smug villain could think of no words to gloat over me.

I lifted my shoulders and set my lips. I left him standing there alone, as he would be for all the days of our married life. It was a very small comfort.

Chapter Thirty

I told my mother I would not leave my room till my wedding day. I could bear to see no one, not my father, not my mother, not Viola. I suspected that even if Lucrezia had come, I would not have had the stomach for a visit.

I said I wanted to spend my last days in prayers and quiet contemplation, and no one questioned that.

On the morning of the last day before the marriage there came a knock at my door. Mama peeked in and with the shy look of a girl said I had a visitor. She moved aside to admit him.

Friar Bartolomo.

A moment later we were alone. I should have fallen at his feet then and asked God's forgiveness, but so many hours of silent solitude and despair left me mute.

Instead he came to me. He spoke gently.

"What have you done, my lady? Unless I am misinformed, you have signed a marriage contract with Jacopo Strozzi."

"I have no excuses, Father. I have failed to prevent this marriage despite my best-laid plans. My letter to Romeo asking him to come and fetch me away went astray." I could not hide the bitterness in my voice. "And he—my true husband—has made no attempt to write me. Neither has he come for me of his own volition." I fixed the friar with my eyes. "Why has he not come?"

"I cannot say," he replied slowly. "But listen to me, Juliet. I know in my heart that he wishes to come."

"In *your* heart?"

"When Romeo came to beg me to marry you two in secret, I met a man so consumed with love, so undone with his passion for you, with joyous hopes for a future family, with"—the friar struggled for the words—"the highest regard for the woman he would make his wife, I was overcome. He spoke, not only of your beauty—though he waxed ecstatic at the perfection of your features and the way every sight of you made him weak—but he made much of your thoughts, which he believed profound."

"My thoughts?"

"Yes. And poetry. He admitted ashamedly, but proudly, that yours was superior to his own. He loved the sound of your voice. Your philosophies, your many virtues that, while strange for a woman, were virtues nonetheless. He felt a better man in your presence."

"He told you all this?"

"Oh, much more. And I can say with all certainty that Romeo was sincere. These were not the ravings of a love-addled boy. He believed he had found in you his personal angel, much as his father had found in his beloved mother."

I turned away from the friar, angry tears stinging my eyes. "Why are you telling me this? There's nothing to be done." I wheeled on him. "Hear my confession, Father, and then you should go."

"Perhaps there is . . . something . . . that can be done."

I shook my head, baffled.

"I need to know if you have faith in Romeo's love."

I stared at him. "I told you, I have some doubt of it."

"And what of that which I have told you today?"

I pressed my lips tight to keep from sobbing.

"Do you not believe me?"

"Actions speak louder than words," I said, more harshly than I intended.

Now the friar spoke gently, as he might have done to a small child. "Might you give your true husband benefit of the doubt? Allow that something—I know not what—has prevented him from a heroic rescue thus far?"

"And what if I did?"

Bartolomo's face lit and flared like a torch in a dark chamber. "If you did, I would give you a secret place and time to meet again."

I stared at him uncomprehendingly. "Tell me." My voice was hard and demanding.

"Lady Juliet . . . this plan is fraught with danger."

"What could be more dangerous than married life with Jacopo Strozzi?"

Friar Bartolomo smiled crookedly. His teeth were white, but crossed one over the other, top and bottom.

"Romeo told me you were brave. He saw as much in your coming out in the middle of the night with him in a boy's disguise. And I must agree. No other ladies I know would carry themselves to the top of the cathedral's dome."

"What is it you want me to do?"

With one final hesitation he drew from the pocket of his robe a small green glass vial—something that would have looked at home on the apothecary shelf of his cell.

He held it between our faces but did not speak. He closed his eyes, trying to find the words.

I felt my mouth go dry, for despite his silence I knew—if not the name of this potion—its terrible nature.

"If you drink this tonight, you will not wake up on your wedding morning."

"You wish me to take my own life?"

"No, no, my lady. Quite the contrary. This will allow you to *live* your life . . . with Romeo. Come, let us sit. My knees are shaking."

We put ourselves down on my bed.

"It is a sleep like unto death," he said, "but not death. You will grow cold and pale. Your breath will become shallow, so shallow that no physician can detect it."

"What will I feel? Will I dream? Or is it all blackness?"

He shook his head helplessly. "I cannot say."

"You cannot say!"

"I would lie if I said otherwise."

"This is a mad scheme. You tell me to drink poison and pretend to die."

"Well, of course there is more to it."

"You'd better tell me quickly. Where is this 'time and place' you promise me and Romeo?"

"Ah, that is the magic of it."

"So I'm giving myself over to *magic*?"

"No, no. It is medicine. Just a deep sleep. Long enough to

see you pronounced dead, mourned, and buried. That is the 'time.' "

"Oh, Father, I do not much like the sound of this."

"Hear me out. You will be taken to your family's tomb. . . . That is the 'place.' " He saw my expression. "I know, I know . . . but here is where you call upon your courage."

"So I am to be buried alive?"

"Yes. But a courier will ride swiftly to Verona. . . ."

"No!"

"Why 'no'?"

"There is no trustworthy courier. The last I sent was bribed and betrayed me."

"This one will not betray you." He set his face, determined.

"You?"

"Yes."

"On a mule?"

He laughed. "No. I am a good rider. At least I was in my youth. San Marco has a fast horse. I will tell them my mother is ill."

"Friar Bartolomo . . ." I was overcome. "You would lie to your order for Romeo and me?"

"It is not a lie. My mother has been ill for years."

Now it was I who laughed. But a moment later I grew serious.

"Why, Father? Why would you do such a thing? And why suggest that I pretend the mortal sin of suicide?"

He looked away; his smile vanished. He fingered the crucifix at his chest, then suddenly let it drop as though it had burned his hand.

"I once knew love," he whispered. "I was very young and

she was . . ."The friar looked away, his sad shaking head the only description of the girl he could manage. "In our flights of passion, lost as we were in the pages of *Vita Nuova*, I had forgotten I was a second son." His fist covered his mouth. "Destined for the priesthood. There was nothing could be done. I entered the church. She was betrothed to another. The prior of my order saw how deeply torn I was in my faith. So he had me marry them."

"Oh!" My heart quaked at the still evident pain this man suffered.

"So will you do it?" he asked.

I stared at this wild cleric. Thought for a final second about the prospect of life under Allessandra Strozzi's roof and of Jacopo's bony fingers on my bare flesh.

"Yes."

"Good." Bartolomo pressed the vial into my palm. "It is bitter. They say it tastes like cold death. But you must drink it all. Then lie yourself down as if you'd gone to bed. And you mustn't be afraid. Because Romeo and I will be there when you wake. *Before* you wake. Then he can spirit you away and take you far from here. The rest is your doing."

"You will tell this to Lucrezia Tornabuoni?"

He nodded.

"Wait! Perhaps she should not be told. She will disapprove. She'll fear for my life. Try to stop me."

"Would you rather she believed you dead?"

I thought hard about this. "For now perhaps. It is better that way. She will be grieved, but later, once Romeo and I are settled, I will write to her. Through you. Will you give her my letter?"

"Of course."

Suddenly the warm flush of this mad plan chilled me. "How

do you know . . . how do I know for certain of Romeo's accord in this?"

"You cannot know," he said simply. "Very little is certain in this life, my lady. What I am sure of is your husband's love for you. What you must find before you drink from that bottle is whether *you* trust in that love." He pressed my hand. "Now I must go. I will await news of your death." He went to the door and grinned back at me with his crooked white teeth. Then he was gone.

News of my death. The words were strange and awful. And yet, I thought with a smile, they were the most hopeful I had ever heard.

I would die in order to live.

Chapter Thirty-one

Romeo, O Romeo, shall I place my faith in you?
Mover of mountains, Lord of the River's flow.
We had lived, one heart between us,
that gift sweet Heaven bestowed.

Can I place my faith in you
when only silence comes from yonder hills?
No sight, no sound at my door,
no tap at my windowsill.

O Romeo, send the smallest sign
from Verona you'll come.
Take me home to your heart,
make a place on your throne.

Your stars, shape of the mighty bull,
elude me tonight, oh why?
They would give me strength, I know,
the strength I need to die.

But here am I, green vial in hand,
choice of deathlike slumber or life like death
in a harridan's house, the
Beast's icy fingers on my breast.

God of Love, hear the prayers
of a faithless child, faithful wife.
Overwatch our stumbling trials,
let us never come to grief.

I close my eyes and there he stands,
bright spirit in my room,
figs in hand, hands of blood.
Will he come to my tomb?

I laid down the quill beside the page of new verse and sat still as stone, all but my eyes. They swiveled right and I saw the moonlit garden, to the left set upon a wooden form my wedding dress in all its obscene splendor.

Freedom, I thought, *or tyranny.* The choice was mine. Spoken thusly, it was an easy election. But choosing Romeo assumed that Romeo would come.

Friar Bartolomo, without hesitation or doubt, believed he would. Even Lucrezia presumed that her letter would find a husband ready and willing to steal back into the city of his banishment, with certain death should he be caught, to carry me away from my father's house.

At first I had believed in his resolve. I had leapt at Lucrezia's plan to call him back from Verona. Why had Jacopo's sabotaging of our scheme also wounded my faith in Romeo's steadfastness? How could a simple evil act have had such insidious power over me?

Romeo had done nothing, not a single thing, to incite my mistrust of him or his love for me. Yet I had begun to think him weak for failing to come of his own volition, or to find a way for his letter to reach my hand.

But it was I who was weak. I who was faithless. I who, having been thrown down once, refused to stand up again and face my tormentor.

Shame rose in me, flushing my face red.

Jacopo was clever and was now provoked to action by the one emotion whose strength rivaled that of love—jealousy. Should I, my resolve unnaturally weakened, give license to this despot and allow his unholy sentiment to prevail? Allow to unravel the whole precious cloth of Romeo and Juliet that the God of Love had so flawlessly woven?

All at once the courage that Friar Bartolomo reminded me I owned burst through my skin and straightened my spine. My will hardened, and joy came flooding in great waves onto the shores of my battered soul.

I went to the small wooden casket under my bed and unlocked it, pulling forth my many poems. I unfurled the sketch Romeo had given me of the God of Love. I shuddered when I saw the woman draped in red, lying in his arms, for to my eyes she looked limp and dead. I flattened the paper and, gathering it and all my writings into a single sheaf, tied it with a string. I pulled over my night-robe and gown a warm cloak and, grabbing my dagger, opened the balcony door.

I was glad for the moonlight so bright it cast shadows, for without it I might not have found the edge of the floor stone

I sought near the balcony's center. It was one I had many times felt as a small ledge under my feet, an imperfection I avoided so not to trip.

Now I knelt at it, feeling its height with my fingers. With the blade I found its weakness and began frantic digging into the mortar. It was loosening! A moment later, using all my strength, I raised it up and slid it aside. Rain in the cracks had happily softened the thick mortar beneath it, and this I carved away with the flat of the dagger, making a space the size of my sheaf.

I put it in its hiding place, replaced the stone, and bore down on it with all my weight till it was even with ones near it. With fingers gone numb I pressed the dried mortar into the spaces to hide my handiwork, then scooped up piles of remaining stone dust, heaving it over the balcony wall.

I swept the place with my hand and walked on it till it was flat and I was satisfied that it looked no different than it had before. I stood and looked up at the sky. Somewhere there was Taurus, proud bull. Romeo's stars. Romeo's House. The stars that had promised me to him. But this night clouds hid all sight of the stars. The constellation eluded me . . . and there was no time to spare.

Inside again, I was perspiring beneath my cloak and threw it off. I removed my night-robe as well and stood at my family's jewel box, pulling it open to reveal the gems that glittered in the torchlight.

The green glass vial was in my hand. I did not hesitate. I did not question. I drank the liquid down, hardly tasting its bitterness, for its purpose was so sweet. I pushed aside the heavy necklaces that lined the box's bottom and found a place to set the trinket. With our family's jewels piled atop the thing, it disappeared, nothing more than a costly emerald's fragment to an unsuspecting eye.

I was still strong and steady on my feet as I walked to my bed. I kept as a constant vision the face of my Romeo, bright eyes, sharp-angled jaw, that mane of hair as it had been the night we'd met. But as I lay me down and drew the covers over my chest, I felt the first cold fingers of the potion in my veins. Weariness came upon me quite suddenly, and I thought, *This is not a fearful thing. It is just a long slumber at whose end I shall see the face of my beloved smiling down at me.* Then utter darkness fell, like an enveloping velvet curtain over my head. No light. No sound. No feeling.

And all at once I was gone from this world to another.

Romeo

*T*ime dragged, and no word back from my love was nearly my undoing. Certainly she had received my letters. Once a trusted courier, Massimo would prove one again. And the friar, my friend and adviser in love, he who had risked all manner of punishment for overseeing our clandestine marriage, would he not be sponsoring the correspondence between Juliet and myself?

Why had she not written?

Had Marco's killing been, despite my innocence in an act of murder, too much for her to bear? Had my weakness and tears at our last meeting been repulsive to her? Had her apparent bliss in our marriage bed been no more than a kind deception?

No! I refused to believe such perversions of our faith in each other. If I had had no word from Juliet, then some evil force was at work to prevent it.

Still I was uneasy. How could my scheme unfold without her complicity, her consent? Without knowledge of my time of arrival to rescue her, she would be forced into preparedness every moment of every day and night.

I revised my arrangements without any word from Juliet. She would know, of course, that darkness was our ally. I must assume, too, that she had procured her male disguise and would bravely come as she had on our wedding night, down the ladder from her balcony. All that was needed now was our conveyance.

My uncles Vittorio and Vincenzo must be convinced to assist me. I would ask them for the use of a wine cart and a team of two horses. When I parked beneath the Capelletti's garden wall, Juliet would climb down and hide beneath some rugs, and I would drive the cart at full speed from the city.

But I had to move quickly. I had to move now. For the present she and I could live happily in this house, away from prying eyes. Our bed was almost finished. Then perhaps I could come to some arrangement with my father—to receive some part of my inheritance before his death. Juliet and I would need little for a happy life. Perhaps we would, as she'd always dreamed, travel to the far corners of the world.

Thus fortified with my plan, such as it was, I left the crone's house as night descended and made my way to my uncles' villa. As always I extinguished my torch within a hundred yards of the place, this night struggling with only the dim quarter moon for illumination.

I became alarmed at my first sight of the villa from a distance, for no lights shone at the walled gates' lanterns, nor in the second-story windows that could be seen above the wall. I felt my stomach churn, but told myself the servants must be lazy or forgetful, though I did move stealthily as I approached, straining to hear the familiar sounds that would tell me all was well within.

But all I heard was the wind singing eerily in the pines and a single hound baying mournfully. When I found the gate ajar and no lights shining from the ground-floor windows, my worst fears gripped me with terrible force.

Then I stumbled, having tripped over something soft yet solid lying in the drive. It was my uncle Vittorio's favorite dog, stone dead. Even in the dim moonlight I could see its belly had been slit and its bowels sprawling obscenely on the ground.

Suddenly I was paralyzed, not with fear, but with rage, for I knew with no small doubt what horrors lay within my uncles' house, and the cause of it.

With all the fortitude I owned, I willed my legs to move and made for the front door. This, too, was half-open and upon entering, I found myself standing in a pool of gore, though no body from which it had flowed. I lit a lamp and saw at once that whoever had been savaged at the door had dragged himself away into the house. Farther on I found Francesco, who lay in a heap near the stairs, too much blood covering his torso to see where he had been stabbed.

Now I saw that the house had been ransacked—tapestries torn from the walls, furniture toppled, my uncles' prized Venetian urn in a hundred pieces on the floor.

It took no time to discover my father's brothers. The attack had come as they sat eating their midday meal, the assassins rushing in so quickly and unexpectedly in broad daylight that Vittorio still sat at the table, the napkin at his neck caked brownish red, and his soup bowl overflowing with the blood that had gushed from his slashed throat.

Uncle Vincenzo, it seemed, had put up a fight, as his hands and arms were covered in deep gashes. He lay on his back near the table. I fell to my knees beside him and covered his body with mine, tears beginning to well, howls of rage forming in my throat.

But then I heard a sound from beneath me. I took Vincenzo's hand and found that while it lacked warmth, it did not have the feel of icy death. I put my face close to his and felt the softest rush of air on my cheek, and heard an unnatural hiss from his chest.

"Uncle," I whispered. "I am here."

"Romeo . . ."

It was hard for him to speak. I saw now that his doublet front was heavy with blood.

"I did not tell them where you were . . . even as they held the knife at Vittorio's throat."

"Strozzi's men?" I uttered, horrified at my own words.

"Who else?" Now he groaned and I held him closer, tears falling.

"Nephew . . . ," he managed, blood trickling from his mouth, ". . . a confession."

"I am no priest, Uncle." I was agonized by my helplessness.

"No priest . . ." His words were more difficult to hear. "Confession to you . . ."

"Me? What?" I pulled back to see his face more clearly. "You have done nothing but love and protect me."

"The letters . . ."

I shook my head uncomprehendingly.

". . . letters to your wife . . . unsent."

"Unsent?"

"Too dangerous for you."

Now it was dawning—the reason for Juliet's silence.

"She never received my letters?"

"Forgive us, Romeo. . . . The family . . . our blood . . . our blood." I groaned at the irony of his choking on the blood he had wished so fiercely to protect.

"You do forgive us?"

"Forgive you? You must forgive *me*! I am the cause of this. I am the cause!"

I hugged him again and kissed his face, but then the long final rasping breath was expelled and settled him into death's ease.

I sat numb by his side for a space of time, then took my uncle Vittorio under his arms and lowered him to the floor, dragging him with regrettable gracelessness to his brother's side. I laid them out in as dignified a fashion as was possible in this circumstance. I steeled myself to find the cook and their body servants in the house, who were all most certainly dead, but as I stood, I heard a sound at the door . . . footsteps.

I rose and reached for my dagger, but before I could spring into action, the figure of a man appeared in the dining room doorway. He was unarmed and held a torch that illuminated his face. He was young, wearing the simple garb of a messenger, and he expressed in his features a look of abject horror at what he had seen, and now fright at the sight of me, covered in blood, standing over the mutilated bodies of my uncles, enraged, and clutching a dagger.

He turned to bolt but I shouted at him, "Stay, stay! I am Romeo. My uncles have been murdered. I thought you were their killer, come to finish me!"

He turned back, trembling and openmouthed with shock. "You are Romeo?"

I nodded. "And you are . . . ?"

"A page in the house of Medici."

Word from Juliet! A glimmer of light in this ghastly scene around me.

"Tell me," I said, going to him. I grabbed him with such force he recoiled.

"I am come to say . . ." He stopped as though to refresh himself of the words he was meant to recite. His face hardened and his eyes went cold, avoiding my gaze entirely.

A chill rattled through me in the moment before he said, "Lady Juliet Capelletti is dead, having succumbed on the eve of her wedding to Jacopo Strozzi."

The rest I do not remember well. I moved slowly, as though ice were in my veins. Disorder and bewilderment reigned inside my head. My uncles and their servants needed burial—of that I was sure—but the thought of remaining at the villa, overseeing their funerals, was untenable as long as their murderers were at large.

And Juliet. How was it possible she was dead? Dead, and "on the eve of her wedding to Jacopo Strozzi"? The Medici courier was useless for any further facts than those that he had been sent to deliver, all but that the planned marriage of Lucrezia and Piero de' Medici had taken place, though without celebration— a mere formality, the exchange of rings and the dowry given, everyone dressed in mourning black.

Before he rode back to Florence, he asked if there was any message I wished to send back to Lucrezia. I had none.

I had not a single coherent thought in my head.

I did find that though the stable hands had been killed, the horses put out to pasture in the afternoon had been overlooked. I took one and must have saddled and bridled it, for I rode it back to the crone's house, low branches scratching at my face, though I felt nothing. I did not hear the birds, the sounds of the forest. I did not smell the moist ferns or moss as I crossed the stream. Was blind to the sight of sun-dappled ground that had always cheered me so. My senses were altogether absent. Those joyful perceptions in which I had reveled my whole life and with which I had courted my wife were far beyond muted.

They were lost. As dead as she was.

I gathered what little I owned from the cottage and began my journey home.

I rode like the Devil was chasing me, though in truth he was before me—in the city of Florence. Jacopo Strozzi. Evil incarnate. I spurred my horse faster.

What is the hurry, Romeo? a cold voice whispered in the wind at my ear. *Juliet is dead. There is nothing can be done.*

Nothing but revenge her death. And the others, I answered. *Tearing Strozzi limb from limb, watching him writhe with agony in an ever-widening pool of his own blood.*

Here on the road from Verona to Florence, farmers with their carts full of onions and cages of squawking chickens jammed the track, forcing me time after time to gallop around them, kicking up clods of dirt and clouds of dust, causing all manner of cursing at so rude a traveler.

Farther on a coach had broken down and a distressed family, their small children squalling, gestured for me to stop and help. I did not. Even a monk who knelt by the side of a fallen horse shrieking with the pain of a badly broken leg moved me not at all.

Instead I spurred my mount unmercifully. For I had no mercy left in my soul, and no love either, save that of revenge and the sight of Jacopo Strozzi's heart, still beating, impaled on the tip of my dagger.

My first sight of Florence, one that I'd believed would soothe my soul, did nothing but anger me. Here was the seat of all my sorrow, all my pain, all my loss.

It was midday, midweek, and I knew where I was most bound to find the object of my loathing. But when I dismounted round the corner from Capelletti Silks, I came upon a scene most unexpected. No one was working. The street in front of the factory—much rehabilitated since the fire—was crowded with Florentines. An entire bolt's worth of twisted silk, black—in honor, I assumed, of the recent deaths in the family—was draped the whole length of the building.

It was a strange gathering, ceremonial in nature, though all those in attendance were, too, in black. Among the throng I found Capello and Simonetta Capelletti, grim and shrunk by their loss. The weavers, dyers, and spinners employed within were there, looking uncomfortable, shifting from one foot to another. Don Cosimo and Piero de' Medici, and Piero's new bride, Lucrezia, were just descending from a coach with Poggio Bracciolini.

Coming to greet them, oozing with deference and gratitude, was Jacopo Strozzi.

My first sight of him roused a fury in me, but I held myself steady, certain that for the ending I desired for him, my own cool head was necessary. I further assessed the scene before me.

On a table was displayed an official-looking contract, an inkpot and a quill, and a pair of giant-bladed scissors meant to cut the thick ribbon, signifying, I assumed, the legal commencement of the partnership of Capelletti and Strozzi.

With everyone of importance now in attendance, an obsequious Jacopo led Don Cosimo and Poggio forward and beckoned to Capello. Joylessly, he kissed his wife and joined the three men at the table.

Don Cosimo gazed at the assembled but was silent for a long moment. He was never a man at a loss for words, but this day it appeared he could not find a sentiment that pleased him.

"What a happy day this would have been," he began in a sorrowful voice, "had our sister, daughter, friend"—he fixed Jacopo in his sight—"wife, Juliet, been here to celebrate with us. The joining of two families in commerce and matrimony is a wondrous thing."

I saw Lucrezia's expression, mournful to begin with, twist tight into fury.

"Some counseled against this occasion so soon after Juliet's loss . . ."

Simonetta's face revealed that she had been one of those counselors.

". . . but Jacopo believed that his bride-to-be would have wished for the contract to be promptly signed and the partnership legally sealed. Therefore, with heavy heart I stand as witness, and Poggio Bracciolini—Notary of the Republic—will officiate the joining of Capello Capelletti and Jacopo Strozzi in their mercantile enterprise."

Cosimo stood aside as one and then the other man took up the quill and signed the document, followed by Poggio adding his signature below theirs.

Jacopo held out the great scissors to Don Cosimo, gesturing for him to cut the silk draping, but the Medici had come to his limit of celebration, and demurred. So, too, did Capello, who went back to stand with Simonetta and hold her hand.

But this important moment was not one that Jacopo was willing to sacrifice. With no hesitation he took up the shears himself, and with the long blades cut the twisted fabric in two.

The pieces fell fluttering away, revealing the office's revitalized facade and Maestro Donatello's grand new sign proclaiming CAPELLETTI AND STROZZI SILKS AND WOOLS. There was modest applause, befitting the somber occasion, but from where I stood, I—and only I—could see the expression on Jacopo's face.

It lacked any shred of sadness for Juliet's death, remorse for the cold-blooded murder of Marco or the butchery of my uncles' entire household. Indeed, it was triumphant, even joyful.

I could stand no more.

I flew from my hiding place into the center of the gathering like a well-aimed arrow, shot straight and true at Jacopo Strozzi.

We collided and fell to the ground together, rolling over and over on the cobbles, I pummeling him with my fists and he repelling my blows, landing several of his own. But my rage empowered me to such an extent that in moments my fingers had tightened around his throat, and his face had begun bulging a purplish blue.

A sharp knee to my groin sent shards of pain ripping through me, and I sprawled backward. Jacopo skittered away like a crab, calling hoarsely to the dumbfounded onlookers, "Will you not help me?! This is Marco's murderer, Romeo! Exiled on pain of death! Will someone come to my aid?!"

All at once the brawniest of the weavers and dyers came rushing at me, grabbing me, several holding my arms outstretched, another gripping my head in an elbow vise. Blows began to rain upon my face and chest and back till taking a breath was hardly possible.

Jacopo regained his feet and some semblance of dignity, and now, brandishing his stiletto, he came forward to where I stood. If I did not speak and speak quickly, my life would soon end in the place, and by the same method and man that Marco's had.

Remembering the sights of my uncles' dining room, I found strength within me and shouted, "Good, kill me, Jacopo! That is what you wished to do from the first moment you saw me!"

Capello strode forward, confounded by my words. The knife was poised inches from my eye.

"The Devil speaks through him," Jacopo snarled. "Let me put an end to it."

"Like your henchmen put an end to my uncles in Verona? And their servants? And their dogs?"

Now Don Cosimo moved to my side and, with him, Lucrezia, her eyes flashing angrily.

"What does he mean, Jacopo?" Don Cosimo demanded.

"Tell them," I said. "Tell them whose blood it is I wear on my doublet."

"He lies," said Jacopo. "He'll say whatever he will to save himself."

"No."

The word was simply spoken, but everyone turned to attend Lucrezia.

"He does not lie," she said quietly, but with great authority. "He does not murder." She paused, to great effect, and said, "Jacopo Strozzi does. He set fire to your factory, Signor Capelletti. And he pushed Marco onto Romeo's blade."

Jacopo's laugh was high and shrill. "What is this?" He glared at Lucrezia. "How dare you speak to me so?"

She remained composed and held his eye with unnerving

calm. "I speak it as the whole truth. You are a despicable creature, Jacopo Strozzi. My dearest friend, Juliet, risked a suicide's hell rather than a marriage to you."

I saw Simonetta's knees buckle at these words. Nothing drew more shame to a family than suicide.

Jacopo faced Don Cosimo. "I say again, would you take the word of any woman over that of a man—and a pillar of Florentine society at that?"

"Perhaps not," said Don Cosimo mildly. He paused, as if to consider the choice.

Jacopo's lips bowed into a slow smile.

"But," Don Cosimo continued, choosing his words carefully, "Lucrezia is not 'any' woman." Now his face hardened and he glared at Strozzi. "She is a Medici, and her word is her honor." Don Cosimo gestured to the factory workers. "Disarm him and take him away—the Signoria Prison. They will deal with him presently."

To me Don Cosimo said, "I will send my men to Verona to your uncles' house for proof of your claims."

I looked to Lucrezia. "Your messenger will bear witness to everything I've said."

"No! No!!" Jacopo shrieked as four weavers surrounded him and began marching him away.

But fury, flashing from his eyes and straining every sinew of his body, turned suddenly to inhuman strength. He wrenched free from his captors' grip and dived unaccountably onto the table on which the contract lay signed, half-covered by a length of the black silk that had fallen there.

When he arose, we all saw Jacopo's purpose for falling on the table. In his two hands he held the giant scissors, their blades outstretched to their fullest in a wide V, and he was running at me, full speed, with the razor-sharp blades at the level of my neck.

I was still surrounded by the men who had held and beaten me, and they, in confusion of what they were now seeing, were slow to move. Jacopo and his shears were nearly upon me before the men scattered, giving me breadth to move.

I swiveled and ducked.

Jacopo missed his target and overshot his mark, and by the time my enemy had turned to find me again, I had unsheathed the only weapon I had—my dagger.

The scissors, blades unwieldy in their V, were now closed, yet with their heavy length of steel and blunt-pointed tip they were still a formidable weapon. I could see that Jacopo was that most dangerous of all opponents—a man humiliated with nothing to lose.

Seeing me suddenly armed—although with an instrument but half the size of his—inflamed him even further. With a grip on both handles he slashed at me from low to high, aiming to land a blow on my chin.

With each slice I backed away another step, but I saw that each attempted cut came slower and slower as the weight and odd shape of the weapon weakened him.

For a single moment Jacopo's chest was exposed and I lunged hard with the point of my blade.

He was yet agile, and to my dismay jumped back and avoided the stab. And then in a move I had scarce expected, Jacopo spun in a full circle, smashing the closed scissors to the back of my neck.

I fell flat to the ground, facedown, stunned by the force of the blow. But this was not how I wished to die. I felt the hasty welling of my wits and my strength and rolled on my back in time to see my opponent had once more opened the scissors. Their two sharp points were even now descending to doubly impale me.

The moment had come.

Punching my arm in a high, triumphant salute to revenge, I plunged my dagger hard into Jacopo Strozzi's chest. He gasped with shock and fury as the strength drained from his hands, causing the shears to slip harmlessly to the cobbles. As he fell to his knees I rose to mine, kneeling face to face, connected only by the sharp bridge of steel. I saw with pleasure that the mad gleam in his eyes had faded to unspeakable agony.

"For my uncles," I said, and wrenched the dagger upward. Jacopo's mouth widened in a silent scream. "For Marco." When I pulled higher, I could hear the ripping of sinew and bone. My face was wet with tears as I pulled him into a closer embrace and whispered the words that only he could hear. "For Juliet." With that fiinal thrust, the blade pierced his heart. Blood erupted from his lips and death took him. He toppled to the street in a graceless heap.

I scrambled quickly to my feet, unsure of the crowd's disposition to an exiled man—perhaps once exonerated for a murder on this street—who had now, with violent certitude, taken the life of another.

I spent but a moment committing to memory the faces of those whose lives had intertangled with my own—Simonetta and Capello Capelletti, who had given Juliet life. Don Cosimo, who had been my partner in peacemaking. And Lucrezia—now and forever a Medici—who had courageously spoken to my honor. Then I turned and walked from the crowded street, my head held high.

Chapter Thirty-two

*B*lind and dumb. The wrapping of my skin numb. Limbs, digits, eyelids, lips, altogether paralyzed. A steady white hissing in my ears, this retrieving me from the depths of dreamless dark. Then a faint thumping of my heart deep within my chest.

The hissing became a rumble that coalesced into beats of solid inflection. Speech. A voice I knew well, as if from a distance. The Poet's familiar words.

"'I seem to see the sun darken in a way that gave the stars a color that would have made me swear that they were weeping.'"

It was Romeo! He was speaking of Dante's Beatrice. Of her death.

"'The tender soul, perfectly filled with grace, now lives with glory in a worthy place. She has ascended to high heaven into a realm where angels live in peace.'"

Why does he speak of unhappy death when we will soon go from here to our life together? I thought, weariness still subduing me.

"'The ladies had covered her face with a white veil, and it seemed that her face was so filled with joyous acceptance that it said to me: "I am contemplating the fountainhead of peace."' "

Yes, I silently cried, I, too, am at peace knowing that you are here, come to take me out of this dark place and into the light. I was longing to speak, to offer some verse of my own. Romeo, O Romeo . . .

"'So much grief has become the destroyer of my soul,' " he went on reciting. "'My sighs can hardly relieve the anguish of my heart. Indeed, I grieve so, that whoever were to see me now could die of pity.' " Romeo's voice was dull and piteous. "'He sins who witnesses my desperate state and does not try to comfort my torn heart.' "

"His" torn heart?

"'I went to see the body in which that most trustworthy and blessed soul had dwelt,' " he quoted, altogether morose. "'Oh, my lady lies dead!' "

What? He seemed to speak for himself and me!

"'I called upon Death and said, "Sweet Death, come to me and do not be unkind. Come take me now, for I earnestly desire you. You can see that I do, for already I wear your color."' "

Perhaps it was alarm at Dante's words too heartily claimed by my husband, or the slow receding of the potion from my veins, for now I felt Romeo's lips on my face, and warm tears. Moved by his suffering and determined to fully wake, I threw all my intention downward to my right hand and moved my pointing finger once, a single small jerk.

He cried out sharply and pulled away. When he spoke again, it was with trembling voice.

"What is this?" he said in a low tone of horror. "Just a miserable man's wishful thinking?"

Wait, I silently said, my strewn and addled thoughts reassembling

themselves. Why is Romeo mournful and distrusting of my reanima-
tion? Should this not prove a joyful moment—my awakening? And
where in heaven's name is Friar Bartolomo?

Romeo sounded close again. He was angry and disbelieving. "Juliet's finger moving on my thigh? Self-pitying fool!"

That was enough. I must make myself known.

With all my resolve and all my strength I pushed open the stone-heavy lids of my eyes.

Now he shrieked, and though my sight was yet blurred in the dim, flickering torchlight, I saw the shape of him propelled back and away from me.

"Unnatural apparition! Unholy ghost! What foul creature has inhabited my poor wife's body?"

"Romeo . . ." That hushed word escaped me like a long sigh.

"'Romeo'? The wide-eyed monster speaks my name?"

"My love, please . . . ," I managed, a supreme effort.

He came closer, looming above me. With all my might I held his terrified gaze. I saw him desperately searching for the human soul behind my eyes.

"Juliet?" he whispered.

The ugly rasping sound that came from my throat I regretted. It would have thrown the fear of God into a priest. But Romeo recalled his courage and steadied himself.

"Are you alive?" he asked.

"Alive. Your Juliet."

He ventured nearer and kissed me on the mouth.

"Your lips are *warm*." There was wonder in his voice. "Not so when I arrived here. You are alive. Oh, Juliet, blessed Jesus!"

Then he was all a flurry of hands, unsure how to touch me,

move me, lift me. Where I had been stiff as a corpse, now I was melting and helplessly limp. When I groaned, he hugged me to him so tightly, with such sweet possession, I would have wept if I had had tears.

He gently arranged me to sitting, albeit leaning heavily on him, one arm around the back of me, the other bracing me not to fall.

I drank in the sight of him. His hair, still short and badly shorn by me, was tousled, as if from a long ride. He wore a modest doublet badly stained, and sturdy boots.

"Where is the friar?" I said, the faculties of my tongue thankfully returning.

"The friar?"

I tried to clear my mind, but his question had thrown me into confusion. Certainly our scheme had succeeded, for Romeo was here and in good time for my waking. Now I looked about and saw with too much clarity all the dead around us. Poor Marco under his sheer veil lay on a marble bier within a man's length from mine.

"Can we leave this place soon?" I asked. "Where will you take me? The south of Italy?" The words were tumbling out happily now. "Your mother has a brother there. A farm?"

"Yes, a farm."

"It will be sad to leave my family, but we'll start again. Our 'many strong children' will bring us joy." I smiled at my own small jest, then lifted my face and kissed him, my hunger reigniting, the promise of our life together feeding the flame.

But how strange. Romeo's return kiss was mild. Almost meek. In all our joinings—fumbling embraces in the shadow of his villa wall, our wedding kiss at San Marco Chapel, our full thrust in the marriage bed—he had never held back. I knew him. He was a man of untamed passions.

I swallowed hard, suddenly afraid to utter the words.

"What is wrong, my love? What has happened?"

He was long silent, collecting his thoughts. "Of what friar did you speak?" he finally said.

I went cold again. "Bartolomo," I whispered. "Did he not come to you in Verona?"

Romeo shook his head, a steady no.

"Then how do you come to be here in my tomb?" I was sure I would not like his answer.

"A messenger did come," he said, "from Lucrezia de' Medici, with news that"—Romeo's features fell into grievous form—"Juliet Capelletti had succumbed on the eve of her wedding to Jacopo Strozzi."

I was struck dumb.

"I died then, Juliet. I died." His eyes filled with tears. "All my letters to you had gone unanswered. . . ."

"They never reached me, love."

"I know, I know. . . ." The look on his face was haunted.

"Romeo, oh God. The friar was meant to come to you and tell you my death was feigned. A way to avoid my marriage to Jacopo Strozzi. It was nothing but a long sleep, a potion I took. You and the priest were to come here and fetch me away."

Romeo was shaking his head again.

"But all is well, my love," I said. "Despite the crossed messages you came."

"I rode like a madman, even believing you dead. I stopped for nothing." Romeo looked away, remembering. "There was on the road—I remember now—a brown-robed monk who knelt at the side of a horse whose leg was broken. But even for this I did not slow. Bartolomo?" He looked back at me. "I tell you I was crazed with grief."

"My sweet husband." I caressed his cheek with my hand.

"Juliet . . . I thought you were gone from the world. I did not want to live without you. I took some poison from an apothecary's shelf."

"Well, there you are," I said, and gave him a cheerful smile. "You need not take the poison, for I am clearly not dead."

He took my hand in his and brought it to his lips. Then he looked at me. "But *I* am, love. It is already done."

I stared at him in horror. "Vomit it out!" I cried, pushing him off my bier. "Let me help you. I can help you." I found the strength in my legs to stand.

"Too late."

Romeo fell to his knees.

I dropped down before him and gently set him with his back against the marble bench.

"Icy vapors are in my chest. My fingers are numb." He smiled crookedly. "Yet my eyes are clear. Here is your lovely face. Those clever eyes that see beyond the lies of flesh. Ha. That last would have made a good line of verse."

I felt desperation sweeping over me. My voice became hard and strident.

"Where is the apothecary's poison?"

"All gone."

"No!"

"Juliet, sweet wife . . ."

I cried out, "If it does not please God that we should live together, let us die together!"

Romeo's voice was growing weak. "Do not think of following me. I am a suicide. I will exist as a twisted tree stump in the Seventh Circle of Hell, scaled harpies flying overhead."

"Then let me be a twisted stump beside you."

"Oh, my love, no. Your life is too precious. You have poetry left to write. Children to birth and love."

"My life will be torment! Jacopo threatened to sign my name to the marriage contract, then rape me. Dante's Inferno is a heaven compared to marriage with him!"

"Have no fear of Jacopo. He is worms' meat."

"Jacopo dead?"

"I took my revenge for Marco's death. For my uncles . . ."

"Oh no . . ."

"But most of all for you. Oh, the Fates were unkind in breaking that horse's leg."

"Unkind? The Fates must have chosen us as their deadliest enemies! And do not dare tell me that God is merciful, or works in mysterious ways."

"I will not tell you that. It is my stars that most disappoint me. By their promise, we were to be together."

Romeo slumped and a terrible sound came from deep in his chest. I sat beside him, my back against the bier, then laid him down, his head cradled in my lap. He was dying.

"My love," I moaned.

"Listen, listen . . . ," he whispered.

> *The stream, hearing her laughter, races faster*
> *Her kindness teaches clouds to be soft,*
> *Her breath the rose to be fragrant,*
> *Her hair the grasses to wave.*

She is Juliet.
She is mine to save.

He smiled. "It is good, is it not?"

"The best you have ever written."

I searched frantically for words of comfort. Something, anything, of hopeful cheer must be said. It came to me suddenly.

"The God of Love will intervene," I said.

"What?" I could see his sight was dimming.

"The God of Love . . . he is our personal savior. When someone takes his own life for a sentiment as pure as ours, he goes to a special heaven over which our god presides. A heaven for those who die for love."

His laugh was weak. "I think our poet would approve . . . of this heaven." Romeo's heavy-lidded eyes closed. "I see it. It is indeed beautiful. A huge walled garden with soft carpets of flowers, and rows of vines. Glorious trees—olive and walnut and fig. A two-sided marble fountain there in the center, one part of cool, clear water, the other of wine. The sky overhead is deep blue with clouds . . . endlessly changing their shapes into faces and fabulous creatures. A great entertainment."

He gasped a breath.

"Romeo, stay with me!"

I kissed him then, with all my might and all my fervor. He raised his head and kissed me back, and I thought the mad thought that I might somehow kiss the life back into him. But then his head fell limp and heavy into my lap. He lay looking up at my face with love and desperation.

"Forgive me," he whispered.

In the next moment I saw the light that was his life flicker . . . then fade . . . then extinguish entirely.

So slender a thread, I thought, and closed his eyes with my hand. I sat still as a statue and death, like fine dust, rose around me. The torch crackled on the wall. Oh, this tomb was cold!

It came suddenly to mind that perhaps *if I willed the breath out of me,* I, too, might expire. I pushed the air from my lungs and held, held, held . . . but the breath returned in a panicked rush.

I sobbed with my failure.

I felt the weight of death in my lap but held my eyes high, refusing its unbearable sight. Then Dante whispered low in my ear, *"I cannot keep my devastated eyes from looking ever and again at you."*

With the last of my courage I lowered my gaze and took in the sight of Romeo's body, lean and finely muscled. Graceful even in death. I grasped his arms to fold them into a cross on his chest. It was then I saw that he wore our braided gold marriage ring, the same as I had been too cowardly to wear.

Oh, the sight of it!

I cried out and fell on him, weeping and kissing his hands, breast, cheeks, mouth. I kissed his eyelids then, one by one, feeling the moist, delicate skin under my lips' touch.

I prayed for a taste of that oblivion I had recently known. No thought. No pain. But then I would wake to find my love—the whole meaning of my life—gone from me. But there *was* a way! A clear path to oblivion. With a steady hand I pulled the dagger at Romeo's waist from its sheath. I held it up to torchlight, a strange and beautiful artifact. It was sharp, its point narrow and still wet with blood—Jacopo's.

I wiped it clean on my funeral veil.

My fingers touched the place on my breast where I felt my heartbeat below it. I was sure my skin could not long resist such sharp steel. My arms were strong enough for a single hard, downward thrust. The pain would be brief, a trifle compared to the dry, grating agony that already raked my chest.

There is no special heaven, I thought bitterly. Our precious God of Love was nothing but a cruel trickster. One who teased his devoted children with morsels of the most delicious existence, only to revoke them with violence and death.

I grasped the hilt in woven-fingered prayer and held the blade over my heart. I closed my eyes.

"Juliet!"

The echoing voice startled me and the dagger fell from my grasp, clattering on the marble floor at my side. I looked up to see hurrying toward me down the catacomb's aisle a familiar form, a torch held high before her.

Lucrezia.

"Dear friend," she cried as she set her torch on the wall. Then she saw the still form of my husband, his head cradled in my lap. "Oh, oh, poor Romeo!" She knelt across from me and placed her hand on his lifeless chest. Tears threatened, but she refused to let them fall. She looked at me. "Thank God you are back among the living. Come, we must away."

I stayed planted firmly where I was.

"Please," she pleaded. "Friar Bartolomo stands guard outside the tomb door. We cannot be found here."

"Bartolomo is the cause of Romeo's death."

Lucrezia looked stricken. "I know. He arrived in Florence just after Romeo . . ." She stumbled on the words.

"After Romeo killed Jacopo."

Then her eyes fell on the blade that had dropped from my hand. "Juliet, what are you contemplating?"

"An end to my grief."

"I do not think Romeo would wish you to take your own life."

"He said that. He did."

Lucrezia grew hopeful. But then she saw my stubborn expression.

"Do you not fear God's punishment?"

"What worse punishment can he have in store any greater than this?"

Lucrezia's face was full of anger. I needed to make her understand.

"For a moment in time," I said, "a man knew me for who I was and, without reservation, loved me for who I was. How can I now live knowing no one will ever see me again in such a perfect light? Hear me as I wish to be heard? Love me as Romeo loved me?"

"By holding the memory in your heart!" she cried.

"What, exist in memory the rest of my life? That is not living, Lucrezia."

"Then write it. In poetry. Let your love flow through the point of your quill, find form on the page."

"'The Story of Romeo and Juliet,'" I mused. "To bring hope to all that true love can flower in a world as cruel and comfortless as this one. But *you* will have to write it." I managed a smile. "Just be sure to write it as a man."

"Oh, Juliet!"

"Lucrezia, friend, I am done with this life. It is done with me. All that made it worth living is here on my knee. What lies outside this tomb is more a death than what lies within."

She was shaking her head from side to side.

"Would you ask me to live only for the sake of living? Or for fear of eternal damnation?"

She set her lips firm and refused to look at me.

"I begged Romeo to stay with me, but much as he wished, he could not. And much as I will miss your tender friendship, I cannot stay with you. But don't you remember? You have 'an extraordinary life' ahead. A brilliant future of love and children and learning and beauty. Live it with me in your heart. And Romeo. Remember us, and we will live forever. I promise you. Now go, friend, please go. Tell the friar you found us both gone to our maker. Seek help before you enter here again. And one thing more. Take Viola into your house, her husband and child, too. There is another marriage for love to sweeten your life."

"What kind of friend am I to leave you here like this!" she sobbed, her face awash with tears.

"The very best friend. One who truly understands my heart. Here, give me a kiss."

She took my face in her hands and laid her lips on my forehead. I held her fingers to my cheeks, not wishing to release them and dreading the last sight of this beautiful angel. But with a wounded cry she stood and, taking her torch from the wall, strode away into the dark of the catacomb's aisle.

I looked down upon Romeo's face. Strangely, I felt heat flowing into my limbs.

"Here we are, my love, alone at last. No one to harry us. Here in the peaceful calm."

I touched his skin and found it warm.

"Are you still close enough to hear?" I whispered. I bent down and spoke into the cusp of his ear. "I'm frightened. Not of fiery hell or shrieking harpies overhead. Only of failing to find you."

I kissed him one last time.

"If there is any justice in the world, I will."

I fumbled at my side and found the handle of Romeo's blade. I placed its tip above my breast and prayed for strength and grace.

"Oh, happy dagger," I prayed, "take me home!"

"Juliet . . ."

My name was being called. I heard it as if from a distance and I saw a point of light before my eyes.

A star . . . the one at the tip of Taurus's chin. I was speeding through the blackest of night skies, but where it once was filled with glittering points of fire, it now but showed the one constellation—the bull in all its power and glory.

Those fixed points grew larger and brighter, glowing like each was a sun unto itself. But the light did not blind me. No, no. The whole of the heavens had gone from black to white.

White as clouds. Clouds endlessly changing their shapes into faces and fabulous creatures. Oh! Now I could see there was blue sky. Blue as a summer's day. And a wall. A garden wall, ivy tendrils and flowery vines tumbling gracefully down.

Then I saw it. A ladder set against the stone, and I heard my name called again.

"Ju–li–et!"

I began to climb. It was high, this wall, but my legs and arms carried me up and up, my heart bursting with hope and joy.

"Come to me, love. Come to me now!"

His hand reached down, that hand with its woven band of gold. He gripped me tight and lifted me up and into his warm embrace.

Romeo smiled. "See where you are."

Above in the changing clouds I saw for the briefest moment the shape of the God of Love. Below was the Garden of Sweetest Delights. Flowers in the colors of silk danced in the soft breeze on broad meadows. A grove of ancient olives and walnuts and figs shaded a clear rushing stream. And there beside it, contentedly grazing, two white horses.

But the garden, I could see now, was walled on only three sides. From where we stood on high, I saw in the distance lands of great majesty. Mountains. Deserts. A city of golden spires. A sunlit sea. All stretching to infinity.

Romeo came close, his sweet breath caressing my face.

"This is ours," he whispered. "For eternity."

Historical Notes

Cosimo de' Medici, for his extraordinary service to the Republic of Florence, was named at his death *Pater Patriae*—"Father of the Country." Through his singular efforts and investments in learning and the arts, and **Poggio Bracciolini**'s scouting for the lost books of antiquity, Europe emerged from the Dark Ages into the brilliant light of the Renaissance.

Cosimo's daughter-in-law **Lucrezia Tornabuoni de' Medici** became the foremost woman of the age—shrewd businesswoman, supporter of the greatest artists of the day, and primary patron of Sandro Botticelli. Lucrezia's marriage to Piero de' Medici was an unusually happy one, and their firstborn son, Lorenzo—taking up the reins from his grandfather Cosimo—presided over the Golden Age of the Italian Renaissance. For his brilliant leadership and patronage of the arts and philosophy, he came to be known as "Lorenzo the Magnificent." Her younger son she named Giuliano. Two of her grandchildren became popes. But Lucrezia de' Medici's greatest personal achievement had nothing to do with her offspring or the patronage of others.

She became the greatest poetess of her time.

ACKNOWLEDGMENTS

Acknowledging those who have helped me in writing my novels is always a pleasure. But during the course of writing and promoting my last two books, an interesting shift occurred. While each individual assisted and supported me in his or her own particular way, I realized that everyone's efforts had transmogrified into a well-oiled "team effort."

Communication was open, smooth, and easy. Everybody—aside from doing the jobs at which they were experts—all worked laterally, "outside the box," as they say. Agents gave me wonderful story notes; my editor came up with marketing strategies; publicists, my webmistress, bloggers and fellow authors supplied ideas for promotion. Thus enthusiastically surrounded, supported, and protected, I was able to do my job—writing and promoting my books—comfortably and happily.

David Forrer and Kimberly Witherspoon, my agents since the beginning, are simply awesome. Lyndsey Blessing, Alexis Hurley, and Susan Hobson in foreign rights, keep my books flowing out into the rest of the world. Rose Marie Morse and Patricia Burke brought expertise in publicity and Hollywood that beautifully rounded out the agency team and really spiced up the stew.

When it comes to editors, there are none that compare with Kara Cesare—smart, insightful, and compassionate. I can always count on her to be at my side from soup to nuts and never steer me wrong. Editorial director Claire Zion is a veritable lion, and made the promotional phase of the editorial process a dream. While she is not in my everyday purview, I always know that publisher Kara Welsh is covering my back. Publicists Megan Swartz and Kaitlin Kennedy really "worked the room" with *Signora da Vinci*. When it came to *O, Juliet*, Caitlin Brown and Julia Fleischaker in publicity, and Ashley Fisher in marketing knocked themselves out. The folks in the art department, who have designed consistently stunning covers for all my books, went way beyond the beyond for *O, Juliet*.

Many thanks to Roberto Zecca for all his help researching olive growing and pressing in the fifteenth century, the history of Florence, and the hills and villas south of the city.

Thirty-year partner in crime Billie Morton, and dear friend Betty Hammett—my trusted "first readers"—gave me the thumbs-up on this manuscript. Once I had that, I knew I could breathe a sigh of relief. James "the Padre" Arimond again assisted me with all things Latin and religious, and my all-around assistant, Tasya, turned chaos into order.

Special thanks go to my spectacular Web designer, Linda Lazar, for outstanding work on my Web site, and to author friends Christopher Gortner and Michelle Moran, who dragged me kicking and screaming into the new world of online promotion and my first-ever "virtual book tour." With the Internet and the blogging community as a conduit, I am connected with my fans in a way I never was before and now, with some sense of who they are, I can express my gratitude to them for their priceless support.

My sourcebook for all versions of *Romeo and Juliet* wrapped up in one volume was *Romeo and Juliet: Original Text of Masuccio Salernitano, Luigi Da Porto, Matteo Bandello, William Shakespeare*, edited and with an introduction by Adolph Caso (Dante University of America Foundation, by special arrangement with Brandon Publishing Company).

It may be unfair to single Shakespeare out from all the other storytellers, but I must, since *Romeo and Juliet* would never have become so overwhelmingly iconic without him. I have to be honest—I had never read a word of Dante Alighieri until I decided to make him part of my novel—but I was flabbergasted by the beauty of his words, both poetry and prose, on the subject of love. I took great pleasure in finding the right quotes for the right moments in my story.

Last, but never least, I give my deepest love and thanks to my darling Max, who simply makes life worth living.

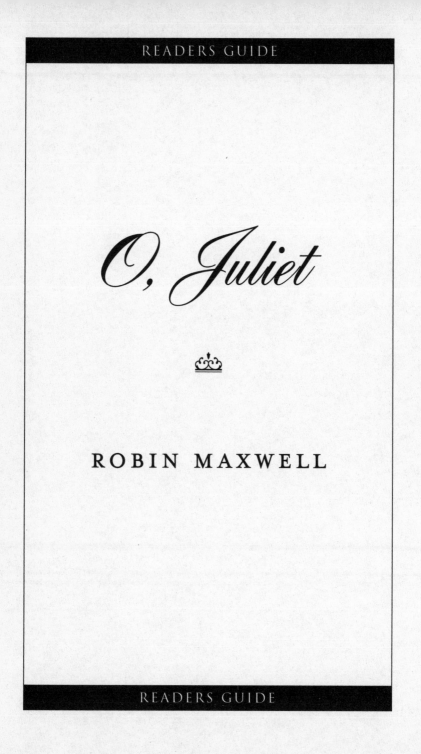

O, Juliet

ROBIN MAXWELL

A CONVERSATION
WITH ROBIN MAXWELL

Q. Why were you drawn to Romeo and Juliet's story?

A. I am a hopeless romantic.

As early as thirteen years old I foresaw myself with a career, and I dreamed of "being friends with the Beatles," which was my way of imagining myself surrounded by extraordinary people. But above all, my future was dominated by a single relationship. I desperately wanted a wonderful husband, someone who understood me and accepted me for who I was—a true "marriage for love." I had no idea what this man might look like or what he'd do for a living. All I demanded—for reasons I'll never understand—was that he possess a pair of "strong, square hands."

On the road to finding my life's partner, I claimed many remarkable men and women as friends. My career, of course, became writing, but the screenplays I began with were broad, bawdy comedies about bawdy broads, ancient civilizations, and extraterrestrials. Later, in my novels, I wrote of the strong, ahead-of-their-time women of history who defied despots in male-dominated societies.

During my search for a soul mate I was always drawn to great love stories, in books, films, and songs. But nothing moved me as profoundly as Shakespeare's *Romeo and Juliet.*

The first time I saw Franco Zeffirelli's version, I sobbed for half an hour after leaving the movie theater.

It was the perfect romantic tale. Beautiful, tenderhearted, yet passionate young lovers, gorgeous language, glorious Italy, family feuds, and a touch of violence. Even the tragic ending wasn't so bad because Romeo and Juliet were reunited in death.

Q. Romeo and Juliet *was famously set in Verona, and yet, you set your lovers in Florence at the time of the Medici. Why?*

A. Of course it's been rejigged a hundred different ways—from Broadway musicals to operas to ballets. Most recently director Baz Luhrmann's feature film starred Leonardo DiCaprio as Romeo and Claire Danes as Juliet. What I didn't know till recently was that Shakespeare's play was not the first telling of "Romeo and Juliet." Since the time of the Greeks and Romans, countless "girl-and-boy-from-warring-families" tragedies have been written. But in 1216 in Florence, two families from opposing factions came to blows when a Donati girl ran off with a Buondelmonti boy, and her cousin was killed at the Ponte Vecchio during the ensuing battle.

This legend apparently took root in Tuscan consciousness, because no less than three writers in the two following centuries decided to commit it to the written word in novella (short story) form. The first, Masuccio Salernitno, set the story in Siena, with Juliet traveling to Alexandria, Egypt, to find her banished husband. Both Luigi Da Porta and Matteo Bandello placed the tale in Verona, with Romeo escaping to Mantua. Those locations "stuck" when, in the sixteenth century, Arthur Brooke wrote the story as a narrative poem, and in 1594 Shakespeare finally took up the gauntlet, immortalizing the lovers in his masterful play.

I had just completed my seventh historical novel, *Signora da Vinci*, the story of young Leonardo and his devoted mother, Caterina, and had become completely immersed in the culture of Renaissance Italy and enamored, in particular, of the glorious Medici family. My divine editor, Kara Cesare, had been urging me to stay in the Italian Renaissance for my next book, an idea I liked, as it meant I could do without long months of monumental, brain-scrambling research once again. She suggested the possibility of using as a character one of her personal favorites from *Signora da Vinci*, the magnificent materfamilias of the Medici clan, Lucrezia Tornabuoni.

Since I dearly wanted a close female confidant for Juliet, a young woman with whom she could celebrate and commiserate, Lucrezia became the perfect "best friend." Having decided on that, I realized I had my place—Florence, where Lucrezia and the Medici lived—as well as the date, a year in which the girlfriends at eighteen were considered ripe and ready for marriage, 1444.

This allowed me the run-up to the social event of the decade, Lucrezia's wedding to the heir of Florence's ruling family, the Medici. It came at a time when the city was at peace, and was prospering with its nexus of bankers, artists, and textile merchants.

And it afforded me another utterly brilliant character—Don Cosimo de' Medici. He was, after all, the man most responsible for the Renaissance happening in the first place, and he would have adored his beautiful, highly intelligent daughter-in-law-to-be. For the family Juliet was meant to marry into, I chose the Strozzi, who were, in fact, second only to the Medici in wealth and power. Allessandra Strozzi was famously fierce when it came to matchmaking for her children. Jacopo—the ignored and bitter "third son"—was a figment of my imagination.

Suddenly I had a perfectly logical, believable, and richly textured setting for my scenario and all my characters.

Today in Verona, "Romeo's Castle" and "Juliet's Balcony" are popular tourist attractions. I hope the citizens of that fine city will forgive my literary license, returning the bulk of the story to its earliest Italian roots, Florence.

Q. What surprised you most in your research of Shakespeare's famous tale and why did you decide it needed a fresh twist?

A. One day, in one of those moments of epiphany that writers long for, and only occasionally in a whole lifetime of writing are afforded, I realized that no one had written a historical novel of Romeo and Juliet. I'd been longing to write a great love story, and while every one of my books included a love relationship, the love between a man and a woman had never been its central theme.

Richly lyrical and transcendentally passionate as the

Bard's rendition was, I'd never gotten a true sense of these two young people who inspired the story. I wanted to know about their inner lives, about their families and the society whose stringent rules and restrictions attempted to keep them apart and brought about their tragic ends.

For research I read the three Italian short stories and used Shakespeare's play as my "skeleton," and as all the writers before me I liberally borrowed, embellished and changed the details to suit my personal tastes. Never did I feel constrained by any of the earlier versions.

I knew that I did not want my Romeo and Juliet to be the fourteen-year-olds as Shakespeare had written them. That age for girls to marry was customary in sixteenth-century England, but not fifteenth-century Florence. Eighteen for a woman and twenty-five for a man was the norm, and that suited me perfectly. I wanted my lovers to have fully formed minds and full-blown passions.

I felt I needed something to tie my protagonists tightly together in a complex way—not simply a case of blind lust, or even love at first sight (though these are emotions that certainly come into play in my version). The conceit I decided upon was Romeo's and Juliet's mutual love of poetry— in particular their reverence for Italy's greatest poet, Dante Alighieri.

In two of the Italian stories Juliet offers to cut off her hair and don men's clothing to become Romeo's page and follow him into exile. Cross-dressing women, it seems, turn up a lot in both medieval literature and history, so as in *Signora da*

Vinci, I was comfortable with my heroine in male drag when the story called for it.

Also in the Italian versions, Juliet does away with herself in various ways, all less violent than with Shakespeare's "happy dagger." She simply *wills* herself to die in one, and holds her breath till she does in two others. The Bard has Romeo expiring in the tomb before Juliet wakes from her self-imposed stupor, but that did not allow for the passionate ending I envisioned. I quite liked Bandello having the lovers reunite one last time before Romeo's poison takes effect, and made it my own.

Q. How has Dante Alighieri influenced O, Juliet . . . *and your life?*

A. The only way I can describe this man's influence with the generations (and centuries) that came after him was that he was a Renaissance rock star—the John Lennon, the Bob Dylan, the Shakespeare of his age. During the bloody feuding between the Guelfs and the Ghibellines in the thirteenth century, the Florentine government executed a political screwup that they would regret forever—they banished Dante from the beloved city of his birth for life. After his death in Ravenna, the Florentine government tried to retrieve his remains to place in a monument they had created for him, but his adoptive town would not release his bones.

In subsequent years, Boccaccio (*Decameron*), who was Dante's first biographer, was paid a small fortune by the Florentine city fathers to give a course of public lectures—the *Cathedra Dantesca*—on the writer he idolized. In the early fifteenth century the most sought-after and highly paid scholar in Italy, Francesco Filelfo, taught the Dante Symposia, drawing huge crowds wherever he went. The tradition has continued in Florence from that time to the present day. My Friar Bartolomo is a fictional character, but you can be sure that if Romeo and Juliet had indeed lived in that city, one scholar or another would have been giving those popular lectures.

That poetry could so inflame two lovers in those days I have no doubt. Alberti's poetry competition in 1441 (the one I have Juliet sneaking her poem into) was a major cultural event. The great historian Will Durant says of Filelfo that he "made all Italy resound with his erudition and vituperation," and that in the Renaissance "scholarship could be passion and literature could be war."

For Romeo—himself an amateur poet—to find a woman who was his creative and intellectual equal, if not his better, would have shaken his world. And for Juliet to discover a soulful, wild-hearted, and secretly subversive young poet determined—as few others were in those days—to be a peacemaker would have been enough to spur her on to great heights of rebellion against a killingly repressive society, even if escape from it meant her death.

Q. Can you share a bit of your own love story?

A. By the time I wrote *O, Juliet*, I had been married to my own Romeo, Max Thomas, for twenty-five years. Handsome, sensitive, and a bit of a daredevil, he took me from my sedentary life of the mind on white-knuckle adventures I'd never dreamed of having. Our version of the ascent to the apex of the Florence Cathedral dome at midnight was climbing to the top of a massive rock formation in Joshua Tree National Park at noon. We committed to our life together on the Hawaiian lava fields of Mauna Loa.

Fortune has blessed me, as it did Juliet, to have found a man to love who "sees me as I wish to be seen, hears me as I wish to be heard, and loves me as I wish to be loved." I have literally followed him through a firestorm. He is my rock and my inspiration.

And yes, he possesses a pair of strong, square hands.

Robin Maxwell would enjoy hearing from you at
www.robinmaxwell.com.

Photo by Skippy Kraus-Sitomer

Robin Maxwell lives in the wilds of the California high desert with her husband, yogi Max Thomas. She would enjoy hearing from you at **www.robinmaxwell.com**.

QUESTIONS
FOR DISCUSSION

1. The role that families played in arranging marriages in fifteenth-century Italy—indeed, in most of the civilized world—was enormous. Children had little or no say in the husband or wife chosen for them. Does it surprise you to know the practice continues even today? In what regions of the world and at what levels of society do you imagine this still happens?

2. Lady Diana Spencer was carefully chosen to be the virgin bride of England's Prince Charles. Discuss how you think theirs being an arranged marriage led to the tragic end of Princess Di.

3. Did your parents have anything to do with the choice of any of your spouses, lovers, or significant others? Did the level of their influence change as you got older?

4. Did you ever openly defy your parents in choosing a lover or spouse? What was the result?

5. Did you ever forgo a love relationship because of parental disapproval? Did you regret it, or did it turn out for the best?

6. Were you familiar with the Italian poet Dante Alighieri before reading *O, Juliet*? Many people know of him as the author of *The Divine Comedy, The Inferno*, but were you aware that he and his Beatrice are considered one of medieval history's great pairs of lovers?

7. Did you enjoy Dante's writing and poetry about love from *Vita Nuova (A New Life)* quoted in *O, Juliet*?

8. Did it ring true to you that Juliet and Romeo would connect so strongly via poetry? Have you ever experienced a love connection that was enhanced by a shared interest?

9. What qualities made Romeo the perfect lover? What were the most attractive characteristics of Juliet's personality to Romeo? What are the traits in a person that make *you* fall the most deeply in love?

10. In fifteenth-century Italy, even friendships between women were constrained and limited, as girls and even married matrons were kept behind closed doors most of their lives. Do you imagine that two young women like Juliet and Lucrezia could sustain a friendship that close and intimate under such conditions? How important did you feel their relationship was to the telling of this story?

11. Were you aware of the importance of the Medici family—particularly Don Cosimo—in the genesis of the Renaissance?

Did you find yourself thinking what a fortunate woman Lucrezia Tornabuoni was to be marrying into such a family?

12. Everyone knows how this story ends. Did you find yourself wishing that the author had allowed one or both of the lovers to live?

13. Do you believe Lucrezia should have been able to talk Juliet out of taking her own life?

14. If you had been Juliet, would you have chosen to commit suicide?

15. Despite Romeo's and Juliet's deaths, was the ending of *O, Juliet* satisfying to you as a reader?

Signora da Vinci

By *Bestselling Author*
ROBIN MAXWELL

In order to watch over and protect her extraordinary son, Leonardo da Vinci, his mother, Caterina, follows him from the tiny village of his birth to Florence. In order to gain admittance into his world—as apprentice to the city's most successful artist—she has had to assume the identity of a man, "Cato the Apothecary." This disguise proves so successful that Cato/Caterina is invited by her new friend Lorenzo—heir to the city's ruling family, the Medici—to dinner at their grand palazzo.

Enjoy this excerpt from *SIGNORA DA VINCI*
and learn about Leonardo and Caterina da Vinci's world
at **www.robinmaxwell.com**
(the Signora da Vinci page).
Click on the gold "BONUS PASSPORT"
icon to learn about cross-dressing women in history,
discover what "The Shadow Renaissance"
is . . . and much more.

"This way," Lorenzo said. "We're dining under the loggia."

At the south wall of the garden we were confronted by three sweeping stone arches separated by ancient marble columns in the Greek style. A moment later we'd passed through the arches to see a high-vaulted chamber and an immense dining table, perhaps the largest single piece of furniture I had ever in my life seen.

It would have easily seated forty, but places were set only at one end—I counted eight. Though the silver filigreed candelabra and saltcellar would have paid for a whole new section of Vinci to be built, the place settings surprised me with their simplicity—terra-cotta plates and goblets, no finer than would be found on my father's table.

The other diners were flowing in through all three archways now. There was a young woman who, I surmised, must be Lorenzo's wife, Clarice Orsini. My gossiping customer had been right—the newest member of the Medici clan had a palpable air of snobbery about her. She was tall, though not as tall as me, with a pale moon face on a long thin neck and a headful of tightly curled hair, more red than blond. She was not unpretty, but the aloof tilt of her chin, and her lips, which seemed perpetually pursed, made me sorry for Lorenzo the instant I set eyes on her.

Giuliano and Lucrezia de' Medici clutched either arm of Piero. First Giuliano seated his mother; then together with Lorenzo the boys helped their father to his chair at the head of the table. The ruler of Florence grimaced as his knees bent to sit.

Giuliano and Lucrezia took places on Piero's right and left, Lorenzo and his wife next to Giuliano, and I across from Lorenzo at their mother's side. Sandro Botticelli sat next to me. Next to Clarice was an empty place setting. No one spoke of it.

"This is my new friend, Cato Cattalivoni," Lorenzo announced, sounding very pleased. He introduced me in turn to his mother, father, brother, and wife.

"Will you make a blessing on our table, Lucrezia?" Piero asked his wife in a voice rough with suffering.

We all closed our eyes as she prayed.

She spoke in a lovely, melodious tone, and suddenly I felt a pang of longing, almost to the point of physical pain, for my own gentle mother, whom I had never known.

The blessing was over and the servers were bringing in wooden platters of steaming loin of veal with sour orange relish, and ravioli in a fragrant saffron broth. The chicken with fennel was equally delightful, and an herb and mushroom omelet was redolent with mint and parsley and marjoram. This would certainly be a feast, but it was, I realized, one of the simplest food, none that Magdalena had not served my father and me a hundred times.

Suddenly I heard my name spoken. Lorenzo was addressing his parents. "Do you remember that fabulous mechanical sun and constellation that Verrocchio and his apprentices erected for our third wedding feast?" His mother nodded. "Cato's nephew, Leonardo da Vinci, designed it. Cato has just opened a wonderful apothecary on Via Riccardi."

"Really it is my master's shop," I demurred. "He'll be joining me presently."

"You are modest, Cato. You yourself refurbished the place and made it a thing of beauty."

"Whosever shop it is, we are delighted to have you at our table, Cato," Lucrezia said, leveling me with a warm and welcoming smile. I could see that her two front teeth crossed a touch at the bottom, but it only increased her charm.

"Oh, I so loved the sun and stars!" Clarice cried, sounding more like a little girl than a woman. "We had three feasts," she told me across the table, "one more splendid than the last. My in-laws built a great ballroom out into the Via Larga, just for the occasion. We had fifty dishes at each feast," and added pointedly, "Served on the *best* gold plate!"

"Clarice thinks us very strange for eating simple fare on stoneware when we dine as a family," Lorenzo told me, trying to suppress his amusement. "In fact, the first time her mother came for a visit, she was insulted by it."

"Well, it is strange, husband. And it was positively embarrassing when, instead of sitting with our guests at the wedding feast, you stood up and *waited* on them."

"That is nothing for you to be embarrassed about, Clarice,"

Lucrezia said. "Lorenzo has a fine sense about what is right and proper in any given situation. He has since he was very young. Do you suppose his father would have sent him at the age of sixteen to visit the new pope if he had—"

"I was seventeen, Mama."

"Sixteen when you went to Milan as a proxy at the wedding of the Duke of Sforza's son," she insisted. "And on the way investigated our banks in Bologna, Venice, and Ferrara. And you are quite right, my darling." She smiled at Lorenzo. "You *were* seventeen when your papa sent you to Rome to wrest a concession from the pope for our family to work the alum mines in papal territories."

"Your brothers advised me all the way," he said to his mother. He seemed embarrassed at the praise being heaped on him in front of me. But Lucrezia was not finished.

"Well, my brothers were not present when you visited that appalling creature in Naples." Lucrezia addressed me directly now. "Don Ferrante, the ruler there, is renowned for his extreme cruelty and violence. He is positively determined to rule the whole of Italy. My husband sent Lorenzo to discover the man's intentions."

"And I never did," Lorenzo demurred.

"But you fascinated the man. Charmed him. And came to an understanding with him that has held Tuscany in good stead with Naples ever since."

"Please, Mama," Lorenzo begged her.

"I know how to silence her," Giuliano said with a wicked grin.

"No, son," she pleaded, appearing to know what was coming. She began to flush pink.

"Our mother," he began, "is the most accomplished woman of the century."

"A noted poetess," Lorenzo went on, pleased that the conversation had veered away from himself. "She has written in *terza rima* a life of Saint John the Baptist, and a brilliant verse on her favorite biblical heroine, Judith."

"That big-boned woman in the garden about to decapitate Holofernes," Sandro told me.

Lucrezia, sincere in her modesty, sat with downcast eyes, knowing she could not quiet the boys and their litany of her accomplishments.

"She is a friend and patron of artists and scholars," Giuliano boasted.

"And a businesswoman of some merit." This was Piero who had chimed in. "Do not forget the sulfur springs at Morba that she purchased from the Republic and turned into a successful health resort."

"Enough! All of you! I shall never brag about any of you ever again," she announced with comic solemnity. There were murmurings of mock approval all around the table. "Though it *is* a mother's right," she added, as if to have the final word.

I smiled inwardly, agreeing with her entirely. It was indeed a mother's right to brag about her children. To glow with the pride of their accomplishments. But here at this table I was witnessing a remarkable happenstance—children that were reveling in their mother's achievements.

I suddenly noticed that despite Piero's enjoyment of this family banter, the patriarch's eyes were closed. Giuliano, too, had observed this.

"Papa!" the younger son cried. Piero's eyes sprang open. "Why were you sitting there with your eyes closed?"

He smiled sadly at the boy. "To get them used to it," he said.

There were cries all around of "No, Papa!" "Don't say such a thing!"

Lucrezia grabbed his sore-knuckled fist and bit her lip. She looked at me imploringly.

"Have you anything for pain, Cato? All of my husband's physicians have thrown up their hands with it."

I looked around, momentarily unsure about talking of so intimate a subject at this table, but I could feel all around me the raw love and concern of family for family, and no less affection in Sandro Botticelli's eyes than in Lorenzo's or Giuliano's. *Manners be damned,* I thought. I leaned toward Piero.

"Is there a repression of urine?" I asked, and he nodded yes. "Frequent fevers?"

"Almost every day," Lucrezia answered for him.

I was silent for a time, recalling a decoction my father had once made for Signor Lezi's condition, one that closely resembled the Medici patriarch's. It had not cured the gout, but considerably lessened the man's fever and suffering.

"If your sons"—I smiled at all the young men, Sandro included—"will come to my shop tomorrow, I will send them home with something that I promise will help you."

Lucrezia bit her lip and blinked back tears of gratitude.

"Thank you, Cato," Lorenzo said. "We all thank you." He grinned. "First thing in the morning we'll be descending on your apothecary like a pack of hungry dogs."

Now everyone was smiling. Even Piero looked hopeful.

"Forgive my tardiness," I heard from one of the garden archways. We all looked up to see a sweet-faced man of perhaps
thirty-five, hurrying to take his place across the table from me,
next to Clarice.

Lorenzo nodded at me. "Let me introduce you to our beloved tutor and longtime family friend, Marsilio Ficino."

I was startled, to say the least. Ficino was a legendary scholar,
one of the greatest writers and translators in the world. "Silio,"
Lorenzo went on, "meet our new friend, Cato the Apothecary."

"I fear I must go back to bed," Piero said suddenly. "The
pain has simply overtaken me." His hands were flat on the table
and he attempted to push himself to standing.

"Wait, Papa!" Botticelli cried, standing in his place. "Please, I
have something to show you."

Piero's face softened, and a pleasant expectation crinkled his
mouth. He relaxed back in his chair.

Sandro stood. "Don't anyone move," he said, and dashed from
the table, "except you, Giuliano. Come help me!" The younger
brother followed Botticelli, and they moved toward a closed
door that appeared to lead into the palazzo from the loggia.

A moment later, to the sound of crunching on the marble
floor, they returned, rolling on a wheeled contraption a huge,
paint-smeared sheet covering a rectangle that looked to be six
feet high and twelve feet across.

Facing us all, the artist beamed. Then he carefully removed
the cloth and stood aside. Every jaw in the room loosened
and fell. Then there was silence as a dozen eyes drank in the
splendor.

"I call it *Birth of Venus*," Botticelli said.

The first sight of it was simply startling. It was blatantly pagan and openly erotic, and an unquestionable statement of its maker's genius.

A woman, magnificent in her nakedness, was stepping lightly from a half shell at the edge of a placid sea onto a fecund shore. Her features were delicate and proportioned as if by the hand of the Creator. The color of her skin was pale, tinged with roses, but so fine in texture that one could almost see through her body. Venus's hair was glorious—red gold and so thick and long and flowing it draped the whole length of her torso, where, holding it with one hand, she modestly covered her pudenda.

So deeply drawn was I to her image that it was only by virtue of a hank of that lovely hair blown sideways from her head that I became aware of other figures in the painting. On the left in the air, amid a storm of flowers, hovered two winged wind gods—one male, one female—entwined in each other's arms, and with puffed cheeks they were creating the breeze around the Goddess of Love.

To the right of Venus was another figure, a woman— perhaps Spring—who in her pretty floral dress held aloft a posy-embroidered cloak with which she seemed to be urging the newborn goddess to cover her nakedness.

But my eyes could not long stray from Venus herself. She was slender, and the one breast not covered by her right hand was small, but her belly and thighs were prettily plump and rounded. Only her left arm seemed oddly shaped—too long, and almost disconnected from her shoulder. But nothing diminished the overall beauty of face and form, and her expression of unutterable sweetness.

I think Botticelli had not expected from the viewers this profundity of emotion, this stunned hush.

"Do you see what I have done?" he said to us, breaking

the silence. "How the image holds a reflection of Idea? How I have used the greens for Jupiter, the blues for Venus, gold for the sun? Is she not a perfect talisman to draw down the power of the planet Venus, the very life force of Heaven, and store that echo . . . that taste . . . that substance of the divine Idea of Love, for our use?" His hand was clutching his own heart, and his eyes were limpid with tender emotion.

But we were all quite speechless.

"My darling boy," Lucrezia finally said, "you have done far more than paint a magical talisman. This is a masterpiece for all time."

"I would venture that she is the most beautiful woman ever painted," Lorenzo offered, "ever in the history of the world."

"What incantations are needed to bring her to life?" Giuliano asked in a hushed whisper. "I want to make love to her. Instantly."

Everyone laughed at that, and the spell seemed all but broken . . . except that I caught, out the corner of my eye, Lorenzo staring at me. He was, I think, unaware I had seen him.

"Come here, Sandro," Piero said to the young man that he and his own father had raised from a boy. His voice was stern and serious. Botticelli went to the patriarch's side and knelt at his feet, laying his head on one swollen knee. The older man's gaze fell on Ficino.

"This is your influence, Marsilio. I see it. I hear it. All your lessons of spirits and occult forces, magi controlling the influences of the stars . . ." Everyone was still. Afraid to breathe. Piero looked up at Botticelli's panel.

"This painting . . ." His voice choked with emotion. ". . . it makes me want to live another day."

A sob escaped Lucrezia's throat, and she clutched her husband's arm. There was a general outcry of relief and celebration. Sandro began kissing Piero's hands in gratitude. The rest of us stood from our chairs and edged closer to the painting to study its perfection.

Clarice was clucking with quiet indignation to her mother-in-law over the total nakedness of Venus on her clamshell. I overheard Ficino and the Medici sons' conversation.

"I've always told you," the boys' tutor said, "that images can be used as medicine."

"Perhaps as strong as an apothecary's," Lorenzo suggested.

"Indeed," their teacher murmured appreciatively. "Indeed."